"I've wanted you f... Hope."

Her lips went soft and plia..., ready to meet and return his impending kiss, but she was unprepared for the searing intensity that flared between them at that first contact between hungry mouths. Raw need flooded through her, unlike anything she'd ever experienced.

Coop was the one who broke the spell, slowly separating his mouth from hers. He stared at her for a long stunned moment.

"Ready to go back?" Coop finally asked.

"To what?"

"Silk sheets? Candlelight? Soft music?"

Hope's instinct for self-preservation kicked in. "I'm not going to bed with you," she blurted. "Neither of us wants to rush into anything based on, well, lust."

"But we'd be good together, Hope...."

Dear Reader,

Welcome to Silhouette **Special Edition**...welcome to romance.

Bestselling author Debbie Macomber gets February off to an exciting start with her title for THAT SPECIAL WOMAN! An unforgettable New Year's Eve encounter isn't enough for one couple...and a year later they decide to marry in *Same Time, Next Year*. Don't miss this extraspecial love story!

At the center of Celeste Hamilton's *A Family Home* beats the heart of true love waiting to be discovered. Adam Cutler's son knows that he's found the perfect mom in Lainey Bates— now it's up to his dad to realize it. Then it's back to Glenwood for another of Susan Mallery's HOMETOWN HEARTBREAKERS. Bad boy Austin Lucas tempts his way into the heart of bashful Rebecca Chambers. Find out if he makes an honest woman of her in *Marriage on Demand*. Trisha Alexander has you wondering who *The Real Elizabeth Hollister* is as a woman searches for her true identity—and finds love like she's never known.

Two authors join the **Special Edition** family this month. Veteran Silhouette Romance author Brittany Young brings us the adorable efforts of two young, intrepid matchmakers in *Jenni Finds a Father*. Finally, when old lovers once again cross paths, not even a secret will keep them apart in Kaitlyn Gorton's *Hearth, Home and Hope*.

Look for more excitement, emotion and romance in the coming months from Silhouette **Special Edition**. We hope you enjoy these stories!

Sincerely,

Tara Gavin
Senior Editor

Please address questions and book requests to:
Silhouette Reader Service
U.S.: 3010 Walden Ave., P.O. Box 1325, Buffalo, NY 14269
Canadian: P.O. Box 609, Fort Erie, Ont. L2A 5X3

KAITLYN GORTON

HEARTH, HOME AND HOPE

Silhouette®

SPECIAL EDITION®

Published by Silhouette Books
America's Publisher of Contemporary Romance

To Lettie Lee, for keeping "Hope" alive, and to Cristine Niessner, for finding her the right home. Thanks.

 SILHOUETTE BOOKS

ISBN 0-373-09942-8

HEARTH, HOME AND HOPE

Copyright © 1995 by Kathy Lynn Emerson

Printed in U.S.A.

Books by Kaitlyn Gorton

Silhouette Special Edition

Hearth, Home and Hope #942

Silhouette Intimate Moments

Cloud Castles #307

KAITLYN GORTON

is a former librarian and teacher who lives in rural Maine with her husband and two cats. She is the author of four books for young readers, a study of sixteenth-century women and several historical romances under the name Kathy Lynn Emerson. She occasionally attempts cross-country skiing and owns a set of snowshoes, and she once built a spectacular snow fort, but most of the time, when she's not writing romances, she's curled up by the fireside and reading them rather that out there playing in the snow.

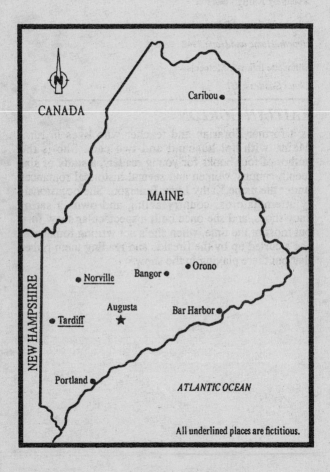

CANADA

MAINE

NEW HAMPSHIRE

Caribou •

• Norville   Bangor •   • Orono

Augusta
★

• Tardiff

Bar Harbor •

Portland •

ATLANTIC OCEAN

All underlined places are fictitious.

Chapter One

Hope Rowan sat in front of a state-of-the-art computer workstation and tried in vain to concentrate on the words on the screen in front of her, but that last telephone conversation with her client still dominated her thoughts. There was only so much she could do with modem and fax and networking. Not every collection of documents she needed to access was on-line. In order to complete several of her commissions, she'd need to visit the libraries and archives in person.

Easier said than done.

Shoulders hunched, Hope sat before the gently glowing word processor screen and ordered her eyes to scan the illuminated green letters in front of her. First things first, she told herself sternly. The Tolliver genealogy was complete. All she had to do was write the cover letter and send the bill.

Ten minutes later she was muttering ominously under her breath. The words on the screen refused to cooperate. No matter how hard she tried, she could not seem to form them into coherent sentences.

Hope rubbed her eyes with the backs of her knuckles. The only sound in the small room was the steady hum of the computer. Even Angel, Hope's obstreperous white cat, was sleeping quietly for a change. No dream mice eluded her today, eliciting squeaks and burbles from the depths of slumber. She was curled into a tight ball in the room's one comfortable chair, oblivious to her mistress's growing frustration.

Hope lifted both arms over her head in a futile attempt to ease the ache between her shoulder blades. Her neck had a crick in it, too, and she didn't need a mirror to show her that her dark blue irises were surrounded by jagged red streaks. The parched-eyeball sensation that had been developing for the past hour meant they'd be bloodshot, just as the light-headed feeling at the top of her head warned her that a headache was simmering, ready to boil over at the least provocation.

Concentrate, she told herself firmly. *Get this done.* Once the pressure was gone she might be able to relax and enjoy the rest of the weekend.

She flexed her fingers, took a deep breath and began to type. She managed five words before she heard the familiar toot of the rural mail carrier's car horn. That meant he'd left a package in her mailbox, which meant Hope might as well give up on finishing the letter until she'd seen what it was. She did not admit, even to herself, that she was looking for an excuse to procrastinate. On the contrary, she concentrated on the fact that it was important that she get out of the house once in a while.

Hope punched the key that saved what little she'd done and stood. She bent her slim, five-foot-three-inch body double, twisting slowly in all directions as she reached for her toes. The exercise eased away some of the kinks, but not all, and it did nothing for her appearance. But it scarcely mattered what she looked like, Hope thought. She was not expecting company. The baggy gray sweat suit she wore for comfort when she worked would do for the evening, too.

Taking a cursory swipe at a wisp of pale yellow hair that had slipped out of its anchoring braid, Hope headed for the door. Young Barry, her next-door neighbor, wasn't due to stop by for another hour. She had plenty of time to get the mail, finish her work and even freshen up, though she was well aware she shouldn't look too good to the sixteen-year-old. He already had a terrible crush on her. Hope was trying to let him down gently.

Hope's office was located on the top floor of a graceful, late-nineteenth-century house. From its bow window she had a splendid view of both the winding two-lane road and Barry's parents' rooftop a half mile to the west. She descended two flights of stairs at a rapid pace, all the while steeling herself for the ordeal ahead. At her heavy front door she hesitated, then took a deep breath.

There was a reward out there. A package was waiting in her mailbox. She only had to go to the edge of the porch to get it. Surely she could do that much without triggering a panic attack. She'd done it before. More than once.

Taking yet another strengthening breath, Hope unhooked the chain, released the dead bolt and opened the door. She ignored the blast of cold December air that greeted her. All her concentration was centered on getting to the railing and the pulley arrangement, which she'd had installed there. With a sense of relief, Hope reached her goal and activated the mechanism that brought the mailbox up from the side of the road to the house.

Feeling quite pleased with herself, she'd just extracted the package and a half dozen letters and bills when she heard a vehicle pull into her dooryard. Curious, Hope stayed where she was, wondering who among her friends would be driving a van with a Pleasant Prospect Ski Resort logo on the side. She watched with only mild interest as the door opened and a man got out. But as soon as he turned to face her, Hope's heart began to race.

Cooper Sanford.

Hope could scarcely believe her eyes, and yet there he was, walking toward her, every bit as big and as blatantly masculine as she remembered.

She blinked, just in case she was hallucinating, imagining him only because she'd forgotten to eat breakfast or lunch. He was still there when she opened her eyes again, far too solid to be the product of a fevered brain. He stopped two feet away from her, on the sidewalk, a rakish grin on his face as he stared at her.

It had been years since Hope had last seen Cooper Sanford. At the least, the man should have gone to fat, or maybe lost some of that dark, wavy hair. Instead he'd just gotten sexier as he matured. The teenage heartbreaker she remembered had grown more devastatingly handsome with the passage of time.

Still stunned by his sudden reappearance in her life, Hope noted abstractedly that the mustache was gone. Together with a ponytail and carefully cultivated beard stubble, that mustache had made him stand out at their small, rural high school. It had been slightly shaggy and thick, and Hope had always imagined that it would be downy soft to the touch.

She ran the tip of her tongue over suddenly dry lips, unable to stop herself from recalling just how often she'd speculated about what it would feel like to find out. She'd often imagined that mouth on her own, that mustache tickling her skin. With an effort of will she forced herself to look away from Coop's bare upper lip. Her gaze shifted to a safe point just beyond his left shoulder.

Get a grip, she told herself, but old habits apparently died hard. Hope knew she'd wasted countless hours as a teenager just daydreaming about kissing this man. She felt a flutter of anticipation start deep in her abdomen and spread rapidly throughout her body and realized with growing dismay that she had no more control now over this frisson of sensual awareness, produced by being close to Cooper Sanford, than she'd had when she was a naive schoolgirl of fifteen. Her face began to flood with color.

That blush delighted Coop.

He'd been right. She was the one he needed, everything he'd hoped for. He'd been worried when he'd heard she'd been married and was now a widow, afraid that life might have changed her, but if she could still blush like that, she was the woman for him.

It had been fifteen years since he'd last seen her. Coop noted with approval that Hope was still as petite as he remembered, but the rather flat-chested tomboy he'd known in high school had long since been replaced by a decidedly curvaceous woman. Wisps of light yellow hair had slipped loose from a braid to frame her pale, heart-shaped face. Ethereal, he thought, and quite lovely.

"You're looking good, Hope."

Her eyes widened slightly, as if she couldn't imagine how he'd think so.

Suddenly self-conscious, she tugged at the bottom edge of her loose sweatshirt with one hand, as if to straighten fabric that was already perfectly aligned over her slim hips. The other hand clutched the mail she'd just collected.

"Clever device," Coop said conversationally, nodding toward the mailbox.

"Handy in bad weather." Hope's reply was automatic and followed by an awkward pause.

When she refused to look at him directly, Coop's eyes narrowed slightly. Awkwardness was to be expected. He told himself he mustn't read too much into her failure to greet him like a long-lost brother. She wasn't like the rest of them. She couldn't be. Not Hope.

She cleared her throat and clasped the letters and a package to her chest, almost as if she meant to use them as a shield. "What are you doing here, Coop?"

"Why don't you invite me inside and I'll tell you," he suggested.

When she hesitated, he knew he could not afford to let her send him away without a hearing. If he had to force his way back into her life, so be it. He climbed the two steps to the porch, cutting the distance between them in half.

"You'll freeze if we do all our talking out here." Coop tried his best to sound nonthreatening, to coax her into doing what he wanted, but he was fully prepared to insist that she listen to him. He was already looming over her.

Hope was aware of him, and she knew it was mid-December and the temperature was frigid. She was shivering in her fleece sweat suit, but when Coop moved toward her she had reacted without thinking, taking a step that had brought her perilously close to the edge of the porch.

Vertigo assaulted her, a warning that she was pushing her limit. She had to make a choice between two hazards, and just now Cooper Sanford was the lesser danger.

"Come in, then," she said, and hurried through the door before he could guess the extent of her panic. For reasons she could not clearly define, Hope did not want practically the first thing she said to Coop after all this time to be a confession: "Nice to see you again. I suffer from agoraphobia." It did not seem an appropriate way to greet an old friend.

Except that he wasn't exactly an old friend. Hope heard him follow her inside and shut the door behind him. If she had any sense at all, she thought, she'd send him packing, but she'd always had a soft spot where Cooper Sanford was concerned, even after he'd broken her schoolgirl heart by eloping with her older cousin, Julie.

"Can I get you a drink?" she asked as she led the way to the living room and put the mail down on the coffee table. "Hot chocolate? I don't have any beer."

"Nothing, thanks."

An awkward silence settled between them. Hope was painfully aware of her disheveled appearance. It shouldn't matter, she told herself. Coop had seen her looking far worse, the time she'd tried mud wrestling, for example. But she'd only been ten at the time. Looking good to Cooper Sanford hadn't yet started to matter.

The room suddenly seemed too warm to her, and apparently it felt that way to Coop, too. He shrugged out of his heavy winter coat and draped it over the back of a chair. The cable knit sweater he wore beneath emphasized his broad, muscular shoulders and flat abdomen. Hope tried not to stare, but found it impossible to look away from her unexpected guest.

14 *HEARTH, HOME AND HOPE*

Cooper Sanford had always been trouble. He'd left a trail of broken hearts behind him when he left Norville, including her own. That memory alone should have been enough to keep her from feeling attracted to him.

It was not.

In spite of the warnings sounding in her brain, Hope's eyes continued their intimate survey. Well-worn, snug blue jeans revealed that his bottom half was in equally good shape. What high school football had begun to develop, activities in the years since had honed to perfection.

Hope realized that she had no idea what those activities might have been. She knew very little about his life since he'd left Norville, and that only as it related to her cousin. Julie's mother had made sure the whole town heard about it when Coop and Julie were divorced. Hope's aunt Penny claimed Coop had abandoned her precious daughter and Julie's child. She'd blamed Coop for Julie's death, too, even though they'd been apart for nearly three years by that time.

When Coop turned away, his attention caught by the entrance of Hope's cat, Hope had to blink and swallow hard. His movement had revealed a back view that nearly took her breath away. *Damn,* Hope thought. *The man even has perfect buns.*

Angel advanced on this newly arrived stranger with queenly hauteur, her snow-white fur fluffed out to make her appear even larger than she was. She took it as nothing less than her due when Coop extended a hand to be sniffed, then began to scratch behind her ears.

Hope's attention shifted to Coop's face. A well-remembered lock of thick, dark brown hair tumbled forward over his eyes as he bent to stroke the purring feline. Angel's rumble of approval grew louder.

In the old days, Coop had been constantly brushing that curl out of the way, or attempting to realign it with a toss of his head. Now he simply let it fall where it would.

At that moment Coop glanced up. Hope was transfixed by his glittering gaze. "I'd forgotten how green your eyes are," she whispered.

For a long breathless moment their eyes locked, jade with sapphire. Hope felt like an infatuated teenager all over again. Part of her screamed that this was a ridiculous situation for a mature woman of thirty to find herself in. The rest of her didn't care.

"It's been a long time, Hope." Coop abandoned the cat and came closer to the woman. He seemed to tower over her and she remembered that he'd always claimed to be just a tad over six feet tall.

Nervously, Hope cleared her throat. In high school she'd frequently been tongue-tied around him. She refused to allow herself to be intimidated into another awkward silence.

"So," she began, pleased to discover that her voice sounded almost normal. "You were going to tell me why you're here." She waved him toward a comfortable chair and seated herself on the sofa.

"Right." Coop sat, stretching those long, muscular legs out in front of him. He studied her intently again as he spoke. "I came looking for you, Hope."

"Why?" Common sense told her it was not to renew a romantic relationship they'd never quite had, but she could not stop a little flutter of hope from stirring.

His expression softened. "I've brought Maureen home. I want her to have all the advantages of growing up in a small town."

Maureen. Julie's child. Coop's twelve-year-old daughter.

Hope had never met the girl and had, she supposed, blocked out the fact of her existence along with most of the rest of what she'd heard about Coop and Julie over the years. "I was sorry to hear about Julie," she murmured.

Some strong emotion twisted Coop's features but Hope was certain it was not the pain of losing a beloved wife. "Are you?" he asked. "Funny. I don't remember seeing you among the mourners."

"I couldn't get to the services." Hope did not elaborate on her failure to appear at her cousin's funeral and was relieved when Coop dropped that particular subject.

"After Julie died, I got custody of Maureen. That's when I realized that I didn't want my daughter growing up in a city. She'll have a better life here in Maine, away from bad memories and bad influences."

"I'm not sure this is the safe haven you remember," Hope murmured, thinking of her own experiences, "and you certainly can't claim that living in a small town kept either you or Julie out of trouble."

"But Maureen isn't at all like her mother. She's more like you were at that age." Coop leaned forward, reaching for Hope's hand. "I'd like nothing better than to have her turn out just the way you did."

Hope jerked away before he could touch her. "You don't know anything about the way I turned out."

"I know enough, and I knew you pretty well back then."

"You knew nothing! You were too busy getting into trouble to pay any attention to me." Irritated, Hope glared at him.

Coop's lips curved into a cocky smile. "I remember that you had a crush on me in high school."

Hope bristled defensively. "I was three years younger than you and very dumb."

"Sweet and innocent little Hope Bellamy."

He was teasing, but she couldn't relax and banter back. Too much had changed, whether he was willing to admit it or not.

"I'm hardly innocent these days. I've been married and widowed." The words sounded bitter even to her own ears.

Coop's expression instantly became contrite. He reached for her again. "Hope—"

She cut short whatever he meant to say and evaded his grasp by springing up from the sofa and crossing to the window. "You don't know anything about me as I am now," she repeated, staring out at the distant landscape, "just as I don't know anything about you." In particular he did not know about her little problem with leaving the house, that since shortly after her husband's death she'd been subject to severe panic attacks that had altered her life.

"Hope—"

She jumped, for he'd come up close behind her without her realizing it. When she turned, she very nearly collided with him. His broad chest was barely an inch away from the end of her nose when she caught her balance.

"You always did tend to run into things," he murmured.

For an instant, Hope was carried back to another time, another place. They were both backstage at their high school, negotiating a corridor of papier-mâché pillars. Seven students comprised stage crew for the annual dramatic production. There were six boys and Hope Bellamy.

She'd been so shy in those days that she'd jumped whenever anyone spoke to her. More than once, she'd turned around too rapidly and plowed right into one of the pillars. Coop had taken to walking with his arm around her, thrilling her to the core of her teenage soul. Unfortunately for that adolescent daydreamer, he'd only been touching her because he wanted to make sure the scenery stayed intact until after the performance.

He could take credit for her dedication to set building, Hope thought ruefully. She'd have scrubbed the floor with a toothbrush to work side by side with him. She didn't think he'd ever noticed because, except when he was playing football or working on stage crew, he'd always been out raising hell.

Even when he was supposedly busy with worthwhile pursuits, he'd still managed to get into trouble. A reluctant smile surfaced as she remembered how, when the director of the play had told them that he needed a stained glass window for one scene, Coop and his buddies had promptly gone out and liberated one from a church sixty miles away. By the time the curtain fell on their single Friday night performance, Norville's chief of police had been waiting in the wings to make an arrest.

"You look like your thoughts are a long way away," Coop said.

Hope came back to the present with a jolt. "Long ago and far away," she admitted.

"Pleasant memories?"

"Bittersweet. The teen years are vastly overrated. I think I liked being ten better. And now that I think about it, you weren't so bad yourself back then. It was only after you discovered girls that you got so obnoxiously full of yourself."

"Ouch." He winced convincingly at her assessment but he didn't deny it. "We were friends once," he reminded her. "Good buddies."

"I remember. Then we started to grow up."

"Hey, that part wasn't all bad, either."

He seemed strangely hesitant. Hope waited, expectant but not quite sure she wanted to hear whatever confidence he planned to share with her.

"The closer Maureen gets to puberty," Coop said, "the more I've been praying she'll stay sweet and innocent, just like you were, instead of taking after her mother."

"Julie had help," Hope snapped. Even after all this time, it hurt to be thought the plain, boring Bellamy cousin. "And for your information, good girls aren't usually good by choice."

Maybe she had been lucky he hadn't noticed her back then, but at the time, Hope remembered, she'd been envious of her older, prettier, bolder cousin.

Coop's eyes narrowed into twin jade daggers, sharp as the words he spoke. "She had help," he agreed, "but let me give you a few facts, Hope. It was Julie who wanted to elope, and it was Julie who walked out on me twelve years later, not the other way around."

This time when Coop reached for her he caught her arm, unaware he was setting off sparks as his fingers curled around it. The headache that had been threatening Hope earlier now arrived full force, adding to her difficulty in thinking clearly. Her reaction to Coop's touch confused her. Anger warred with an alarmingly sensual heat as she tried unsuccessfully to twist out of his grip.

Instead of releasing her, Coop brought the other hand up to grasp her shoulder. He didn't hurt her, but his fingers slid relentlessly along her collarbone to capture her braid and forcibly tilt her head until their eyes met.

"Listen to me, Hope. I've made my share of mistakes, but I'm not as bad as Julie and her mother have painted me."

He'd sounded sincere when he'd spoken of his desire to do what was best for his daughter, but now his face was hard, unyielding and ultimately unreadable. Hope wondered if she should be afraid. At the same time, she found herself sympathizing with him. She'd been the victim of her cousin's vicious conniving more than once when they were children. She knew Julie had been capable of lying when it served her purpose.

Coop closed his eyes, as if his thoughts pained him. "I know it's going to be an uphill battle for me every day that I live in this area, but I'd hoped I still had a few friends here. I need our old friendship, Hope. If not for myself, then for Maureen. She needs to have a sense of belonging somewhere, to know she has a family, flawed though it may be. There are only three of us left now. Julie's mother and me . . . and you."

This close to him, Hope was made forcibly aware of the heart-stopping physical appeal of the man. The faint, elusive scent of his after-shave had started the erotic images flowing again. To combat the weakening in her knees, Hope struggled to seem indifferent. He'd only come to her for his daughter's sake. He couldn't have made that much plainer. He had no more interest in her personally than he'd ever had.

As if he could read her thoughts and was put off by them, Coop abruptly released her. She would have fallen if he hadn't caught hold of her again, his hands surprisingly gentle as he righted her. When he released her the second time, he raked all ten fingers through his unruly hair in obvious frustration. A hint of apology lurked in his eyes, and his rueful voice mocked them both.

"You were right earlier, Hope. We don't know each other anymore. Could we start again? I'll even take you up on that offer of hot chocolate."

"Yes. Fine." What choice did she have but to agree? No matter why he'd come looking for her, Hope didn't want to lose Cooper Sanford again. Not just yet.

As he followed her toward the kitchen, she made a concentrated effort to regroup. Bright and chatty would be best, she decided. After all, he was looking for a friend for a twelve-year-old.

"So, you've returned to Norville," Hope said cheerfully. "I haven't spent much time over there lately, and I haven't lived there since I left town to start college."

"We've been back just over a week," he said. "Maureen's already making new friends. In fact, she's going to a sleep over tonight with some of them."

"I noticed the van you were driving. Does that mean you work at the ski resort?"

"Right. Best damn ski instructor they've got."

"Ski instructor," she repeated, trying to take that in as she heated water in the microwave. She remembered that he had skied in high school, though not a lot. It was an expensive hobby, and his family had not been rich.

In the past fifteen years, Pleasant Prospect had gotten even more exclusive, catering year-round to well-heeled, out-of-state tourists and employing local help only in the most menial jobs. "I heard the place changed owners again last year," she said aloud, "but that doesn't seem to have done a thing for the local economy. Ever since they built those ugly time-share condominiums next to the golf course and put in a second restaurant and a gift shop, no one bothers to leave the resort and shop in the village anymore. Even the gas stations aren't getting much of the tourist business."

Coop frowned and started to speak, then seemed to change his mind.

"Where are you staying?" Hope asked. "Are you living at your parents' old house on Seger Street?" She remembered the place very well. Her family had been the Sanfords' next-door neighbors all the time she and Coop were growing up.

Coop shook his head. "Maureen and I are in one of those ugly condominiums. Comes with the job," he added quickly, and went on before Hope could apologize. "I'd been back in Norville only twice since I left, till now. Once to sell the house after my father died and then to bury Julie."

Hope's remarks left Coop feeling uncertain. As she opened two premeasured packets of cocoa, emptied them into ceramic mugs and added boiling water, he pondered the differences between Hope Bellamy, the one girl he'd known in his misspent youth who had been special to him, his friend rather than a potential conquest, and Hope Rowan, the woman that girl had become.

There had been a spark between them years ago. Coop could admit that to himself now, even admit that he had gone out of his way to make sure no fire got started. At eighteen he'd been afraid of what might happen, afraid he'd end up dragging Hope down to his level.

She'd been an innocent in rose-colored glasses in those days. His little buddy. The girl who lived next door and tagged along after him from the time she started grade school, until the day she informed him that she was tired of being treated like one of the guys on stage crew, and asked him to be her date to a church picnic.

He'd turned her down. He'd had to. He'd tried not to hurt her feelings, but he'd said no and he'd walked away from her. Not too long afterward, later that same summer, he'd walked away from everything.

And now he was back.

Coop knew that most things were different. He was no longer a hell-raiser. Hope no longer lived in Norville, Maine, but in Tardiff, the next town over, some twenty miles from his condo. He'd had little trouble tracking her down, though. Everyone still knew everyone else's business in these parts.

The other thing that hadn't changed was that spark. It was still there between himself and Hope. He was being drawn to her again, and again it was almost against his will.

He blinked. Hope Bellamy Rowan, widow, didn't need to be protected from that randy teenager she'd had a crush on. Not anymore. There was no reason he couldn't—

"Coop?"

Hope's voice startled him out of his musings and when he looked at her, he realized he still didn't have her figured quite right. She might have grown up and even been married, but there was still an unmistakable aura of the innocent about her. She could be hurt.

So could he.

They'd both changed. Yet they were both the same.

That very contradiction intrigued Coop even as it made him wary. She was right. He didn't know the woman sweet little Hope Bellamy had become. But he wanted to.

She was sitting at the table now, the two mugs full of hot chocolate steaming in front of her. "Have a seat," she invited. "Tell me what it's like to be ski instructor to the rich and famous. Did you have similar jobs somewhere else before you came here?"

Frowning, he took the proffered chair. Hope's tone was almost too breezy. Coop wasn't sure what to make of her attitude and that made him reluctant to reply with complete honesty.

"On and off," he drawled. "There are worse ways to make a living than being a ski bum."

"I'm sure there are. Still, I expect Maureen would be glad to settle down in one place."

Irritation now kept Coop from revealing the full extent of his connection to Pleasant Prospect Ski Resort. Did Hope, like the majority of those who had known him fifteen years ago, judge him? It seemed she did if she thought a man of thirty-three could consider the seasonal job of ski instructor sufficient to provide for a child.

She pushed one of the mugs his way and he noted how careful she was being not to touch his hand. The bowl of fruit she used as a centerpiece now constituted a makeshift barrier between them, too.

Keep it light, he warned himself. This visit hadn't been for him, anyway. He'd come on Maureen's behalf.

Coop looked around him as he sipped the hot chocolate, taking in the cat decor of Hope's cheerful green and white kitchen for the first time. The walls were hung with pen and ink sketches by Kliban, except for the one titled "Fat Kitty," which hung directly over Angel's food and water dishes.

Inevitably, the direction of Coop's gaze shifted to Hope. The intensity of his stare seemed to disconcert her. She took a nervous sip from her mug.

"You're surprised I came back," he said bluntly.

"Of course. Why should anyone who knew you then think you ever intended to return to Norville? You hated the place. Couldn't wait to get out." She took another sip of the chocolate, then glanced up at him again. "No one blamed you for wanting to leave here, though, no matter what they said about your prospects at the time."

His laugh was short and humorless. "I know what people thought. They were sure I'd end up in jail, like my uncle Brad, or turn into a mean drunk, like my father. Well, both of them are dead now and, for better or worse, my roots and Maureen's are here. That's why I had to come back."

"So how exactly do I fit in to this picture?"

"I want you to spend some time with my daughter. Let her get to know you. You may not like being remembered as sweet and innocent, but you were and are the sort of person who'd be a good role model for Maureen."

"I'd like to meet your daughter," Hope said carefully. "She is my cousin."

"Great. Why don't we all go out somewhere for dinner? Or you could come to our condo. As a cook, I'm not half bad."

Hope's fingers clenched on the handle of her mug. She avoided his eyes even as she made an alternate proposal. "Why don't the two of you come here for supper some evening instead?"

There was something wrong here, in spite of Hope's willingness to meet Maureen. She had tensed up at the thought of going out with them.

"Fine." She relaxed instantly, her relief that he'd agree to bring Maureen here so obvious that it made Coop wince. A nasty uncertainty nagged at him, a suspicion that Hope had made her alternate suggestion because she did not want anyone from Norville to know she'd agreed to befriend him. He drained his mug, scarcely taking the time to savor the rich chocolate flavor.

"How about next week?" Hope offered. "Wednesday?"

"Done." Coop stood abruptly, deciding to quit while he was still ahead.

The saying went that it only took five minutes to get a reputation...and twenty years to live it down. He'd come home prepared to accept that as true and be patient and work hard to redeem himself. But he hadn't counted on the possibility that Hope might share her aunt's opinion that he was worthless and irresponsible.

He hadn't counted on anything about his reaction to seeing her again. Being with Hope had triggered an excess of contradictory impulses. Coop didn't feel ready to deal with any of them just yet, especially not the one that was urging him to pull her into his arms and kiss her.

"I've got to be going," he said aloud.

He'd accomplished his purpose. It seemed best to get out of Hope's house before he said or did something to screw things up for Maureen.

By the time he'd retrieved his coat from the living room and shrugged into it, Hope was waiting for him by the front door.

Don't think about her as a desirable woman, he warned himself. *She's Maureen's cousin. That's the important thing.* But he was unable to resist entirely. On his way out, Coop dropped a light, almost brotherly kiss on Hope's forehead.

"See ya," he said . . . and bolted.

Chapter Two

"See ya," Hope echoed as she watched Coop cross her dooryard to the van. She came very close to following him, at least out onto the porch.

Memories flooded into her mind when she stopped in the doorway. Only after he'd driven off did she close it firmly and once more whisper, "See ya."

That was the way Coop had always said goodbye. Even the last time she'd seen him, when he'd given her the brush-off, when he hadn't planned to see her again at all, he'd left with a "See ya!" and a wave.

Shaking her head at the roller-coaster ride her emotions were on, Hope returned to the kitchen and concentrated on washing out the two mugs they'd used. By the time they were drying in the dish drainer, she felt more in control.

It was not, she decided, the prospect of meeting Julie's and Coop's daughter that had her worried, though that was certainly going to be a disconcerting experience. No, it was Coop himself who troubled her. Even in the worst throes of an adolescent crush, she didn't think she'd ever felt so awkward with him as she'd been today. It was not knowing what his feelings toward her were, she supposed. There had been no real doubt in the old days. He'd always regarded her as the kid sister he'd never had. She'd been the one to change the equation by developing a crush on him. Unrequited love. What a waste of time!

And now? Hope realized that she had absolutely no idea what Coop really thought of her. More to the point, she couldn't begin to guess how he'd react when he learned the truth, when he found out about Elliot, and discovered what she had become since her husband's death.

As that afternoon faded into evening, Hope tried—really tried—to contain her curiosity, but it was no use. She had to find out more about Cooper Sanford. There was one person guaranteed to know something. At ten minutes past eight in the evening, she finally overcame her qualms about prying and dialed the number of Penelope Bellamy, Coop's former mother-in-law and Hope's uncle's widow.

When the phone began to ring in Norville, Hope reminded herself that this was all going to be hearsay. Gossip. She shouldn't believe a word of it without proof. Still, forewarned was forearmed. She sincerely wished someone had made her stop and listen to rumors about Elliot Rowan before she'd gone and fallen head over heels in love with him.

Fifteen minutes later she hung up wondering what had possessed her to think Julie's mother would have anything to offer but venom. To hear Penny Bellamy tell it, Cooper Sanford was worse now than he had been at eighteen. "Once a bum, always a bum," Aunt Penny had declared. She was even talking about taking him to court to get custody of Maureen by proving him an unfit parent, though she hadn't offered a single solid fact to back up her accusation.

Hope weighed what she knew of the two of them. Aunt Penny was a tireless club woman and volunteer organizer, ruthless when it came to raising money for her favorite charity but frequently insensitive to the feelings of the very people she claimed she wanted to help. She was the ultimate in respectability, but in some ways, Hope decided, Aunt Penny had to bear part of the responsibility for Julie's wayward ways. She'd alternately spoiled and badgered her daughter until Julie rebelled.

She'd do the same thing to Maureen.

Then there was Coop, who had been a wild kid and still didn't seem to be particularly respectable, but who had wanted his daughter to have a family so badly that he'd been willing to come back to the one place on earth that was least likely to welcome him.

The more she thought about what Coop had done, the more admiration Hope had for him. In the end her decision was easy. Whatever she could do to help him succeed, she would.

With a lighter heart, Hope went to her office to put the final touches on the Tolliver genealogy.

On Sunday evening, Deputy Sheriff Dennis Long invited himself over for supper at Coop's condo. Maureen, who had spent the day with her grandmother, took to him at once. With little urging, she was calling him Uncle Dennis and treating him as if she'd known him all her life. Delighted to have an audience, she began to regale both her father and his friend with her adventures at the slumber party the night before.

Maureen had inherited Coop's features and his height. Her green eyes danced and her shoulder-length brown hair bounced as she described what fun she'd had. The only reminder of Julie that Coop could find in his daughter's face was that turned-up nose. He hoped it was the only thing she'd inherited from her mother.

"Do boys have slumber parties?" Maureen asked.

"Not exactly." Fond remembrances had Coop and Dennis exchanging a sheepish grin. At fourteen or so they and their buddies had never given up on the possibility that they might catch a glimpse of female flesh scantily clad in baby dolls and lace. "I do, however, remember going uninvited to a few of the parties the girls in my class gave."

"Daddy! You went on a panty raid?"

He tried to look stern. "Did boys crash this all-girl party you were at?"

"Of course not," Maureen assured him with as much twelve-year-old dignity as she could muster. Then she sent an impish look his way. "We just hoped they would."

Before Coop could think of an adequate reply to that comment, Maureen changed the subject on him. "Tell me about my cousin Hope."

"When I first met Hope, neither one of us was as old as you are now."

"So, she wasn't your girlfriend?"

Was that disappointment in Maureen's voice? Coop couldn't tell, but he watched his daughter's face closely as he tried to explain what Hope had meant to him back then.

"She was too much younger than I was to be my girl-friend," he said. "So, she was just a friend who happened to be a girl."

"How much younger?"

"Three years."

"Daddy! That's not so much."

"It was then, Maureen. Trust me on this one."

She looked unconvinced.

"So, Hope was just a friend. Actually, if you want to know the absolute truth, she was mostly a pest. When I was your age, she was around nine, and Hope used to tag along after me when I went to the park to play baseball with my friends. It was pretty embarrassing." He indicated Dennis. "This guy used to tease me unmercifully. Right, old buddy?"

"Oh, yeah," Dennis agreed. "We hadn't gotten to the point yet where we appreciated having girls follow us around."

"Boys mature later than girls," Maureen informed him.

Coop had to give Dennis credit. He didn't laugh out loud. But the thin little mustache he was so proud of started to twitch and he gave in to a sudden need to cough. As he bent forward to hide his face from Maureen, Coop saw that Dennis's light brown hair was starting to get a little wispy on top.

"You're right, Maureen," he said with real regret. "Most girls do mature earlier, and most of them manage to keep their looks longer, too."

Maureen looked thoughtful. "Was Cousin Hope pretty? Is she still?"

Dennis made a strangled sound. Coop assumed it was another stifled laugh.

"I think you should decide that for yourself," he told Maureen. "We're going over to her place on Wednesday."

"Okay," Maureen agreed. Then she yawned and surprised him by declaring it was time she went to bed.

"It's only nine."

"I have school tomorrow," Maureen explained in a solemn little voice. Then she spoiled the image by adding, "I need my beauty rest. Grandmother Bellamy said so."

Grandmother Bellamy was full of hot air, Coop decided, more convinced than ever that he'd done the right thing in recruiting Hope to help him with Maureen. Hope would provide the perfect antidote when Penny Bellamy tried to promote her misguided notions of what a young girl should consider important.

When Coop returned to the living room after saying a private good-night to Maureen, he found his oldest friend's short, stocky form sprawled comfortably on the sofa in front of the big-screen television. Dennis held a diet cola in one hand and was fishing in a box of fat-free Fig Newtons with the other.

The faint, aromatic smell of the lasagna Coop had baked several hours earlier still hung in the air, but it was a pleasant reminder of a satisfying meal. He saw no reason to turn on the vents or open a window to air out.

"The little minx did it to me again," Coop complained good-naturedly as he settled into his favorite chair. "After all that foolishness about beauty sleep, she turned around and talked me into letting her go to the basketball game tomorrow night, even though that will keep her up way past her normal bedtime. She claims the Falcons won't be able to defeat the Hilldale Bulldogs unless she's in the crowd cheering them on."

"She's a good kid," Dennis said, but most of his attention stayed fixed on the hockey game he was watching.

His friendship with Dennis went back a long way, Coop thought, and the two of them had the doubtful distinction of being the only ones from the old gang who were still alive and not in prison. Unlike Coop, Dennis had never left Norville. He'd straightened himself out and done a complete turnaround with the eyes of the entire town glued to his every move. Coop couldn't help but admire him for that.

Small towns neither forgave nor forgot easily, as he was still finding out. Newcomers, including most of the staff at the ski resort, accepted him as he was now. Old-timers, at least the ones he'd run into so far, all remembered him as that wild kid who'd tipped tombstones over in the town cemetery and spray-painted graffiti on the outside of the school building, and they seemed to assume that he hadn't reformed any in the years since.

He'd been home less than two weeks. He knew he shouldn't expect miracles, but he was impatient. Every time Maureen spent the day with Julie's mother he felt as if salt had been rubbed in an open wound.

"I'm real glad you came over," he told Dennis. "It's nice for Maureen to know I have a few old friends left."

"You'd have plenty of company if you let the cat out of the bag."

"I don't want to buy respect, Den. I'm still hoping I'll be able to earn it on my own."

"People are bound to learn the truth eventually."

"Why should they? I've already owned Pleasant Prospect for nearly a year. You only found out about it because you came out to investigate that series of break-ins we had in the fall."

"Someone will let it slip. Your employees know you're the boss."

"But they don't know my background. The ones I deal with directly aren't from around here and they keep to themselves." Hope's comments still stung. Was his hiring policy hurting the economy? He'd never intended that.

"I don't see what the big deal is," Dennis said. "It's no crime to be rich and successful."

"Let's wait and see how rich and successful I am when the season's over," Coop suggested. "Running a ski resort may be respectable, but it isn't exactly a no-risk business."

Dennis shrugged, his attention drawn to the action on the television screen.

Coop couldn't focus on the game. Had he made the right decision when he'd resolved to keep his ownership of the resort quiet? He'd thought at the time that he had good reasons. In the past he'd spent too much time with people who judged others by the jobs they held. He knew he'd made his acceptance in Norville harder than it had to be, but he'd been reluctant to capitalize on the trick of fate that had turned him into a CEO overnight. Besides, it wasn't likely to help his reputation if the precise details of that trick ever got out.

He was doing the right thing, he told himself. So far, the only person he'd really wanted to level with had been Hope, and he still wasn't sure what to make of her reaction to him after all these years.

Or of his reaction to her.

"What do you know about Hope Rowan?" he asked abruptly.

The question succeeded in distracting Dennis from the game, no small feat when the University of Maine Black

Bears were playing, but there was a speculative gleam in his eyes when he turned to look at Coop.

"Well, well," he said. "Why do you ask?"

"Don't be cute, Den. Obviously, we've renewed our acquaintance. I ran into her yesterday."

"You don't just 'run into' Hope Rowan. You had to have gone to her house. The lady doesn't, ah, get out much." Before Coop could ask him what he meant, Dennis winked and went on. "Grew up nice, didn't she?"

An understatement, Coop thought as he remembered just how attractive she had looked. He stared out the window, unable in the dark to see the snow-covered golf course or the ski slopes beyond. From this angle he couldn't even see the other condominiums, and he was suddenly glad of it. Hope had been right. They were uniform and ugly—some modern architect's idea of linked ski chalets. "Hope has turned into a fine-looking lady," he agreed. "What happened to her husband?"

"He died."

"That much I know."

With a resigned sigh, Dennis reached for the clicker and pressed the mute button. "No great loss," he said. "The guy turned up one day about ten years back. Big city fella from California, or so he said. Called himself an entrepreneur." Dennis's grimace as he said the word told Coop a lot about his friend's opinion of the man who'd used it to describe himself. "He had fingers in a lot of pies, and some of them smelled pretty bad."

"A crook?"

"We never had enough to arrest him on, but he was involved in some land deals that didn't look right. If he'd lived, there could well have been prosecutions."

Coop was liking the sound of this less and less, but he felt driven to find out more. "How did he die?"

"Car wreck. Driving too fast on icy roads. Plowed into a tree. That's all she wrote."

"Was Hope with him?"

"No. I was the one who had to tell her. Drove out there in the middle of the night. That's her grandparents' old place she lives in. Did you know that? She and Rowan moved in there when they got married. He lived off her inheritance, from what I could see. Anyway, Hope took it plenty hard when she found out he was dead."

"She loved him."

Dennis gave another shrug. "She married him, so I guess she must have, but toward the end? I just don't know." He ate another Fig Newton while he considered that idea. "She didn't cry or scream or anything when I told her. Just got real quiet."

Coop realized he knew very little about the events in Hope's life after his departure from Norville. Through Penny Bellamy he'd heard that Hope had gone off somewhere to college, and he knew that Hope's mother and father had sold the house on Seger Street and moved to San Antonio a year or so after that. He and Julie had still been married when word came that Julie's aunt and uncle, Hope's parents, were among the victims in a plane crash. A freak accident, he remembered, caused by wind sheers at a small Texas airport. He didn't recall hearing much else about Hope over the years. Julie and her cousin had not kept in touch.

"Seems odd she'd come back here and marry," Coop said aloud. "I mean, she'd gotten out, hadn't she?"

Dennis nodded. "Had a job in Boston. She met Rowan on a visit home. She came back when her grandfather died, met him again, and they tied the knot two weeks later. Wouldn't think she'd be so fussy after that, would you?"

Coop turned to stare at him. "What's that supposed to mean?"

"Hey, don't get all defensive." Dennis lifted both hands as if to ward off an attack, but his grin got wider. "If you've got something going with her—"

"I don't have anything going."

Dennis started to chuckle. "Froze you out, too, huh? There were two or three of us who wouldn't have minded spending some time with the lovely Widow Rowan, but she turned us down flat. Won't go out with anybody. Stays right at home, keeps to herself." He shook his head regretfully. "You'd think she'd be lonely, right? Anyway, more than one man tried to...comfort her. She wasn't interested. Not even in yours truly, and *my* intentions were strictly honorable."

Dennis caught sight of Coop's skeptical look and winked.

"Are you sure you've reformed?" Coop's tone was dry but he could hardly condemn Dennis for having the very same thoughts he himself had entertained about Hope.

"Hey, old buddy, Hope turned into a fine-looking woman and there aren't that many around, in case you haven't noticed."

"Her husband had just died, Den."

"Yeah, well, like I said, that was no great loss."

"She couldn't have known what he was up to." The Hope that Coop remembered had always been honest. She'd have accepted nothing less in a husband, unless he'd managed to deceive her.

"No, she probably didn't," Dennis agreed. "To this day I don't think she's guessed there were other women."

"Damn. He cheated on her?"

"Oh, yeah."

Dennis's calm acceptance annoyed Coop and made him wonder why no one had tried to warn Hope about this lowlife before she married him.

"Probably everybody in Norville and Tardiff except for Hope knew that Rowan was spending a lot of time with Ginny Devereux right before he died."

Coop felt like he'd been punched in the gut.

Ginny, of all people. Ginny, the out-for-a-good-time cheerleader he'd been seeing when he first realized little Hope Bellamy had a crush on him. He'd never forget the embarrassment he'd felt when he'd looked up from the hammock where he and Ginny had been necking and seen his young neighbor staring down at them from her bedroom window. Hope's stricken expression had been a revelation.

He cleared his throat. "You're sure Hope didn't know Ginny was the one her husband was catting around with?"

Dennis's attention had shifted back to the screen and he answered only after the next goal had been scored. "I told you—she didn't know about any of them. Hope and Ginny were both at Rowan's funeral but I didn't see any fur flying."

Sweet and innocent, Coop decided. Maybe some things hadn't changed, after all.

Coop hesitated on the verge of asking Dennis more questions about the late Elliot Rowan. Hope probably wouldn't appreciate his prying into her personal business. Then again, there were few secrets in a small town, and he felt an overwhelming need to know the truth.

How could he avoid touching on subjects that might upset Hope if he didn't know what they were? Reaching for the clicker, Coop turned the television off entirely.

"Tell me everything you know about Elliot Rowan," he ordered.

Coop's phone call on Wednesday to say they were on their way over as soon as he picked Maureen up at school left Hope nervous and on edge. She tried to tell herself that she was reading too much into the event. Coop's voice had sounded businesslike, almost brusque. "Don't cook anything," he'd added. That meant they weren't going to stay too long, so why on earth should she think there was any more to this upcoming visit than his desire for his daughter to meet her cousin?

He'd never felt as strongly about her as she had about him. There was no reason for her to think that time had changed that fact. This time she'd be smart enough not to set herself up for a fall.

In the four days since she'd seen him, Hope had convinced herself that Coop wasn't interested in her at all and that it was for the best since he'd probably be turned off by her condition once he knew.

So, he was going to stop by with his daughter. She'd try to make Maureen feel she had family who loved her, and that would be that. Neither friendship nor puppy love could be expected to survive fifteen long years of separation.

Hope sighed, suddenly feeling very sorry for herself. After a few visits, she might never see Coop again...unless she could conquer her phobia.

"That could take years," Hope told a disinterested Angel. "I'm not being pessimistic. I'm just facing facts."

Angel, who had opened one eye at the sound of Hope's voice, now yawned, closed it again and went back to sleep.

The next hour found Hope taking more than usual care with her appearance. Coop had seen her at her absolute worst. She felt driven to show him that she could look presentable. She'd never been one to fuss over her clothes or hairstyle and she didn't ordinarily wear much makeup. She didn't intend to overdo now, but her hair was clean and shining and she put on what she considered a flattering casual outfit. Snug white jeans and a soft blue velour top with flowing sleeves made her feel both feminine and sensible. The color exactly matched her eyes.

Hope's nervousness disappeared the moment she opened her door and realized that Maureen Sanford reminded her of herself. The girl was shy at first. She didn't seem to know what to say to Hope once her father had introduced them. Then Angel put in an appearance and the ice was not only broken, it shattered.

"You have a cat!" Maureen advanced into the living room, her face eager. "I love cats, but Mama wouldn't let me have one. She said she was allergic to them, but she wasn't really, because once there was a cat right behind the chair she was sitting in, when we were visiting someone's house, and she didn't know it was there and she never sneezed even once."

Hope's heart went out to the girl. "If you haven't been around cats much, go slow," she advised. "Extend one hand, slowly, so that Angel can sniff your fingers."

Hope exchanged a quick smile with Coop when Angel, having assessed Maureen's potential, permitted herself to be lifted.

"Why don't you hold Angel on your lap while we talk," Hope suggested. She sat down and patted the sofa beside her.

"I thought we could all go out for pizza," Coop said.

For just a second, Hope froze. Then she forced a smile onto her face. "Great idea, but I have a better one. Call the order in from here and then go pick it up. I'm hungry enough to eat supper early. How about you, Maureen?''

"Me, too. Does Angel like pizza?''

"Loves it.''

"You can't get rid of me that easily," Coop said. "I'll call, but they can deliver it.''

"You've been away too long. No one delivers pizza in this neck of the woods. And now that you mention it, getting rid of you for a while isn't a bad plan, either. Maureen and I will have a better chance to get to know each other if you aren't hovering in the background.''

"Girl talk?''

At the sarcastic note in his voice, Maureen giggled. "I want to hear Hope's version," she said.

Hope and Coop both spoke at once. "Of what?''

Maureen giggled again. She didn't answer the question until her father had left.

To Hope's relief, Coop hadn't told his preteen daughter about that painfully embarrassing moment when Hope had gathered up all her courage and asked him out. Girl to boy, on a date. She sincerely hoped Coop had forgotten all about the incident.

What he had shared with Maureen were the early days, when Hope had been tolerated and allowed to tag along.

"I think they regarded me as a mascot," she confided to Maureen. "They'd probably have been happier with a dog.''

"Dad likes you better than any dog," Maureen assured her. "Do you like him?''

"Almost as much as a cat," Hope quipped, just in case Maureen was getting any ideas about matchmaking.

She'd always taken refuge in humor, joking around to cover up her insecurities. For the first time, as she thought back on what Coop had been like when they were

younger, it occurred to Hope that he might have been d[...]
ing exactly the same thing.

There were worse ways to cope, as she well kne[...]
Firmly, she concentrated on Maureen, reluctant to let h[...]
thoughts dwell on other methods of evading reality.

"Do you like me?" the girl asked.

"You," Hope said in a mock serious tone, "are [...]
equal footing with Angel. You're one of the family, ju[...]
as she is."

"Does that mean Angel's my cousin, too?"

"Precisely."

Maureen thought that was just fine. Then she asked [...]
she could see the rest of Hope's house. A quick tour too[...]
them through every room. From various windows, Hop[...]
pointed out features of her grandparents' farm, and to[...]
stories from the time when she'd been Maureen's age an[...]
younger.

By the time Coop got back with two enormous pizza[...]
Hope and Maureen were fast becoming friends. Maybe [...]
had been reading too much into Hope's manner, [...]
thought as they ate, but her refusal to go out with him ha[...]
left him with a bad taste in his mouth. He couldn't qui[...]
shake the feeling that something was going on here that [...]
didn't understand.

At the same time, he knew he wanted to spend mo[...]
time with her without Maureen. In spite of his reserva[...]
tions, there was a powerful attraction at work here. At th[...]
least he had to find out if Hope felt it, too.

"Did you know there's an Indian cave on Hope[...]
land?" Maureen reached for the last slice of pepperor[...]
and onion, whisking it out from under her father's fir[...]
gertips.

"That's the legend," Hope qualified, "but even if it isn't true, it's an interesting place to explore."

"I'd like to see it," Maureen said. "Can we go there now?"

Because he was watching Hope's face, Coop caught the flash of panic at his daughter's question. Hope quickly masked her reaction, but he waited with as much anticipation as Maureen for her answer.

"It's already too dark out this evening," Hope said. "Maybe you can see it the next time you come over."

"When?"

"Let's entertain Hope at our place first, Maureen," Coop suggested. "Social obligations and all that."

"Don't be silly," Hope scoffed. "You're family."

She wished she'd kept her mouth shut. Maureen was going to be expecting a guided tour of the back forty and Hope knew she couldn't manage that now. Perhaps not ever.

Coop would have to take her. Hope glanced sideways at him. Maureen plainly adored her handsome father, but she had a generous nature. The smile she gave her new-found cousin touched Hope's heart and tore at it at the same time.

She had all but lied to this child, letting her jump to the conclusion that they'd go adventuring together. Too late, Hope realized that she shouldn't have mentioned the cave at all. She knew firsthand just how fascinating such a place was to girls Maureen's age. She'd been through that stage herself.

Shape up, she lectured herself. *What's done is done.*

Tomorrow, Hope decided, she would get back to work on the desensitizing process that was the only sure way to conquer agoraphobia. It wasn't all that complicated. Just a matter of forcing herself to go outside, to get a little farther away from the house each day. She'd been meaning to do that, anyway. The prospect of reaching the point where she could travel freely again appealed to her even more now that it would also mean she could see more of Maureen and her father. They'd be an added incentive to recover completely from the phobia.

Before she was ready for her company to leave, Coop and Maureen were clearing away the paper cartons and napkins and soda cans and putting on their coats. "Why don't you wait for me in the van, Maureen?" Coop suggested. "I want to talk to Hope alone for a minute."

Hope's breath caught. Awareness simmered through her veins, heating her skin. To her horror, she realized she was blushing again.

Fool! she chastised herself as she walked Maureen to the door. Coop only wanted to talk about his daughter.

The boy who ran errands for Hope arrived just as Maureen reached the van.

"That's Barry Green, my neighbor," Hope told Coop as Barry got out of his mother's station wagon and went over to Maureen to introduce himself.

"Kid doesn't look old enough to drive."

"He's sixteen," Hope informed him. "You were behind the wheel at that age."

But Coop was no longer looking into the floodlit dooryard. He was staring at her. He caught hold of Hope's hand, then shifted his grip to her elbow, running his hand beneath the loose fabric of her sleeve as he guided her inside the foyer. When he closed the door, he effectively shut out the rest of the world.

"I'll be back in a couple of days," Coop said.

"I'll look forward to seeing you and Maureen again."

"Who said anything about Maureen?" he asked.

"I beg your pardon?"

He grinned. Even his eyes were smiling. "I'd like to come over on Sunday, while she's at her grandmother's house. Let's say early afternoon. It'll be just the two of us, Hope. You and me."

She swallowed hard. His hand had begun to caress her arm. Long, strong fingers stroked her skin with an erotic, feather-light touch. She was trying to find the energy to protest when he released her.

The broken contact immediately left Hope feeling bereft. She had a sudden mental image of those same fingers moving elsewhere on her body, stroking and caressing other areas of bare skin. A shockingly sensual awareness shot through her.

"I'm not sure that's such a good—"

"If you were to offer me a picnic lunch," Coop said softly, "I wouldn't be such a fool as to turn you down again."

"Hey, Rapunzel," Barry's voice called out, shattering the moment. "Where are you?"

"My groceries," Hope murmured. She was still feeling flustered when Barry came through the door, followed closely by Maureen. Together they carried the bags through to Hope's kitchen and put the heavy paper sacks on the counter.

"I've seen Barry play basketball," Maureen told her father. "He's pretty good." Even though Barry lived in Tardiff and Maureen was in Norville, they both attended the same consolidated school. They exchanged a few more comments about Monday night's game before Maureen suddenly frowned and turned to Barry. "What was that you called Hope?"

Barry glanced at Hope and Coop, then at Maureen. "Uh, Rapunzel," he said. "You know, from the fairy tale?"

Maureen nodded, but still seemed puzzled.

"It's the long yellow hair," Barry started to explain, "and her spending all the time in that office with the bow window, like a tower, y'know? And—"

"It's just a joke," Hope interrupted, cutting Barry off before he could blurt out the truth about her little problem. She intended to tell Coop and Maureen that she suffered from agoraphobia eventually, but not just now.

Ducking her head to avoid Coop's sudden, intense scrutiny, Hope excused herself to go get her purse. Before he could address any questions to Barry, she was back, lugging a satchel-size pocketbook that weighed at least ten pounds. Still refusing to meet Coop's eyes, Hope wrote Barry a check, then busied herself unpacking the grocery bags.

"Thanks, Barry," she said without looking at him, either. "See you tomorrow."

Dismissed, Barry had no choice but to leave. The boy's face had the same look on it that a puppy dog's got when it had been unjustly yelled at for piddling on the carpet.

"I'll walk you to your car, Barry," Maureen offered.

The boy brightened instantly, unaware of Coop's increased interest.

Barry was a gangly kid, his arms and legs still way too long for the rest of his body. Towheaded, he had pale blue eyes and a sprinkling of freckles. Everything about him shouted All-American Boy Next Door. That had never been Cooper Sanford's description and yet, even as Coop noted the many differences between them, he felt a certain kinship. He remembered very well what it had felt like to know Hope was not for him.

But being all grown up had its advantages. Coop shifted his attention to Hope, who was still busily putting groceries away. She hadn't exactly seemed thrilled by his suggestion.

Snobbery? Or just the same ambivalence he was feeling about their relationship?

Once he'd been sure she was too good for him. Maybe she was still too good for him. Maybe he was crazy to want more. But he couldn't deny that he was powerfully drawn to her, or that she'd been on his mind a lot the past few days.

Didn't they both deserve a chance to find out if the chemistry was still there? "So, how about it?" he asked. "Shall I come over on Sunday?"

"You're forgetting. That's Christmas Day."

"You've already made plans. I should have realized."

"Surely you have the day all planned yourself. Christmas should be special when you have children."

He grimaced. "I've been ordered to present myself for Christmas dinner at Maureen's grandmother's house but I was hoping to avoid it. She's only tolerating me for the day for Maureen's sake. I don't suppose that's where you're spending the holiday?"

She shook her head, a trifle regretfully, he thought, but she didn't reveal what she was going to be doing. He thought of all the reservations young couples and singles had made at Pleasant Prospect. Hope was probably going away, off somewhere that didn't remind her that she had neither parents nor husband anymore. And no children. He wished now that he'd thought of the coming holiday in time to convince her to share it with him.

He cleared his throat, suddenly uncomfortable with his own thoughts. Sharing the holiday was something a *wife* did. Talk about getting a little ahead of himself!

Coop backed off. He needed to give her some space, and take a hard look at his own motives, too. Staying

away from each other for a while would be the sensible
thing to do. But there was still a lot of rebel left in him,
even after all these years. His impulsive side took control
even as he warned himself he might be getting into hot
water.

"What about the following Saturday? Are you free to
help me bring in the new year?"

"Sorry, Coop. I won't be able to go out with you on
New Year's Eve, either."

"Well, after that, then. I'm not taking no for an answer."

She put the last can in the cupboard and turned to face
him. "Bring Maureen over again the first part of January," she suggested.

"You don't want to see me alone, do you?"

"I don't think it's a good idea. Let's stick to friendship, okay? We used to be able to do that."

"If that's the best you can offer."

"'Fraid so."

Maureen was beeping the horn to get him to hurry. Reluctantly, Coop went. Maybe a platonic relationship with
Hope would be best but he knew now that it was not what
he wanted. He'd go along with her wishes...for now.
There was Maureen to think of. But later? He made no
promises.

Once again, Hope followed him as far as her front
door. Once again she watched him drive away.

She'd wanted very badly to trust Coop with her secret
and to confess that she'd love to go out with him, on New
Year's Eve or any other time, except that she just..
couldn't. What held her back was the memory of how
badly she'd been hurt the last time she'd allowed herself
to get too close to a charming ne'er-do-well.

Better to play it safe. Coop had let her down once before. He'd probably get tired of coming around soon enough. It was unlikely, even now, that he'd ever ask her to go out with him again.

Maybe it would be best if Maureen came to visit alone in the future. Yes, that would definitely be the safest way to handle this situation.

Hope's smile was a trifle grim as she recalled the conclusion she'd come to that first day Coop appeared on her doorstep. She'd convinced herself that he presented the lesser danger and had blithely invited him back into her life.

She closed the door and sighed. Even after all these years, and in spite of everything Elliot had done to undermine her faith in her own judgment, Hope knew she was still mightily tempted to be "bad" with Cooper Sanford.

Chapter Three

Coop moved slowly over the uneven ground. It was cold and his ears were already tingling. The surface had a thin layer of hard snow on top of it, but it was also littered with half-exposed roots and branches and he'd tripped more than once.

How much farther was this damned Indian cave? The directions Hope had rattled off some twenty minutes earlier seemed to involve tramping over the entire forty acres.

Hope was at the house.

More than three weeks had passed since the last time Coop and Maureen had seen her. She'd put them off twice by phone and then seemed surprised when they finally turned up on her doorstep an hour ago.

"Why aren't you out tutoring ski bunnies on such a nice, bright weekend afternoon?" she'd asked.

"Day off," he'd muttered.

A lie, but not one he could feel guilty about, not when he'd just learned from Dennis that Hope hadn't left town as he'd assumed she would over the Christmas holidays. According to Dennis, who had stopped by Hope's to deliver a fruitcake from his mother, Hope had been right at home the whole time.

He didn't like being deceived, but what he hated even more was the discovery that Hope's promise to Maureen meant nothing to her. She was as bad as her self-centered cousin, and Julie had surely held some kind of record for number of broken vows.

Little Hope Bellamy, Coop decided as he stumbled over the rough contours of an overgrown path, the shy tomboy who'd literally have given anyone the shirt off her back, had grown up to be a woman insensitive to other people's feelings. She'd only made things worse when she'd given Maureen some stupid excuse about how she had to stay in the house because she was expecting a call. Even if he hadn't noticed the answering machine hooked up to her phone, that nervous fiddling with her hair would have given her away.

She'd been listening to Penny Bellamy.

That was the only answer Coop could come up with for Hope's behavior. He grimaced and kicked an offending rock out of his way.

The old Hope wouldn't have believed anything bad about him. He'd overheard her once, defending him to a couple of her girlfriends. He'd been accused of throwing firecrackers onto the math teacher's porch. She was insisting he'd never be that cruel to a poor old lady like Mrs. Kinkle. He'd done it, of course, but Hope's faith in his innocence had pleased him, flattered his ego... and even prompted him to cancel plans for a return engagement.

Coop's scowl deepened as he pushed his way along the overgrown path. He didn't know why Hope's changed attitude should surprise him. From what the few old high school acquaintances he'd run into over the years had let slip, everyone in town thought he was a cross between Casanova and Conan the Barbarian. Dennis had been the only exception, and even he hadn't been entirely sure what to believe at first.

"Daddy! There it is!"

Ahead of them, three glacial boulders rose from the forest floor. They sat in a small clearing that was almost magically quiet. He could imagine it in autumn, shaded by the majestic trees in full fall foliage.

The Indian cave was formed by the two largest boulders, which tipped toward each other to create a crawl space just the right size for a youngster to hide in. Maureen, all twelve-year-old dignity temporarily forgotten, scrambled up the surface of the first boulder, eager to stand on the very top and be ruler of all she surveyed. Lost in the world of her imagination, she crawled through the hollow, emerging triumphant on the other side.

Hope should have been here to share this, Coop thought. She should have kept her promise, and if she'd broken it only to avoid spending time with him, then he needed to have a little chat with her. He wasn't about to stand by and let anyone shortchange his kid.

Less affected by Hope's decision to remain behind than her father was, Maureen explored happily for almost an hour, then chattered all the way back to the house. It was clear to Coop that his daughter idolized Hope, and that only deepened his resentment. She had no call to slight Maureen even if she did believe Mrs. Bellamy's stories about him.

"Look, Daddy," Maureen exclaimed as they crossed the last field. She was pointing toward the top floor window. "Doesn't she look just like a fairy-tale princess?"

Hope seemed unaware of them. She stood in front of a large bow window. She had shaken out her hair, probably to relieve the pressure of a too-tight braid. The long, fine-spun gold strands were captured by the last rays of the setting sun.

In their absence she'd also changed into something soft and clinging, an outfit that revealed to Coop's astonished eyes the full extent of the curves Hope had developed since high school. His body was reacting before his mind could completely absorb what he was seeing. The intensity of that jolt of desire shocked him. He couldn't tear his eyes away from the sensual picture she made. Each movement brought the fabric of a jet black jumpsuit taut, outlining high, firm breasts, a trim waist, hips that curved enticingly and long, slender legs.

"Rapunzel," Maureen said with a delighted giggle.

Or Lady Godiva, he thought.

The presence of his daughter forced Coop to rein in his errant thoughts. During the short walk the rest of the way to the house, his heart rate slowed to normal and his body began to relax once more. With a wicked grin at Maureen, Coop bent to scoop up a handful of snow and moved into position directly below Hope's window. Then he lobbed the loose snow gently upward, so that it barely brushed the panes of glass.

Startled, Hope looked down, her eyes wide. Then, realizing what had caused the sound, she smiled at them and waved.

"Open the window," he called.

Hope hesitated, then bent forward to obey. Coop's grin widened as he realized he was actually contemplating quoting from the balcony scene in *Romeo and Juliet*.

"Rapunzel, Rapunzel, let down your hair!" Maureen shouted.

"Even better," Coop said under his breath.

Maureen was convulsed with laughter. "Rapunzel!" she repeated, and pointed at her own softly curling light brown hair.

Hope laughed with her. Then, imitating the fairy-tale character locked in a tower, forced to offer her long tresses as a ladder for her lover, Hope leaned out and let her pale hair drift toward them.

"Are you going to climb up, Daddy?" Maureen demanded.

"Hope's hair doesn't reach down far enough," he said regretfully, almost as caught up in the fantasy as his daughter was. He wished he could make some romantic gesture, but as he watched her face, he saw Hope's laughter abruptly die. Without warning, every bit of color drained from her cheeks and she shuddered. For a long moment after that she didn't move, didn't speak. Then, very slowly, she began to withdraw.

Once she was safely inside she called out to them. "It's too chilly for this." She closed the window behind her before anyone could say another word.

Puzzled, Coop continued to stare at the place where she had been. Had he imagined it? For the space of a few seconds could the expression in her eyes really have been fear?

Big mistake, Hope thought.

In an attempt to bolster her self-confidence she'd made Cooper Sanford remember that she'd grown up. Now he'd be after her again, wanting her to go out with him. It was impossible. She should have let things be.

She'd decided weeks ago not to burden him with her problems but perhaps, subconsciously, she'd still wanted to attract his attention, the old approach-avoidance thing psychology textbooks blathered about. For just a moment she'd reveled in his appreciative grin. She'd even forgotten caution so far as to lean out the window toward him.

Out there toward him.

What irony. After all this time there was finally something out there she wanted, and she was trapped, just like poor old Rapunzel.

She heard Maureen clatter up the stairs, heading toward the bathroom. If she wanted to talk to Coop alone, Hope realized, it would have to be now.

She had to tell him. She'd explain that the nickname Rapunzel had come about when she'd told Barry that she figured she and that fairy-tale character shared the same little problem, that Rapunzel had really stayed in her tower because she was trapped there. Every time she tried to go out, she had a panic attack, just the way Hope did.

But by the time Hope joined Coop downstairs she'd lost her nerve. She had a social smile pasted firmly in place. "You had a lovely day for a walk in the woods," she said brightly. "I wish I could have gone with you."

Coop's gaze swept down, then up. Suddenly self-conscious, Hope wished she'd chosen a less revealing outfit. She'd been looking her usual sloppy, comfortable self when he and Maureen arrived and in their absence she'd given in to the urge to change. Feminine vanity would be her undoing, she feared. Under the silky teddy beneath her jumpsuit, her body was responding enthusiastically to his bold stare.

"Very nice," he said. "If you'd been dressed this way that first day I'm not sure I'd even have recognized you."

She ought to feel insulted, Hope thought, but his grin was knowing and his eyes were dark with an intensity that held her still even when he reached out to touch her hair. Unbound, it cascaded down her back, reaching nearly to her waist.

"Whatever happened to that skinny kid with braids?"

"I was a late bloomer." Hoping to dispel the charged awareness between them, she said the words in a phony Southern belle accent and batted her eyelashes with outrageous abandon.

"It was worth the wait." Reluctantly, he released the strand of hair he'd been fingering. His gaze dropped to the ring at the top of her front zipper.

Hope danced away from him. "Why, thank you, sir," she said. She escaped into the kitchen and busied herself with preparations for Angel's supper.

"I'm taking Maureen to the potluck supper at the fire station tonight. I thought I'd expand her education in rural life. Want to come with us?"

"I've been to potluck suppers. Besides, I'm still waiting for that phone call."

"Are you?"

Something in his tone made her stop with the can of cat food still in her hand and look at him. He was glowering, all traces of approval gone.

"Maybe you're just reluctant to be seen out in public with me. Is that it, Hope? Worried about your reputation?"

"Don't flatter yourself," she snapped, and jammed the cat food can into the electric can opener. Angel magically appeared to wind herself around Hope's ankles, complaining loudly when a filled bowl failed to appear immediately.

"What's the problem, then, Hope?"

Her laugh was humorless. "Not a big problem. Just a little one."

She steeled herself to confess, but before she could say a word, Maureen bounded into the kitchen. "Daddy! I'm ready! We've got to go right now if we want to sample the best chowder. Grandmother Bellamy said so."

"Sure you won't come along?" Coop asked.

Hope refused to meet his eyes, and had scooped twice Angel's normal portion into her bowl before she realized what she was doing. "I ... can't."

"You mean you won't."

"I mean I can't," she whispered. She didn't know whether he caught the words or not, but a moment later she heard her front door open and close and turned, only to find that Maureen had gone but Coop was still in her kitchen.

"Go on," she told him. There was no time now to explain. "You'll have more fun without me, anyway." She put Angel's supper down on the floor, refusing to look at him again.

Her voice seemed strained to Coop, and in spite of his irritation at her and his confusion he was still beset by a compelling attraction. With every movement of her body, his reacted. The dark cloth outlined the curves and dips of derriere and thigh as she carried the cat's water dish toward the sink to refill. Coop followed her, waiting only until she'd dumped the stale contents down the drain before he reached for her.

Startled, Hope swung around, moving into his embrace before she realized how close he was. Coop made no apology for taking advantage of the alignment of their bodies. His lips captured her mouth, already open in futile protest. At the same time, he pinned her between the counter and the cradle of his thighs, and caught her wrists with manacling hands in case she intended to fight him.

She didn't.

Coop felt as if he'd walked into a furnace. She caught fire in his arms, her passion hot and melting. Never before had a kiss consumed him as this one did. He forgot everything but the erotic pressure of her lips. Off balance, he clung to her and angled his mouth over hers to deepen the kiss. The first touch of her sharp little teeth against his exploring tongue sent ripples of pleasure throughout his already aroused body.

Against his chest, he felt her nipples harden, exciting him still more. The warm smell of her skin seeped into his senses until he knew he'd never forget her uniquely feminine scent.

"We've got to stop," she murmured when they drew apart far enough to breathe in ragged gulps of air. "This is crazy."

"This is heaven," he whispered, but he forced himself to release her. "Now you've got no choice. Come with us to the supper and later we can—"

He broke off at the look of sheer panic on Hope's expressive face. A moment later it was gone, but she was stepping away from him and avoiding his eyes again. His unease quickened, combined with an almost painful sense of loss.

"I'm not ready for this," she said.

"No pressure, Hope. Just come with me tonight and we'll play it by ear."

"You don't understand. I can't go with you. And you'd better leave now. You and Maureen want to get there early, so she'll have the full experience."

Her voice suddenly sounded so calm and disinterested that Coop wouldn't have believed passion had flared between them only moments before if it hadn't been for the swollen look to her well-kissed lips. The aftershocks of their embrace still tormented his aroused body.

"Hope—"

"You'll have to hurry." When he would have protested again, she said the only thing guaranteed to send him on his way. "You don't want to disappoint Maureen."

Penny Bellamy bore down on her ex-son-in-law with the determination of a bulldog, and something of that animal's angry expression. "Sit down, Cooper," she ordered, "and we'll both try to pretend we're enjoying this conversation."

The potluck supper was being held above the fire station. Chairs had been set up in the dimly lit corners and unless someone came too near, Coop knew he and Penny would appear to be enjoying a pleasant chat. A hometown combo was providing music at a level that made it difficult for anyone to overhear even if they were standing nearby.

"To what do I owe this honor, Mother Bellamy?" Coop used the title deliberately, aware that she hated it.

For the first time since he'd known her, Julie's mother looked a trifle unsure of herself, but that situation didn't last long. Coop waited, his curiosity engaged, while Mrs. Bellamy harrumphed and glared.

"Maureen tells me you tried to convince Hope Rowan to come here with you. As your date, I assume. Leave her be, Coop."

Coop stared at her. "Why should I? Your opposition alone is almost enough to send me back to Hope's place to try again."

"That poor girl has enough to contend with without you complicating her life."

"She's hardly a girl any longer."

Penny ignored that comment. "My niece married one loser. She doesn't need another taking advantage of her. It's bad enough Maureen has to be exposed to your scandalous life-style without—"

"Maureen is doing just fine, thank you."

"Yes. Well. I know she won't say a bad word about you, but I know what you are, Cooper Sanford, and I'm not likely to forget it. You thwarted all the wonderful plans for Julie that her father and I had."

Coop waited. That last was one charge he could not deny.

Penny Bellamy's florid complexion changed to an odd mottled shade. "I hold you personally responsible for my daughter's death. If she hadn't married you, she'd still be here today."

Coop wondered why he wasn't getting angry. By the time the local rumor mill had finished grinding up his reputation after the divorce, people had apparently been speculating that he beat his wife and neglected his daughter. If he'd still lived here at the time, the public censure probably would have been enough to drive him away.

"Don't you just love small towns," he muttered under his breath.

"My Julie was a sweet girl, sensitive and—"

"Please! I was married to her, remember?"

Mrs. Bellamy's face hardened. "How can I ever forget? You—"

"Maureen is coming this way, Granny. Do you really want her to hear us discussing her mother?"

Mrs. Bellamy did an abrupt about-face, both literally and figuratively. "Hello, darling," she called to Maureen. "Are you having a good time?"

After his ex-mother-in-law went off with Maureen, who for some inexplicable reason wanted to introduce her to Barry Green, Coop had little time to dwell on her accusations or her warning. Taking her private conversation with him as a signal that they'd patched up their relationship, that Coop was now at least marginally respectable, other people wandered over. The older ones were cordial, and seemed curious about what he was doing now. He was close to enjoying their reminiscences about his youthful pranks, which differed a good deal from his own memories of them, when Ginny Devereux suddenly appeared at his elbow.

"Hey, lover boy," she greeted him, and gave him a noisy smack on one cheek. Then she made a production out of wiping her lipstick off his skin.

The town librarian, who'd actually been smiling at Coop, changed her expression into a censuring frown and excused herself. A little knot of people gathered around her as soon as she reached her table.

Ginny had gotten louder with the passage of time. At five-eight and red-haired, she'd always stood out in a crowd. Now she seemed to dominate her surroundings. Her dress was both five times more expensive and five inches shorter than anything any other woman there had on. Coop hid his amusement. On this evening in mid-January, she'd have shown better sense to do as most of the others did and wear wool slacks.

Ten minutes after she sat down and started talking to him, Coop knew all about Ginny's successful real estate business, her regular sessions at the county's only athletic club and her brand new BMW. She commiserated with him over the scarcity of job opportunities in a depressed economy, obviously having heard he was employed as a ski instructor. In spite of his apparent lack of wealth or position, she let him know she was available.

Coop wasn't interested.

It was no greater hardship for him to part company with Ginny Devereux than it had been to watch Mother Bellamy walk away. The evening had taught him one thing. He knew now that there was only one person, aside from Maureen, whose opinion of him mattered. What Hope thought had always been important. Her hero worship had meant more to him than she'd ever realized back then. Her approval counted now, too.

Coop decided to allow a little time to elapse, to give them both a chance to do some thinking. Then he was going to have to see Hope Rowan again. He wanted her friendship. He needed her respect. And he hoped for much, much more.

Without Maureen to distract him.

Hope was feeling rather pleased with herself as she went out after the mail. She could do this particular chore now without a qualm, and yesterday she'd even gone to the barn and back, albeit with Barry present to talk her through the trip.

She was making progress. Slow progress, but better than none. She only hoped her efforts hadn't come too late to salvage a good relationship with her cousin. She hadn't heard a word from Maureen or her father for nearly a week. Not since that mind-blowing kiss, a kiss she was trying very hard to dismiss. She didn't need the complications that romance would bring into her life. Or so she'd been telling herself ever since Coop walked out the door.

Hope activated the mailbox.

A long moment passed before the anticipatory smile faded from her face. The box had started toward the house but now had stopped moving. It was jammed at the halfway point.

"Damn."

Hope knew she could wait for Barry, but her frustration at such slow progress ate at her. How was she ever going to get over this agoraphobia if she couldn't manage to go a few feet away from her own front porch? The absurdity of the situation was not lost on her. She told herself she was foolish to hesitate. Unsticking that mailbox could be exactly the challenge she needed. Chances were she'd have no difficulty at all. Nothing terrible would happen to her.

Hope knew there was no logical reason she couldn't go out onto the terraced hillside herself. Right next to her end of the pulley was the broom Barry used to sweep snow off the porch. She hefted it experimentally. Using the handle, she should just be able to reach the mailbox and jiggle it loose.

"It isn't far," she said aloud, hoping that by speaking the words she could make herself believe them. The rolling, snow-covered expanse still seemed to stretch forever.

"Five minutes," she muttered.

Surely it wouldn't take more than that to dash off the porch, crunch across the crusty white surface, which was only a few inches deep, knock the box loose with the broom, and sprint to safety.

"I can do it," Hope whispered. The trick was not to spend too much time thinking about it beforehand.

A determined gleam in her eyes and the broom held tightly in one hand, Hope stepped off the porch. She reached the spot directly under the stuck mailbox without any difficulty, but when she stretched upward, attempting to knock the ice loose from the pulley wire, she discovered that the handle wasn't quite long enough. She reached again, and abruptly lost her footing.

Hope's panic began even before she landed heavily in the snow. She tried to struggle to her feet but only slipped again. After that she stopped trying. Her heart was racing far too fast, banging in her chest so forcefully that she was certain it was trying to batter its way out. Her breath began to come in short little gasps. She knew the last thing she should let herself do was hyperventilate, but she didn't have enough control left to stop herself.

Nameless fears multiplied, closing in with a paralyzing intensity that left Hope's limbs rigid and her mind numb. Her eyes stayed open but she no longer saw anything. The only sound she heard was the violent rhythm of her own heart.

A few miles away, Cooper Sanford was heading home after a Friday afternoon business meeting when he caught sight of the road sign and applied his brakes. Columbia Hill Road. Since he was so close it only made sense to stop in.

He checked his watch, then remembered that Maureen wasn't waiting for him, anyway. After school she was going shopping with Amie, her new best friend, the same one who'd hosted that slumber party. He had plenty of time for a side trip.

Coop made a cautious U-turn, though the traffic was light, and headed back the way he'd come. The main road, Route 2, was only two lanes in this part of Maine, but Columbia Hill Road was a narrow, twisting byway. The houses along it were few and far between. Other cars were nonexistent.

Driving slowly, he soon came to the post labeled Rowan in fancy script. The mailbox must be on the porch, he realized, though he couldn't see it from where he was.

The house and barn sat back from the road, shaded by trees. They could only be reached by a driveway that crossed a small bridge as it wound its way uphill toward the dooryard. Coop squinted at the house as he pulled in, half blinded by the sun glinting off the snow on either side of the narrow way. It was a nice-looking place, he decided, well aware that once he would have called this site lonely. Only now could he recognize it for the quiet haven it was.

Coop parked his car, got out and was halfway up a recently sanded flagstone sidewalk before he spotted her. He came to an abrupt halt at the sight of Hope sitting bolt upright in the middle of a snowbank.

Coop blinked once in surprise. Then he was sprinting toward the motionless figure on the terrace. She was still as an ice sculpture, out in the frigid cold with neither coat nor hat on to protect her from the elements. He wasted no time trying to figure out how she'd gotten into her present predicament. She obviously needed help.

Coop slowed at the edge of the hill. He'd have to inch his way down the steep incline, edging cautiously closer to the immobile form, for the footing looked treacherous. Coop felt the flat surfaces of four narrow steps set into the bank as he started down. Their coating of ice only made the going more precarious.

She was not lying unconscious, but that fact failed to reassure him. There was nothing normal about her statuelike stillness. Her back was to him, so he could not be sure, but she seemed to be staring off into space.

"Hope?"

She didn't turn, didn't acknowledge him in any way. He wasn't sure she even knew he was there. Struck again by the fact that she wore no warm outdoor clothing, only another of those fleece sweat suits she favored, Coop shivered in sympathy. A frigid wind eddied out from behind the house, hitting them both full force. If she'd been sitting there long she might already be suffering from hypothermia. That could be serious, even life-threatening, if it wasn't treated in time. He broke out in a cold sweat at the thought.

Coop glanced at the pulley arrangement overhead and saw at once what had happened. She'd fallen trying to knock a jammed mailbox loose. Still, there had to be more to the story than that. Had she hit her head? Broken something? He couldn't imagine anything less would keep an able-bodied woman in this outdoor icebox.

Reaching her at last, Coop sank onto his haunches in front of her. There was no obvious cause for her condition, but she seemed to be in shock. She stared blankly at him. Her bare hands were icy to his touch, and equally unresponsive.

There was no help for it, he decided. Whatever hidden injuries she might have, his first act had to be to get her inside the house where it was warm. Praying he wasn't doing any permanent harm, Coop slid one arm around her shoulders and started to lever the other under her knees.

"Good thing you're only a little bit of a thing," he muttered as he struggled to his feet with the woman in his arms.

Coop took a closer look at his burden as he clasped her tightly against his broad chest. Under other circumstances, Coop realized he'd have been enchanted by the opportunity to sweep such an attractive female off her feet. In the present situation, he could only grit his teeth and ignore the idiotic fancy that he might be able to kiss her out of her trance, like some modern-day Prince Charming to her Snow White.

Careful of the dangers underfoot, Coop began to climb toward the house. Hope stirred in his arms. Her eyes blinked closed as she whimpered and squirmed against him, burrowing into the warmth of his shearling jacket.

"Hope? Are you hurt? I can take you to a doctor."

His softly spoken words provoked an unexpectedly violent reaction. Brilliant sapphire-blue eyes shot open again, still unfocused but now reflecting sheer panic. Her struggles nearly tumbled both of them into the snow.

"No!" she cried. "No, I won't leave here. Let me go!"

Her sudden, violent attempt to break free caught Coop off guard. He maintained his balance but it was a near thing. When she began to pummel his chest and arms with furious fists he lost his temper. Most of the blows landed harmlessly, but one clipped the side of his head and made his ear ache painfully. It was abundantly obvious that she was not seriously hurt. She didn't seem to have much control over her aim, but her arms and legs clearly worked just fine. Abruptly, Coop bent forward and deposited her on the topmost terrace step, holding her there with one hand on either side of her hips.

"Settle down or I'll leave you on your butt in the snow till you freeze to death!"

Hope stared at him, wide-eyed and bewildered. Her face was only inches away from his but he couldn't tell if she recognized him or not.

"You need to get back inside the house where it's warm," he said. "I won't hurt you. I just want to help. Do you understand me?"

He got no answer, but she stopped trying to escape. Cautiously, mindful of the damage one hysterical female could inflict on a man, Coop took her hands in his and tugged her to her feet. She didn't resist as he helped her regain the sidewalk, but her steps faltered. Impatient, Coop picked her up once more to climb the steps to the porch.

Inside the house he found welcome heat and the smell of freshly perked coffee. He hoped that meant she hadn't been outside very long.

Coop kicked the front door closed behind them with one foot and carried Hope through the foyer to the living room. He deposited her on the sofa and deftly, carefully impersonal, ran hands over her, checking for broken bones or any other obvious sign of injury.

Lord, she was soft to the touch.

He found nothing to alarm him, unless he counted the disconcerting effect of discovering that she wore no bra under her sweatshirt. There was no indication that she'd struck her head. There was no blood anywhere. Nor were there any lumps, bumps or broken bones.

It was the bemused expression on Hope's pale face that brought a new and very ugly suspicion into Coop's mind, one that could certainly explain her odd behavior.

"What's the matter with you, Hope?" he demanded sharply.

She murmured something under her breath, but it made no sense to him.

"What are you on?" he demanded.

Bending closer he sniffed her breath. Only the faint wintergreen scent of toothpaste wafted his way.

That ruled out alcohol but left him with a host of other possibilities. The idea that someone he'd once thought was very special could have been stupid enough to have gotten involved with drugs infuriated him. He'd seen far too much substance abuse when he'd been married to Julie to feel tolerant about it.

Coop jerked Hope upright and shoved roughly at the sleeves of her sweatshirt, pushing them up as far as they would go. There were no needle tracks, although that didn't prove much. He subdued Hope's struggles easily to check again and make sure he hadn't overlooked some kind of medic alert necklace or bracelet. He hadn't. That meant he couldn't attribute her symptoms to diabetic shock or epilepsy or any of the other medical conditions he knew of that had symptoms that could be mistaken for signs of drug overdose.

A shiver racked Hope's slender body as he released her.

She needed warming up, no matter what was wrong with her. Coop glanced toward the fireplace, wondering if it would help to light the wood already laid in the hearth, but the room seemed a comfortable temperature to him. With impatient movements he flipped open the brightly colored afghan she kept rolled up at one end of the sofa and covered her with it, then stalked off toward the kitchen.

"Coffee," he muttered as he went. It would be hot, and the sobering effect of caffeine wouldn't hurt her any, either.

Chapter Four

Hope's sense that disaster was imminent began to subside as soon as she was carried in through her own front door. The numbness took longer to fade, and she was confused by the fact that she could hear someone rattling around in her kitchen.

Too warm, she tossed aside the soft wool cover and took several deep, restorative breaths while she tried to order her thoughts. With each passing moment the effort became easier. By the time Coop came back from the kitchen with a mug of coffee in each hand, Hope's scattered wits had regrouped.

Her hard-won composure shattered the instant she saw the irritated look on his face. She accepted the coffee but couldn't seem to stop staring at him over the ceramic rim. She took a sip of the hot brew and burned her tongue. Her hands were trembling so badly that she had to wrap them both tightly around the mug to keep from dropping it.

Slowly, the feel of the heated surface had a calming effect.

"Drink up," Coop said gruffly, and took a long swallow from his mug.

She obeyed, finishing the coffee quickly, hoping it would clear her head. With exaggerated care, she set the empty mug on the end table.

The aftermath of this attack seemed different from the norm. Not that there really was a normal pattern, but Hope knew she should have felt more rational again as soon as she got inside. Instead, Coop's presence was keeping her pulse racing and her mind bemused.

Above all else, she was aware of regret. This was not the way she'd wanted him to find out about her little problem. To be truthful, she'd hoped he'd never have to hear of it at all. She wasn't usually so unrealistic, or so reluctant to face up to things, but now she had no choice. She'd have to tell him everything and be prepared for his disillusionment, maybe even his pity. To have him feel sorry for her, Hope realized, might be the most difficult thing of all.

She sighed.

"What happened?" Coop asked.

The deep, resonant tones she knew so well were underscored by an equally familiar impatience. He sounded as irritated as he looked, and a fierce scowl marred otherwise handsome features. Coop's gaze swept over her from head to toe and back again. If his expression was any indication, he did not particularly like what he saw.

Hope frowned, then drew herself up straighter and glared back. She knew he must be confused by what he'd just seen, but she didn't understand why he was acting so hostile. She tried to tell herself that his mood was only affecting her this strongly because she'd just suffered one of her panic attacks and hadn't quite come out of it yet. And that she'd been overtired before that.

Rationalizing didn't help. She resented his attitude. What did he have to be so superior about, anyway? He'd once dealt with his problems by running away.

Hope squared her shoulders. It was time to get herself off this emotional roller coaster. To stand up for herself.

"I didn't expect to see you today," she said.

It was an inane remark. She conceded that to herself the moment after it came out of her mouth, but she also knew it was the best she could manage at the moment. She was glad she was able to speak at all. After one panic attack she'd been reduced to stuttering for hours.

"I cannot believe that the reason I moved back here, the reason I wanted Maureen to know you, was to cut down on the chances she'd be exposed to bad influences."

"I beg your pardon?"

She already knew that he was a protective father, but just what threat he suddenly thought she presented to Maureen, Hope could not begin to fathom.

"I just want to know one thing," he said. "Why couldn't you get yourself out of that snowbank? Why were you just sitting there?"

Hope felt her face flood with color. He'd rescued her from a potentially dangerous situation. Naturally, he was curious. And it was her own fault that he didn't yet know about her little problem.

She tried to make light of it. "I never even thanked you for bringing me in—"

"You made a quick recovery," he interrupted. "What did you take?" He leaned toward her, regarding the decorative covered dish on the end table between them with suspicion.

"I beg your pardon?"

Coop was at her side in an instant. One callused finger slid under her chin, holding her head still so that she could not avoid his searching gaze. In the depths of those jade green eyes she saw simmering anger. "I want to know what you took."

"I did not *take* anything," she said through clenched teeth.

"Sure." Looking disgusted he released her and stood. He backed away from the sofa, as if he could no longer bear to be close to her.

"You can believe me or not, but I happen to be telling you the truth."

His eyes blazed. "Don't get on your high horse, lady. I saw you out there. You were out of it."

Hope was on her feet in an instant, fists clenched tightly. She kept them at her sides with an effort as she glared at him. "You have no right to jump to such offensive conclusions. How dare you assume I was high on something? Even a criminal isn't condemned that fast."

"I know what I saw, and because of that I don't think I want my daughter anywhere near you."

"Now I'm going to corrupt your child? Coop, you're overreacting. I told you before—you don't know anything about my life or the way I live it."

"I can guess." He turned his back on her and headed for the foyer.

He'd taken only one step before she followed him. Hope was still annoyed by his attitude, but she was trying to hold on to her temper. This was so typical of a reformed hell-raiser! Fatherhood had made him protective. She couldn't really fault him for that. But she could not stand the thought that he might leave thinking she'd turned into a terrible person.

"You're being ridiculous, Coop," she said as she caught his arm. "You ask for an explanation and then you cut me off before I can give you one."

There in the narrow confines of the foyer, he stopped short and swung around to face her. "Did you hit your head when you fell?"

"No, I didn't hit my head." Exasperation made her voice shrill.

"Then why in hell were you sitting in a snowbank in the freezing cold? Face it, Hope, that is not the act of a rational person."

"So now I'm crazy?"

Indignant and offended all over again, Hope pulled back on the verge of telling him the truth. Let him think what he liked!

"Fine. I'm crazy." She probably was. For a few weeks she'd actually thought that she was glad to see him again. "So long, Coop. Do drop in again in another fifteen or twenty years."

"Damn it, Hope, how can you treat this so lightly? You're ruining your life. Tell me what you've been taking. Maybe I can help you."

"Maybe it isn't any of your business. Why should I confess all to you? You probably wouldn't believe me anyway."

"You owe me an explanation."

"I don't owe you a thing."

"I saved your butt, lady."

"Okay, I owe you a thank-you. You've already gotten it. Now get out of my house." The more belligerent he got, the less willing Hope was to attempt any sort of explanation. It was difficult enough making people understand her phobia under normal circumstances.

The look in his eyes was one of disillusionment, with a hint of regret. That shook her. Did he really care so much?

"I wouldn't have believed it of you, Hope," he said softly. "You were a nice kid once."

"I'm still a nice kid!" she all but shouted. "My life is about as exciting as dry toast!"

Their gazes locked, hers defiant, his startled. Very slowly, the beginning of a rueful smile lifted the corners of his mouth. Hope stared at his lips, then hastily jerked her eyes away. She felt much too warm, and the small foyer suddenly seemed to have shrunk.

"Hope—"

"If I were to judge you by how quickly you made assumptions about me, then I guess I'd have to think that you must have made some less than straitlaced friends in the past fifteen years. What would they likely be on? You tell me. Are we talking about illegal drugs, or just some handy prescription for Valium?"

He sighed and his warm breath stirred her hair. "Okay, Hope. Maybe I jumped to the wrong conclusion. I've been surprised before by the kinds of people who can become dependent on drugs."

"In your misspent youth, I suppose."

"And after." She felt him look away, then at her. "I've been wrong before, too. When they first told me Julie was dead, I figured she'd overdosed on something. Lord knows there was enough available in her world, and I couldn't think of any other reason a woman her age would just up and die."

Hope sensed his agitation, felt his hands clench on her arms, but she could think of nothing to say to ease it. She didn't know all the circumstances surrounding her cousin's death, only that it had been a fluke, an infection that had not been caught in time.

After a moment, Coop relaxed his grip. He inhaled deeply and exhaled slowly, as if to drive out all thoughts of his ex-wife along with the bad air. When his attention centered on Hope once more, he spoke in a husky whisper.

"You have to admit that what I saw was pretty peculiar. Do you want to tell me why you couldn't get back inside on your own? Why you fought me when I picked you up? How you got calmed down again so quickly?"

"Are you sure you'll believe me?"

"I don't know why, but yes, I'm sure." He didn't sound upset anymore.

Head still lowered, she'd ended up staring at his chest. Now she was remembering how it had felt to be held tightly against that firm surface. He had carried her inside. Under other circumstances, the act would have been incredibly romantic.

"I'm sure of something else, too," he murmured in a voice that sounded so strange it prompted Hope to look up at last.

Coop placed one hand against the wall on either side of her head, trapping her. The intense look in his eyes as he lowered his mouth toward hers robbed her of breath, and drove every rational thought right out of her mind.

The kiss was an apology, gentle, coaxing and as sensual as anything Hope had ever experienced. She didn't want it to end.

At the same time, his generosity made her feel guilty. They wouldn't have quarreled at all if he'd known about her little problem from the first.

Reluctantly, she pulled back from the embrace. He kept a light grip on her forearms, as if he feared she'd run away if he let go. His eyes locked on hers, determined to extract the truth as if it was an unwanted and painful tooth.

"I was out there because I had a panic attack," she said. "I'm agoraphobic."

"Agoraphobic?" Coop repeated, plainly startled.

She nodded.

"Agoraphobia," he murmured.

"The word derives from Latin," Hope blurted. "Literally it means fear of the marketplace."

Coop stared at her, still taken aback by the revelation. He'd heard of the condition, but he'd never encountered anyone who suffered from any phobia before. That Hope had fallen prey to one astonished him.

"This is a little hard to swallow," he muttered. He made no attempt to hide his confusion. For the moment, the promise in the kiss they'd just shared was all but forgotten.

"I should have told you before. It's no big deal. It isn't even that hard for me to talk about, usually. Lots of people know. Barry does all my shopping, except what I get by mail order. And he clears out the driveway and takes things to the post office for me."

"But...how did it happen? You were never afraid of anything when you were a kid. Shy sometimes, yes, but brave enough to try just about any stunt we dared you to."

Coop was still trying to absorb what she'd told him. He'd already admitted to himself that he'd accused her unfairly. She was not popping pills, like so many of Julie's high-powered, stressed-out co-workers.

Hope had a phobia.

Trouble was, Coop didn't find that explanation very reassuring. How could the girl he'd once known, the girl he'd admired and put up on a pedestal, have fallen prey to an irrational fear of leaving the safety of her own home?

She was younger than he was. As a kid he'd more often than not felt protective toward her. He'd talked her
out of taking the really dangerous dares. But never had
Coop thought of little Hope Bellamy as the vulnerable
sort. She'd always had a strength of character he'd admired, a determination to go after what she wanted. Even
him.

"I'm not consciously afraid of much now," Hope told
him.

"None of this makes any sense to me."

"I know. I'm sorry. I should have told you sooner."

"You say you've made no secret of your condition.
Why didn't you tell me?"

She finally met his eyes, but sheepishly. "I was embarrassed, okay? Maybe I hoped someone else would spill the
beans. Aunt Penny was a good bet. And Barry almost did,
with that Rapunzel business."

"You stopped him halfway through making the com-
parison," Coop said, remembering. Idly he stroked one
hand along the back of her arm. "But I don't think I get
the allusion."

"Rapunzel in her tower? Trapped there? I don't know.
It just seemed an appropriate symbol at the time. Good
for a few laughs. I even considered having a logo put on
my business cards."

"How can you joke about this?"

"Better to laugh than to cry."

She was being flippant again. Just like the old days.
Coop shook his head, unable to comprehend how anyone could stand to live that way. If she really thought she
was trapped in some Rapunzel-like tower, why wasn't she
moving heaven and earth to free herself?

Hope's heart sank as she watched Coop. He had released his grip on her arms, but what bothered her more

was that he seemed to be withdrawing from her emotionally. She could not guess his thoughts, but she suspected they were unflattering.

"It isn't a disease," she said sharply. "I'm not some kind of a pariah, either."

"No. You didn't need society to cast you out. You did that to yourself."

"You're angry."

"Yes."

"Only because you don't understand what it's like for me."

"All right. Tell me. How could something like this happen to you? What caused this phobia? More important, what are you doing to get over it?"

She sighed. "I've always been as forthcoming as possible about my reasons for staying at home. I refuse to treat the whole subject like some dark, dirty little secret."

"Right. That's why you didn't tell me right away. You've fed me one lie after another to cover up, lies about waiting for phone calls and not wanting to go out for pizza. What else have you lied about?"

"Nothing important," she said honestly. "And I guess I know the reason now. I must have suspected, deep down inside of me, that you'd act just the way you're acting right now. You don't even know the first thing about phobias, do you?"

"I've never had one, if that's what you mean."

"Then you cannot possibly comprehend what—"

"Try me," he challenged her. "I know that phobias are fears. Powerful fears. Some people are abnormally afraid of heights. Some panic at the thought of flying. Others are terrorized by cats."

Maureen's story about her mother's supposed allergy was in both their minds. Hope was sure of it. But Coop didn't smile, and her pessimism increased.

"Come back into the living room," she said, resigned to an uncomfortable discussion. "We might as well sit down, because this will take a while."

For one tense moment she thought he might leave. Then he shrugged and motioned for her to precede him.

When they were seated again, with her on the sofa and him in the chair, Hope took a deep breath, knowing before she began that she'd probably sound like she was quoting from a textbook. "Agoraphobia is a fear of open places. In extreme cases, someone suffering from it never leaves a single room, and sometimes she even stays in bed all the time."

"She?"

"Statistically, far more women are afflicted than men."

"Okay. I follow that," Coop said.

"Don't get sexist on me," she warned. "It's probably the fault of society rather than gender. If women weren't pushed into thinking they only belonged in the home—"

"Spare me," Coop interrupted, holding up one hand to stop her. "I have never objected to women doing anything they wanted to."

The bitterness in his voice gave Hope pause and convinced her that Julie had really done a number on him. She wished now that she knew more about his marriage. She also wished he'd stop staring at her, especially since his expression was so enigmatic. She didn't have a clue as to his real feelings about her condition.

"Could you please explain to me," he said, "how an intelligent woman like yourself could get into this situation in the first place."

"It wasn't deliberate!"

He lifted one brow at her heated defense.

Easy, Hope warned herself. This was no big deal. She only had to talk to the man, answering his questions calmly and clearly.

"Sorry," she mumbled. Carefully, she unclenched her fists and smoothed her open palms over the sides of her sweatpants.

"Take your time," Coop said.

"Don't patronize me."

An eloquent silence followed her unwarranted warning.

"I acquired this phobia pretty much the usual way," Hope finally said. "I've done some reading on the subject since, and it turns out I'm almost a textbook case."

"Is that something to be proud of?"

In the face of the almost angry glitter in his eyes and the sardonic tone of his question, Hope hesitated. She'd been prepared to be totally honest, but now she wondered just how much she should tell him. She wanted him to understand what suffering from a phobia was like for her, but she had no desire to discuss the events that had taken place immediately before its onset. She didn't want to talk about Elliot Rowan, her late husband, at all. Most of the time she even avoided thinking about that phase of her life.

But she was committed now. And she did not want Coop to end up feeling pity for her. There was no longer any point in trying to hide the fact of her agoraphobia, not when he'd already witnessed what could happen to her because of it. Moreover, she owed him at least an edited explanation.

"I was at the grocery store," she said as she toyed with the edge of the afghan. "I was waiting in line at the checkout. All of a sudden, I couldn't seem to get enough air. My chest felt too tight."

Before Hope could contain them, memories of that terrifying experience assaulted her, surfacing so vividly that she stopped speaking entirely. In her mind she was back in Mike's Market, feeling waves of heat rush into her face and thinking that she was way too young to start having hot flashes.

All around her was the normal everyday activity of a small rural market, but for Hope her surroundings suddenly began to fade in and out. The sound of the old-fashioned cash register was too loud one moment, almost inaudible the next. Hope heard the cashier's voice, even understood that the woman was talking about her, but she was incapable of speech, unable to answer a spate of worried questions as other people in the line noticed that something was wrong with her and crowded around.

A woman's perfume nearly choked her with its cloying scent. Then she caught a whiff of fresh blood as Mike of Mike's Market himself came to see what was going on. He'd been cutting meat, and when he fanned her with the edge of his butcher's apron it was all she could do not to scream. Mike was more worried that she'd sue him if she fainted and hit her head than he was about what ailed her.

Hope clutched her chest and tried with trembling, frantic fingers to loosen the collar of her blouse. She was certain she was having a heart attack. Then, when she felt nausea begin to overtake her, she had the even more horrible conviction that Elliot had gone and died and left her pregnant.

"Hope?" Coop's worried voice penetrated the vision, calling her back to the present.

She blinked at him, then drew in a deep breath. "Somehow, I managed to stay upright," she whispered, "but I dropped all my groceries." Cat and dog food cans had rolled everywhere. She'd heard something in a glass container break. A can of coffee had landed on her foot and left a bruise, but at the time she'd barely felt the pain. "I watched a head of lettuce bounce away, and for a moment there I was wondering if my own head might be about to fall off and roll after it."

She tried to smile reassuringly at Coop, but the effort failed miserably.

It had been nothing short of a miracle that she'd been able to stagger out of the market and into the parking lot. The sun had seemed too bright, but at least she'd been able to breathe again.

"As soon as I got out of the store and into my car, everything was fine," Hope finished.

Coop left the chair to sit beside her on the sofa. He pulled the afghan out of her grip and took her icy hands in his warm ones. She resisted the temptation to curl against him, absorbing his warmth and strength and comfort.

"Damn it, Hope," he muttered in a gruff voice. "You've lost every bit of your color."

"I don't usually get this flustered when I talk about it," she apologized. "I've accepted that this happened to me. I'm dealing with it."

Who was she trying to convince? Coop, or herself? Hope wasn't sure anymore.

"Dealing with it? Not from what I've seen. How—"

She put her finger to his lips to silence him. Her eyes locked on his, willing him to understand what she was telling him. "After that first one, the panic attacks became more and more frequent."

Hope barely controlled a shudder and forced herself to go on, still holding Coop's gaze, still determined to make him feel what she'd felt. Gradually, her voice gained strength. She thought she sounded nearly normal.

"Naturally, I went to a doctor, but nothing seemed to help except avoiding the places that tended to trigger attacks. Pretty soon I just stopped going into town at all. It was easier that way. If I stayed here at home, I could be certain I wouldn't embarrass myself in public. It seemed to me, for a long time, that I didn't have much incentive to go any farther from the house than my own barn."

"Why the barn?" There was no pity yet in Coop's eyes, only genuine concern and a certain amount of curiosity. He seemed to be trying very hard to put himself in her shoes, though she couldn't tell yet if he was succeeding.

Hope managed a weak smile. "There's a doghouse built into the side of the barn. Our dog, Moxie, had his own private entrance. Long chain. Good-size run."

"A watchdog," Coop said, half to himself. "Out this far in the country, that's only good sense."

"He was an old mixed breed, mostly husky. After Elliot died, I had to go out to the barn to feed him and to put out fresh water and give him a run." She shrugged. "But then, after old Moxie died, there just didn't seem to be much point in going even that far. There wasn't anything out there that I wanted badly enough to leave the house for. I was already working at home. I'd established a reputation for meticulous research. I had the equipment to reach out to the rest of the world from right there in my office."

Determined not to make heavy weather of her situation, Hope began to tell him some of the more amusing challenges she'd faced in the past year and a half, a time during which she'd devised numerous ways to stay safe at home and have everything she needed brought to her.

"I have colleagues who exchange information with me. I can borrow books and microfilm on interlibrary loan.

The only real problem has been getting access to material that is kept in special collections."

"So you do have incentive to get out, to visit those locations in person."

She shrugged dismissively. "I could just pay another genealogist to do the work for me. It's only a job, after all."

"Jobs are usually required in order to have a few other things. Money to buy food, for instance. Pay taxes on your house."

"I have enough to live on." Hope managed a weak smile. "I don't need much."

"What about people? Don't you feel a need to see your friends? You always used to be a sociable sort. Volunteered for all kinds of things. Always had friends staying over at your house."

"Most of my high school friends are long gone. If they didn't move away, they changed. I found I didn't have much in common with any of them when I came back here."

They'd been married, with young families. And they hadn't cared much for Elliot. What friendships she might have renewed, he'd discouraged. Their life together had been almost as isolated as her solitary existence was now.

Banishing unprofitable regrets, Hope patted Coop's hand. "Besides, you were my first best friend. None of the girls ever compared."

"I can't see you avoiding people," he said.

"It wasn't people I was avoiding. Just . . . situations. I haven't been unhappy living this way. Most of the time I've been perfectly content." At least she had been until Coop burst back into her life.

"Don't you get tired of spending all your time in one place?"

"I don't suffer from cabin fever, if that's what you mean. And I do have some friends, Coop, friends who come here." That their visits had become fewer and fewer in the past year was a fact she chose to ignore. "And I have Angel. And Barry looks after me."

Coop looked skeptical, as well he should. Her defense of her life-style was beginning to sound pathetic, even to her.

"A cat and a kid." Before she could say more, he added a question. "Has he been working for you long?"

"About four months. Before that his older brother Rodney ran my errands. When Rodney went off to college, Barry took over."

"And how long have you been a widow?"

Hope pulled back, suddenly cautious. She wondered what Coop had heard about Elliot. "My husband died a little over two years ago," she said carefully.

"So, you got out of the house, into town and all, when he was still alive?"

"Yes, I did. And no, it isn't likely there's any connection between his death and my phobia." At least she hoped there wasn't. No one really knew what caused agoraphobia, but widowhood didn't seem a likely cause in her case. If anything, losing Elliot should have made her more eager to get on with her life, to enjoy all that the wide world out there had to offer her.

Coop was staring at the cold hearth. Brooding, she thought. She still couldn't guess how he felt about her revelations.

"What happens when Barry goes off to college?" Coop asked after a moment. "For that matter, what happens when he has to choose between you and a hot date, or a basketball game?"

"He has a younger brother. Jason. By the time Barry goes to college, Jason will be old enough to drive to the store for me."

The pat answer seemed to annoy Coop.

"In other words, you plan to go on like this forever." His hand turned, capturing her fingers. He leaned closer, until their faces were only inches apart. "Surely you don't want that. And there must be some way to get over this... this... thing."

"Go ahead and say it—this irrational fear."

Gently she extracted her fingers from his grip. She needed a little distance. His concern warmed her, but she was afraid to read too much into it.

"In some few cases, the condition disappears as abruptly as it surfaced. People in life-and-death situations, for example, threatened by some greater danger, may be able to overcome their fear. But those cases are rare. The usual cure is a process of gradual desensitization. I have to force myself to go a little farther outside the safety zone each day. Slowly, the area that feels comfortable expands. Eventually, I get back to where I was before the first attack."

"If that's all there is to it, why haven't you done it already?"

"I've been working on it." She didn't add that until recently, the effort hadn't seemed particularly worthwhile, that taking the chance on having a panic attack was an act of courage, the kind of courage she didn't always find within herself.

"Not hard enough, apparently."

Exasperated, she glared at him, but she got control of her temper quickly this time. He couldn't understand. No one could who hadn't endured the sheer panic. "You al-

ways were impatient, Coop. It isn't some kind of a virus.
I can't just go to a doctor and get a shot or some pills.''

"Hope—"

"Anyway, I got the distinct impression just now that
you don't much approve of people taking pills."

"I'd think a psychiatrist—"

"No."

"Why not?"

"Because they don't make house calls?"

Her attempt at humor fell flat.

"Look, Coop, I already know what I have to do. This
does not require analysis. The problem is that one has to
be very strongly motivated to go through the process. I
mean, think about it. Would you willingly do something
that made you physically ill?"

His expression gentled, and she softened her voice in an
attempt to match it. "Desensitization may sound easy,
Coop, but it is devilishly difficult to do."

He continued to look thoughtful, but refrained from
comment.

"I'm working on it," she repeated, and knew she
sounded defensive.

She *felt* defensive. This was her life, after all.

Now that she thought about it, Cooper Sanford had a
hell of a nerve coming back to town after all this time and
making her feel guilty that she'd let this thing take control of her the way it had.

"You'll just have to accept me as I am," she told him,
"and for the present, if you want Maureen to spend time
with me, she'll have to do it here."

Then she waited, dreading his response to the challenge she'd just issued.

What if he thought the agoraphobia changed things?
What if he no longer believed she'd have a good influ-

ence on his daughter? What if he decided neither he nor Maureen should visit Hope's home again?

Her track record with Elliot did not inspire much confidence. She knew now that she couldn't have been more wrong in her understanding of her late husband's character.

What if she'd completely misjudged Cooper Sanford, too?

Chapter Five

She'd stopped going out when the dog died.

Coop heard what she was saying—and what she wasn't—but it was still difficult for him to take in. He stood, leaving her on the sofa, and moved restlessly around her cozy living room. Heavy gold draperies had been pulled back to let in the afternoon sun. The view through the window was perfection itself, a trackless, snow-covered meadow and the woodland beyond. Peaceful. Serene. But only to look at? He shook his head, unable to imagine willingly locking himself away from the world outside.

She must really have loved Elliot Rowan, he decided, to react so badly to his death. It was the only explanation Coop could come up with for the change in her.

But one small corner of his mind sneered contemptuously at the idea. Could he really believe she hadn't known what sort of man her husband was? She was probably still living off his ill-gotten gains. No wonder she wasn't very concerned about her job.

He shook his head, trying to focus his thoughts. What if she had known, and was still this upset at losing him? What did that say about Hope's common sense? What did it say about her charac—

Coop didn't permit himself to complete that thought. Foundering again, desperately trying to take in all Hope had told him, he let his mind drift to his own history, let himself remember just how thoroughly he'd been taken in by Julie's machinations toward the end of their marriage. It seemed to him that he and Hope had both, as the old saying went, loved not wisely but too well.

Of course Hope had loved her husband, and of course she hadn't seen the darker side of him. Sweet, innocent little Hope Bellamy had hidden herself away in this house precisely so that she wouldn't have to face up to the facts about her late husband.

Satisfied that he'd sorted things out logically, Coop knew without a doubt what he had to do next. He had to help Hope get through this difficult time in her life. There was no reason for her to be afraid of anything any longer. From now on she would not have to face her fears alone.

"Do you want me to tell Maureen, or would you prefer to?" he asked. "I think she should know as soon as possible, in case she thought you were turning down our invitations because you didn't want to be seen with her."

"Tell her what? That I have a little problem or that I'm no longer fit company for her?"

Startled, Coop turned away from the window at last. Hope had curled her legs beneath her and sat huddled in a corner of the sofa, eyes downcast, hands tightly clenched in her lap. Three long strides brought him to her side. He lifted her chin with the side of his hand, forcing her to meet his eyes.

"Don't be absurd, Hope. You're the one who keeps saying it's just a *little* problem. Now, do you want to talk to Maureen about it yourself, or should I—"

"I'll tell her. She may have questions."

He nodded and released her. Her relief had been almost palpable. She'd really believed he meant to keep Maureen away from her. With sudden guilt, Coop remembered he'd threatened exactly that, before he'd understood the reason for her erratic behavior.

"I didn't realize Maureen had come to mean so much to you. You've only spent time with her on two occasions."

Hope managed a weak smile. "Quality time," she murmured. "And I like your daughter, Coop. She's a good kid."

"Let's hope she stays that way."

"She's going to grow up, Coop. There's no way anyone can stop that."

Unable to stay still, reluctant to think about his little girl turning into a teenager, let alone a woman, Coop wandered the confines of the living room, pausing to study the fireplace tiles, moving on to corner knickknack shelves loaded down with a collection of bisque figurines.

He couldn't put his finger on why, but somehow the sight of those delicate, very feminine figures relieved some of his anxiety. "Yours?" he asked. "Or something your grandmother collected?"

Lost in her own thoughts until he spoke, Hope looked up, startled. It took her a moment to follow his change of subject. Then she smiled. "They're mine. See the broken one? That started me off. Remind me to tell you the story behind it sometime. You'll get a kick out of it."

"There's another story I'd rather hear first. You haven't told me yet how you met your husband."

He'd heard a person's face could close, but he'd never before witnessed the phenomenon. He'd clearly touched a nerve by mentioning Elliot Rowan.

He assumed that meant his conclusion was the correct one. Hope didn't want to talk about her husband because there were still strong emotions at work when she thought of her life with him. He'd have to coax the details out of her if he wanted them.

But did he really want Hope to confide in him?

Suddenly Coop wasn't sure he did. A sensation remarkably akin to jealousy twisted inside his heart. Hope's feelings were the important thing here, he told himself. Not his. She needed to talk to someone. That much seemed obvious.

"There's a lot we don't know about each other," he said carefully. "Maybe we should try to remedy that. For Maureen's sake," he added. "I don't know much about what happened to you once I left town. You were still in high school then."

"Finished high school. Went to college. Started a career."

"And then?"

Hope came up off the sofa before he could plant himself beside her. "I don't want to talk about my marriage to Elliot or his accident."

Coop held up both hands in surrender. "I don't mean to pry. I just thought it might help to talk. One of the things old friends are good at is listening."

"Can we drop it, Coop? I've told you I'm working on starting over. I'd just as soon not talk any more about my past."

After a moment's thoughtful silence, he nodded. "Yes. You may be right." He didn't want to discuss his divorce from Julie, or his marriage to her, either. Not yet. "I vote we agree to avoid discussing both our former spouses . . . for now."

She opened her mouth but he didn't give her time to say a word.

"I think we've probably said enough serious stuff to each other for the time being." He gathered up his coat and fumbled in the pockets for his gloves.

Hope looked relieved that he was going, but when he turned toward the door she caught his arm. Her voice sounded worried. "You will bring Maureen over again? Soon?"

"Tomorrow soon enough? It's Saturday. How about in the middle of the day sometime?"

"Fine, but . . ." Hope's voice trailed off and she frowned.

"What?"

"Don't you have to work? I mean, the weekend has to be the busiest time at a ski resort. I don't want you to risk losing your job on my account."

Coop knew her bewilderment was genuine, as was her concern, but considering the fuss he'd just made over her white lies, this didn't strike him as the best time to confess to his own little deception. "Don't worry. I can take time off whenever I want. No problem."

"How can I not worry? How can *you* not? After all, you have a growing daughter to support. If you get fired, you won't even have a place to live."

"We could always move in here," he teased.

Hope's frown deepened. "That's an awfully casual attitude."

He was tempted to explain that they couldn't fire the boss, but what he'd said a few minutes earlier was still true. They'd been serious enough for one afternoon. He held on to his light tone, determined to distract her. "You don't like casual? I can do formal." He clicked his heels together and bowed slightly.

The move garnered a reluctant smile.

"Fear not, Lady Rapunzel. I am Prince Charming, the fair-haired boy of Pleasant Prospect Ski Resort. I've got them convinced that I can do no wrong."

"Obviously they don't know you very well." Hope stopped fighting her amusement. "And you remind me more of Peter Pan than Prince Charming."

"Never grow up? The idea has definite appeal."

Hope's eyes were alight with laughter. Suddenly Coop no longer wanted to leave. It took all his willpower to stick to his resolution and walk out the door.

"See you tomorrow," he promised. "Expect us right around noon."

"In that case," Hope informed him, "you'd better stop on the way for pizza."

By the time Coop arrived home, he'd mapped out his entire campaign. From now on Maureen was going to be spending even more of her free time with Hope, and so was he.

Desensitization, Hope had called it.

He and his daughter were going to help her through that process. They'd tempt her to get out more and more. Coop was certain they'd be successful, and that Hope would be back to normal within a couple of weeks. The perfect role model for his daughter had one minor flaw. He intended to do everything in his power to help her overcome it.

He had the time. He'd hired a new ski instructor at the first of the year. Most of his job now consisted of paper-work, and he could do that any time, even at night at home.

Friends help friends, he told himself. For the moment he would shelve the more complex emotions Hope inspired. Belatedly, he understood Mother Bellamy's warning and reluctantly agreed with the point she'd been trying to make at the potluck supper. Hope didn't need anyone lusting after her just now.

There must be some other old friends still around, in spite of Hope's disclaimer. Dennis might know. He'd known all about Elliot Rowan's part in a scheme to sell faulty office equipment. And Dennis had obviously also known about Hope's phobia. Had he been trying to protect her by keeping that tidbit to himself?

Coop got out of the car and let himself into the condominium apartment he shared with Maureen. It was far from sterile, not with a twelve-year-old in residence, but it wasn't really a home, either. Not like Hope's place.

He'd been joking when he'd said he and Maureen could move in with her, but damned if the idea didn't have a certain appeal.

The front door of the condo opened onto a small hall-way with a closet on the left and stairs to the right. Ahead, Coop could see up to the balustrade that set off the living room on the upper level. No, not living room. Living, dining and kitchen were areas in this place, not rooms. The condo had come fully furnished, too.

They needed a dog, he decided.

Then he remembered that pets weren't allowed.

He was tempted to get a pooch from the shelter any-way, then ask Hope if she'd keep it for them at her place. It could be a replacement for the dog who'd died. She'd have to go out and feed it. Or let it live in the house with her and Angel.

Coop found he was smiling. Hope would see right through that ploy. Reluctantly, he abandoned the idea of a dog. Even if Hope did agree to look after one, Angel would never forgive him.

Hope's eyes, clearly reflecting her sense of relief, met Coop's over his daughter's head. Both their lunch, on this bright, sunny Saturday, and her explanations had gone much better than she'd had any right to expect. Maureen had indeed asked many questions, but she'd seemed satisfied with Hope's answers, and had been frankly intrigued by some of the ways Hope had contrived to avoid leaving the house. She'd exhibited particular interest in the fact that Barry Green and his brothers had played a major role in implementing some of them.

"Barry is a very nice person," Maureen remarked.

"Yes, he is." Hope began to gather up the remains of the two huge pizzas Coop had brought. "Anyone besides me like cold pizza for breakfast?"

"Yuck," Maureen said, and shivered.

At the same time Coop said, "Love it."

Maureen giggled.

"Split it with you, then," Hope compromised. By the time she'd wrapped two equal portions in foil, Coop had fetched three coats from the hall closet. He tossed Maureen's at her and began to bundle Hope into the bright yellow parka she'd bought shortly before Elliot died.

"Coop, what are you—"

"We need to work off what we just ate."

"You know I can't—"

"Shh. Trust me. We're not going far."

Their eyes locked.

"Trust me?"

After a long moment, Hope nodded.

The worst that would happen to her was another panic attack. She didn't much care for that possibility, but he'd be right there to rescue her. And maybe it wouldn't happen. This time she was willing to take the risk.

"We're going to go over to that snowbank at the side of the barn," Coop announced when they'd gotten as far as the front porch.

Hope looked in the direction he was pointing. The snowblower Barry had used to clear the dooryard had left a good-size mound on the spot. "Why?"

"To build a snowman, of course."

She studied the distant white surface. A frisson of unease slid along her spine. "No, I don't think so."

"Now, Hope—"

Panic edged closer. Hope willed herself to ignore it. She'd been as far as the barn before. This was not going to defeat her. She blinked. She swallowed. Aloud she said, "I don't think so because that's not snowman snow."

Coop quirked a brow at her.

She sent a brave smile in his direction. "That's snow *fort* snow," she informed him, and stepped out onto the flagstone walk.

Ten minutes later, having collected shovels and a bucket from the barn, the three of them were hard at work. Hope glanced toward the house. She waited for the palpitations to start but nothing happened. Almost dizzy with relief, she bent to the task at hand and was soon enjoying herself every bit as much as Maureen was.

Coop's daughter was obviously having fun. She stopped now and again to lob a snowball at her father, but a structure of blocks of snow steadily rose to defend the top of Hope's driveway.

"Did you and Dad build snow forts together when you were my age, Hope?" Maureen asked when they'd reached the point of adding turrets shaped with the bucket.

"I don't think I ever played in the snow much at my house," Hope reflected. "Your father and I were next-door neighbors on Seger Street in Norville, so we saw a lot of each other in the summer when school was out, but in the winter all my playing in the snow was done right here on the farm where my grandparents lived."

"It was a working farm, then?" Coop asked.

"It had been in my great-grandparents' day. A small one. A few cows for milk, a few chickens. A vegetable garden. But most of that was already gone by the time I started coming here for visits. There's a little man-made pond not too far back in the woods. It was originally dug to water the cows, but when I was a kid we just used it for ice skating."

Hope stopped midway through hoisting a block of snow to the top of the wall and stared off across the meadow. Speaking as much to herself as to them, she murmured, "I'd almost forgotten about the pond."

"We'll have to try the ice some time," Coop said. "Do you have skates or should I bring you a pair from the resort?"

She made a face at him, knowing full well what he was up to, but she didn't reject the idea out of hand. Neither did she answer him. As she finished placing the snow brick to her satisfaction she spoke to Maureen. "I spent every Sunday here on the farm with my grandparents, all year round."

"I spend every Sunday with Grandmother Bellamy." Maureen sounded uncertain if that constituted a common bond or not.

"Your Grandfather Bellamy was my father's brother," Hope said. "These were my mother's parents."

"Grandfather Bellamy is dead," Maureen remarked as she went to work putting the finishing touches on the snow fort. "And so are your grandparents and your parents and both of Dad's parents and my mother. People don't seem to live very long in this family."

Coop and Hope exchanged a startled glance, uncertain how to answer. "If you're worried about inheriting a short life span," Hope said after a moment, "there's no need. Those who didn't die of old age were the victims of accidents."

"What about my mother?"

"Julie wouldn't have died if she'd gone to a doctor sooner," Coop said bluntly, "and I think this discussion has taken a morbid turn. Let's find something more cheerful to talk about."

"There isn't anything wrong with being interested in your ancestors," Hope said gently. "After all, that's how I make my living."

Hope wondered if Coop and Maureen had ever talked about Julie's death. She was hardly the one to suggest they should, though. She'd lost Elliot long before they lost Julie, and she had yet to talk about his untimely demise with anyone. She didn't even like to think about it.

"How did you get started in the family tree biz?" Coop asked. She couldn't see his face. He'd started building an addition on the snow fort.

"My grandfather was a history buff. You never met him, did you?"

He shook his head. "I don't think I ever knew where your mother's parents lived, or where you went every Sunday, though I do remember that you always went somewhere."

She smiled to herself, momentarily lost in good memories, and idly packed a snowball with both hands. "Gramps got me interested in genealogy. It was a hobby at first. Then it just...grew. You'd be surprised how many people want to know about their ancestors but are too lazy to do the research themselves."

"I have to do a family tree for school," Maureen said. "Would you help me, Hope?"

"I'd be happy to, Maureen, but you might want to ask your grandmother first. She knows a lot about the Bellamys, and about her own family, as well. She had to trace them all the way back to Colonial times so she could join the Daughters of the American Revolution."

"Would she know about Dad's family, too?"

Coop winced. "I'm sure she can rattle off the names of all the horse thieves and con men in the lot."

Hope glared at him. Then she threw her snowball, striking him squarely on the arm.

"What was that for?"

"Every family has a few black sheep," she said. "That should never be a reason to avoid looking at the past."

He gave her an odd look.

"There's another school assignment you could help me with, too," Maureen said, apparently oblivious to the undercurrents between her father and her cousin.

"What's that one?" Hope asked.

"We have to evaluate and compare popular exercise programs for a gym project. When you showed me around your house I noticed that you've got a whole shelf full of tapes. Cindy Crawford and Kathy Smith and—"

"If you want to borrow them, that's—"

"Could I come here and try some of them out instead? That way you could tell me which ones you like best and why. That would really help me get a good grade."

"She's got you there," Coop said with a chuckle. "You're now personally responsible if she doesn't get an A."

Ignoring him, Hope addressed Maureen. "Let me get this straight. You want to come over so the two of us can exercise together?"

Maureen nodded eagerly. "My friend Amie has to come, too. We're assigned to this gym project together."

Hope glanced at Coop, who was trying to contain a smirk. "On one condition," she said. "Your father has to stay far, far away on that day."

He feigned hurt feelings. "As if I was the one who always tagged along and made your life miserable."

Maureen giggled.

"He didn't always try to get rid of me," Hope said smugly. She beckoned for Maureen to come closer. "I remember one summer, when he didn't have anything better to do, he came over and sat on my porch steps and we decided that when we grew up we were going to go off to the desert and be archaeologists together."

At the sight of Coop's bewildered expression, Hope laughed aloud. "How soon they forget! Well, I remember. I was reading a book called *Lost Worlds,* all about finding fabulous riches in tombs. And the minute I told your father about all the gold and jewels, he was ready to pack up and go."

"What else do you remember?" Maureen was bright-eyed with curiosity.

Hope grinned at her, aware of a deep sense of enjoyment in this recounting of childhood adventures to Coop's daughter. "One time your father dared me to jump off the garage roof," she recalled. "That was supposed to be our fire escape. My room had a little second-floor balcony attached to it and in case of fire I was supposed to go out the door, onto the balcony, over the rail and onto the garage roof. It was sloped, so the lower edge was only about five feet above Coop's yard. Still, when you're under five feet tall yourself, that's a long way down."

"You never did jump," Coop reminded her. "And I'll bet you never knew that I could make the jump going the other way."

"What are you talking about?"

"From my yard to your roof and over your balcony railing and right up to your bedroom door without you even knowing it."

Hope felt her eyes widen. "You never did!"

"Did too." Unrepentant, he grinned at her.

"When? And what did you see, peering into my bedroom window?"

He shrugged. "Not much. You weren't there. Still downstairs with your parents, I guess. Anyway, it was just one night after play rehearsal. After I walked you home." He turned to Maureen. "The guys on stage crew took turns. This frail little female had to be protected, you see."

They both lobbed snowballs at him.

"Did you have a serious crush on my father?" Maureen wanted to know.

"Unfortunately, yes. We were just friends for a long time, and then, all of a sudden, every time I tried to say anything to him, I'd get tongue-tied. It was awful. And the worst part was that he knew." She shot an accusing glare in his direction. "You flaunted your girlfriends, too. You—"

Hope broke off in midsentence, remembering that Maureen's mother had been one of those girlfriends. Hope knew she wasn't ready to deal with questions about Julie. Not just yet.

Fortunately, Maureen didn't seem to notice Hope's abrupt silence. She was too busy putting the finishing touches on the new wing Coop had added to their snow fort.

Five days later, Coop pulled into Hope's dooryard just as the UPS truck was leaving. The fort was still standing and there had been two more successful outings since.

The gym project had been postponed until Maureen's friend Amie was free, but the three of them had tried out skating on the pond after school on Monday. Yesterday Hope had accompanied Coop and Maureen to the Indian cave, traveling on cross-country skis. Today, without Maureen, Coop planned to coax Hope into taking a short drive. It was past time she got off her own land for a change.

"Why aren't you at work?" Hope asked first. Then, "Is Maureen all right? She's not sick or—"

"She's fine. She's in school. I took the day off. Want to come out and play?"

"I can't." She hefted the bulky package she'd just signed for. "I have to see if this contains the information my client is looking for."

Coop nudged her toward the kitchen, still hoping to change her mind. "Leave it for later. What's the point of working for yourself if you can't have a flexible schedule?"

"I'm psyched up to do it now. Besides, people who are self-employed can't allow themselves to be irresponsible. Bad habits are hard to break."

"So you keep telling me," he reminded her. At her wince, he lightened up. He wasn't here to lecture but to cajole.

"Everybody needs a coffee break." Coop produced a bakery bag full of fresh doughnuts from concealment behind his back and waved it under her nose. "Coffee breaks are an American tradition."

"No fair tempting me." She wavered a moment longer, inhaling the tempting bakeshop aroma, then compromised. "I'll take a short break in a few minutes. Just let me take a quick look at these films. In the meantime you can make yourself useful by putting on a fresh pot of coffee."

"Ah, the thrill of victory." He shrugged out of his coat and reached for the percolator. "Hurry back."

"I'll be down in a little while," she promised. "Fifteen minutes, max."

An hour later, Coop had polished off a cup of coffee and three doughnuts and was running low on patience. If the lady wouldn't come down from her tower, he decided, then he'd just have to climb up to her.

Since he'd missed the tour she'd given Maureen, Coop had never been upstairs in Hope's house before, but it didn't take long to find his way around. The most interesting parts of the second floor were a locked door and what was clearly Hope's bedroom, a delightfully feminine boudoir that smelled as fresh and delicate as Hope herself. He found it curious that there were no pictures of Elliot Rowan around. Perhaps, he told himself, they aroused memories that were too painful for Hope to deal with.

Up another flight of stairs he found a different world, this one all business, but it had a surprisingly cozy atmosphere in spite of that. Even more disconcerting, Hope didn't hear him come in. Not only was she oblivious to the fact that she was being observed, she had obviously forgotten there was anyone else in the house.

The office was a small one, and every corner was filled with the tools of Hope's trade. Everything a genealogist could want or need was there at her fingertips—computer, fax, machines to read microfiche and microfilm, copiers. She even had a small refrigerator and another coffeemaker in her aerie. As Coop watched, Hope ran a reel of microfilm through the reader, stopping every few turns to check the backlit screen.

Coop waited for Hope to notice him. She did not. She was totally engrossed in her work.

Finally, intrigued in spite of himself, he moved a step closer. He was not a vain man, but he was accustomed to being able to catch a lady's eye without too much effort. Trust Hope to be the glaring exception. Coop stared hard at the figure before him, trying to fathom the effect this woman had on him, an effect that was as powerful as it was puzzling.

He hadn't cared much for such dedication to a job when it had been Julie working so hard. His late wife's determination to succeed in her chosen profession had been a grim thing to watch. She'd had a love-hate relationship with the business world that had kept her in a state of continual frustration and constant stress and had made her pure hell to live with. In spite of that, Julie had come to crave the competition, and she'd relished the rewards of victory. She'd thrived on the long hours and, in the end, come right out and told Coop that her career came first, her family a poor second.

Hope's preoccupation with her work was an entirely different experience to watch. Her body language was eloquent. Possessed by a growing excitement, completely absorbed in the discoveries she was making on the screen in front of her, Hope reacted with almost sensual enthusiasm to what Coop knew to be no more than dry, historical records.

Hope's delighted laughter rippled through him like an electric shock. "Got it!" she exclaimed. Her elation and relief were infectious. Coop felt a bit triumphant himself as he moved close enough to look over her shoulder at the screen. He couldn't stop himself from wondering if she'd bring that same joy to making discoveries of a more erotic nature.

"What have you found?" he asked. From the way she was acting, it had to be at least as important as the missing link.

Hope jumped and let out a little yelp. Her hand went to her heart. "You gave me a start, Cooper Sanford! How long have you been in here?"

"Not long. I got tired of waiting downstairs."

Her attention returned to the screen. "I get involved in my work," she murmured by way of apology. She began to make notes on the material in front of her.

Coop watched without comment, but he picked up one of the boxes scattered across her worktable and read the label. Census records from 1860 and 1870. Not a thing many people could get so excited about. Then again, he'd always known Hope was different.

He glanced at what she was reading. It looked like heavy going to him. The spelling exhibited a great deal of variety, to say the least, and it was executed in a spidery handwriting that had to make deciphering it an even greater challenge. As he watched, it occurred to Coop that genealogy bore a strong resemblance to detective work, and that Hope Rowan was one relentless investigator.

She'd also forgotten all about him again.

Resigned to wait, Coop settled into a deep, softly cushioned chair that had a view through the bow window.

Hope changed reels. A few minutes later he had a second opportunity to witness her exuberant reaction to success. It was all there—the increasing excitement, the little burst of delight. The jolt of desire Coop felt was stronger than before.

Down, boy, he warned himself.

Features still glowing in triumph, Hope meticulously translated several more pages of nearly illegible nine-teenth-century script before she glanced up from the screen and caught Coop staring. He managed a shrug and an apologetic smile, but he couldn't feel sorry that he'd intruded on her during working hours. It had allowed him to see a side of Hope no one else had . . . except, perhaps, her late husband.

Why didn't she keep any pictures out?

"I really didn't mean to get so involved again," Hope apologized when she saw his frown. "It isn't good to go too long at a stretch, even if I don't have company wait-ing. The dreaded VDTs will get you. That's—"

"I know the term. You stare too long at a video dis-play terminal and you develop all sorts of nasty symp-toms."

She nodded. "Hence the exercise tapes Maureen no-ticed."

"And the invention of the coffee break."

"Oh, that definitely predated the computer age," she said with mock seriousness.

"Before you launch into a lecture on the history of the office, I should warn you that Julie wasn't the only one who had a degree in business."

She hadn't known that. He could see it in her eyes. Coop didn't know why he should be surprised. It was only natural that Julie's mother wouldn't bother to pass on any positive gossip about him.

Hope turned off the reader. Before she could slide her chair away from the table, Coop was behind her again, ready to play the gentleman. One hand came to rest on the back of the chair. The other strayed to her shoulder.

When he inhaled, Coop breathed in the fresh clean scents of shampoo and soap. She wore no perfume. She needed none. And her hair was incredible.

He was looking down at the top of her head. All those long, luxurious tresses, he suddenly realized, were held in place by a single, cleverly placed ivory clasp. Transfixed by his discovery, Coop did not move for a long moment. Then, unable to resist the temptation, he caught the clip in his fingers and tugged.

Her hair spilled over his hand, drifting toward her shoulders. Hope bit back a gasp and turned to stare at him. When he felt her involuntary shiver, he smiled.

Carefully, Coop stepped away from her, giving her room to swivel the chair. When she looked at him, his hands were extended with the palms up in front of him. "No harm meant," he said softly. "You have beautiful hair, Rapunzel. I couldn't stop myself."

"No harm done," she whispered, but she sounded a bit dazed.

Coop's lips twitched as his smile threatened to turn into a grin. His gaze returned to her cascading hair and he gave up any effort to sound contrite. "You must admit that was an effective way to get your attention."

Hope abruptly stood. "I was already going to break for that coffee."

"Just coffee?"

"Coffee and doughnuts," she amended.

Coop was tempted to take her into his arms and tell her to forget the damn coffee. They were alone. They had the rest of the day to discover—

Chapter Six

When Hope opened her front door on Sunday she found Coop standing there holding up two sets of snow-shoes. "Want to show me some more of your back forty?" he asked.

"Do I have a choice?" She knew what he was up to, and to her surprise it seemed to be working, but she was still a bit wary, especially since Coop had pointedly avoided making any direct reference to her agoraphobia.

His slow grin enticed her. "Sure you have a choice," he said. "We can go for a drive instead."

Hope made a face at him. She'd already turned down that particular suggestion twice in the past three days. She tried to see beyond him to the van. "Is Maureen with you?"

His chuckle was as rich and delicious as a cup of hot chocolate. "Nope. Just you and me today. It's Sunday. Remember? Maureen spends Sundays with her grandmother. Besides, this is only fair. It was just you and Maureen, skating again, on Friday."

"Yes. You actually did have to work for a change." Hope's eyes narrowed suspiciously. "Did you arrange for Barry to show up on Friday? Just in case I freaked out and had to be carried back to the house?"

"Not a chance. That kid has a crush on you, you know."

"I know." She also suspected that Maureen had a crush on Barry, and that Coop still hadn't realized it.

"So, what do you say, Hope? Snowshoes? One size fits all."

Hope knew she also had two other options, choices he'd not bothered to mention. She could invite him in, which might turn out to be a little too cozy for comfort without Maureen to chaperon. She could also send him on his way alone, but she enjoyed his company, with or without his daughter present, too much to contemplate that last alternative very long.

"Snowshoes, huh? I don't know, Coop. I've never tried them before."

"No sweat. I'm an expert."

"Of course you are. And modest, too."

"That's my girl. Go get your coat and boots. I've got everything else you need." He waggled his eyebrows and gave her a mock leer.

When Hope reappeared a few minutes later she was dressed in layers and wearing a pair of earmuffs with a Santa Claus face on each ear. Coop smiled at the latter, but made no comment.

"Remember—be gentle. I have no experience whatsoever on snowshoes."

"Think of them as very wide cross-country skis."

She took a deep breath of fresh, cold air and remembered the joy of their last excursion, of gliding through a silent woodland. They'd spotted a rabbit on their way up to the Indian cave. It still amazed Hope that she had made such wonderful progress. She'd expected the desensitizing to work, but not this quickly. The key, obviously, was Coop's matter-of-fact attitude about helping her. She just hoped he'd be as supportive when the inevitable setback came. She'd made almost this much progress once before, only to find herself back at square one following a particularly virulent panic attack.

Coop helped her strap her boots in place, then proceeded to give her a lesson in what seemed to Hope to be the fine art of moving forward with two large tennis rackets attached to her feet.

"You know," she grumbled, "I used to consider myself graceful." Moving a few steps ahead nearly defeated her.

Coop caught her elbow to keep her from falling face first into the snow. "You have to lift your feet straight up," he said, "and balance forward a little."

"I don't suppose I could use a pair of ski poles," she grumbled.

"Nope. That's against the rules."

"Since when have you bothered to obey rules?"

"I keep telling you, Hope. I've turned over a new leaf. What's the matter? You chicken? Come on. I dare you to make it to that stand of birch without falling down."

"You used to tell me I was a good sport," she reminded him. "Of course, when I got to be a teenager I disliked that handle almost as much as I disliked being called one of the boys."

"Trust me, I'm never going to mistake you for a boy again."

His intense gaze swept over her snug jeans and the slate blue sweater she wore under her open down vest. The turtleneck pullover was loose, but suddenly she felt as if he could see the teddy beneath, a silky garment that clung to her breasts like a second skin.

"Let's go," she said, her words suddenly too breathy, too fast.

He chuckled softly, but obliged.

Keep it light, Hope reminded herself. She was reading too much into the occasional heated look. Coop was just kidding around. He wasn't really attracted to her. And even if he was, they both knew getting involved in that kind of a relationship would be a mistake.

Friendship. That was what was best for everyone— Coop, and Maureen and herself.

She concentrated on following his lead across the hard-packed snow. The effort was intense enough to distract her from all her incipient fears, and in a short while they had reached the small cluster of white birch trees at the far side of the meadow. By then, Hope was growing accustomed to the rhythm of walking on snowshoes.

"This isn't bad," she told Coop. "Not once you get the hang of it."

"Want to go back to the Indian cave again?" he asked.

"We're headed the wrong way."

"All right. Where, then? You know you're not ready to go back to the house just yet."

A slow smile came over her features. "You're right."

She studied the contours of the land. The snow lay in pristine whiteness, sculpted into artistic drifts by the shifting winds. On snowshoes they could make paths through it with greater ease than if they'd been on skis. On the other hand, she knew one area nearby where there should already be a packed-down trail. Some days she could hear the snowmobiles from the house as they made their way through the woods.

"Come on," she said. "I want to show you something special."

"Lead on," Coop told her.

Hope set off, cutting through the trees toward the low stone wall that divided her property from that of her neighbor on the north, but when they stopped beside it to rest, she frowned, reminded for an unsettling moment of Elliot.

"What's the matter?" Coop asked.

"Nothing." She did not want to bring up Elliot's name or blight what was turning into a nearly perfect afternoon, but when Coop gave her an exasperated look, she relented.

"We had a little problem over this three-acre triangle we're about to cross. It was recorded on both the Hendersons' deed and mine."

"A little problem?" he echoed.

Elliot had made a huge fuss, but it hadn't really been important. She'd never understood what all the shouting was about. Aloud she said only, "Quarreling over who really owned this land never made any sense to me. The parcel has no value as a woodlot. It's too close to a stream to be harvested."

"Is that all it was, Hope?"

He was perceptive. She'd give him that. Too perceptive.

"Come on. Just step over the boundary." There was already a gap, where snowmobiles had followed the same trail she and Coop were on.

"How did you settle your border war?"

"I declared peace when—" *When Elliot died,* she finished silently. She swallowed hard. "I settled it by signing the land over to the Hendersons."

"Then aren't we trespassing?"

"They won't mind. The Hendersons even allow snowmobiles, which aren't always popular with landowners. No one objects to skis and snowshoes, though. They don't pollute the air or make a lot of noise."

Elliot had objected, of course. And he'd been even more impossible about the snowmobilers. He'd told the local snowmobile club that if they wanted to cross his land they'd have to pay a fee. They'd responded by avoiding Hope's grandparents' farm the next time they laid out trails.

Coop didn't ask any more questions, to Hope's immense relief. That allowed her to dismiss Elliot's unsuccessful scheme from her mind.

They struck out toward her goal once more and made steady progress. The exercise loosened up muscles Hope hadn't used in a long time, which felt surprisingly good. She worked out fairly regularly, to those exercise tapes Maureen had spotted, but she'd realized during this past week that she'd been missing the fun that could go along with physical exertion. When it took place outdoors and in good company, getting a workout was especially pleasant.

As they followed the woodland path, Coop began to talk about Maureen, relating some of her experiences settling into a new school and telling Hope about Maureen's new friends. Hope relaxed even more, enjoying this undemanding company.

"Have you noticed, Coop?" Hope asked when he paused for breath. "Maureen seems to like my young neighbor a lot."

"Barry's a nice kid. What's not to like?"

"I mean I think she has a crush on him."

For a moment Coop said nothing. Then he scoffed. "Don't be ridiculous, Hope. Maureen's too young to be thinking about boys. Besides, Barry is way too old for her."

Hope let the subject drop. Coop obviously had a blind spot where his daughter was concerned. He might even be right. Maureen was only twelve.

The splendor of the view made their long trek worthwhile when Hope and Coop came out of the woods to stand at the top of a low ridge. Side by side, they looked down at the tranquil scene in the valley below.

"I've always thought this would be a perfect picture to put on a Christmas card," Hope confided.

"Nice," Coop agreed.

"Now look more closely, in particular at those animals by the barn," she instructed. "What are they?"

Coop studied half a dozen four-legged creatures. "Too small for cows. Goats?"

"Guess again."

He shaded his eyes and squinted. Then he started to chuckle. "Is this for real? Llamas?"

"Right. That's the Henderson place. Mac Henderson uses them for pack animals and takes hikers on overnight trips in the summer and fall. It's quite a booming business, or so I understand."

"A Christmas card with llamas. Well, why not?"

Coop was standing directly behind her. His words were a warm breath against her cheek. Then his hands came up to cup her shoulders and, as she had that time in her office, she felt the contact all the way to her toes.

Rattled, Hope tried to put some distance between them. She meant to sidestep, to take herself out of his reach. But she forgot she was on snowshoes. She succeeded in breaking away, but then she was slipping, sliding, falling down over the first low rise. As the snow gave way beneath her, she gasped in alarm and reached for Coop.

She missed.

Ice-cold snow sprayed into her face and insinuated itself under her cuffs and into her mittens as she tumbled head over heels. She landed a foot or so down the bank. She was unhurt, but smack in the middle of a deep drift.

His eyes full of laughter, Coop scrambled down after her. "Must I always be helping you out of snowbanks?"

Hope glared at him. "I can manage on my own."

But the more she struggled to stand upright again, the deeper she sank. Snow worked its way beneath the back of her vest and up under her sweater, chilling her skin as she continued to flounder. It was hopeless. She was wedged in by her own snowshoes. One had somehow twisted under her. The other stuck straight out, half undone. She'd have slipped it off entirely, except that the buckle had buried itself, out of reach, in the drift. Defeated, Hope finally stilled.

"A gentleman would have insisted on offering a hand," she grumbled, still huffing and puffing from the exertion. She could no longer see Coop, but she knew he had to be nearby, watching and undoubtedly laughing his head off at her futile efforts to extricate herself.

"No gentlemen here. Only me."

Snow crunched behind her as he navigated the treacherous surface to grasp her under both arms. With one tug, he pulled her free.

"Piece of cake," he informed her smugly as he set her on her feet and dusted her off. "In fact, I quite like coming to your rescue. Does wonders for my ego."

With a disarming smile, Hope turned. Alarm flashed in Coop's eyes a second before she shoved, sending him over backward into the snowbank in her place.

"Rescue yourself, then!"

Hope's smile widened into a grin. She felt wonderful. She hadn't experienced even the flicker of a panic attack just now when she'd been trapped in the snow. That singular fact left her amazed and pleased and suddenly more alive than she'd been in months.

"Do you think you could give me a hand here?" Coop demanded. He was flopping about, cursing softly, apparently as helpless now as she'd been a few minutes earlier.

Hope started to extend a hand to him, then pulled back. He owed her one and she didn't trust him, not one little bit. "No way, buddy."

He growled.

She laughed.

Coop's hand snaked out and caught her ankle. Hope landed right on top of him, in a tangle of snowshoes and flailing limbs. Her earmuffs went flying. One of his gloves disappeared under the snow.

Then they were both laughing, so full of mirth and sheer delight that for a time neither realized just how intimately entwined they had become.

Hope sensed the danger first. She shifted her legs, breaking contact, but Coop was stronger and he wasn't yet ready to let her go.

He maneuvered their positions until his face was level with hers. His clever, gentle fingers stroked her arms, the balls of his thumbs caressing her with a slow, sensuous rhythm. The look in his eyes changed subtly, evoking dark, erotic images Hope wasn't sure she dared acknowledge. She felt mesmerized by that heated gaze and by the skilled movements of his fingers.

Their snowy cocoon no longer seemed cold to Hope. In fact, she wondered why steam wasn't rising all around them.

"I like you, Hope Rowan," Coop said.

"I, uh, like you, too," she whispered.

One strong hand smoothed up her arm to stroke her cheek with the back of a gloved finger. The leather felt soft and supple against her skin. Her fingers came up to the nape of Coop's neck and she could feel the texture of his thick, wavy hair right through her woolly mittens.

Frightened by the electrifying impact of touching him, Hope sucked in a great gulp of cold air. She'd never reacted this strongly to any man before. Nerve endings she hadn't even known existed were suddenly humming with anticipation.

She saw, in the jade green depths of his eyes, a reflection of her own rapidly escalating desire. His nostrils flared. His voice was husky.

"I like you," he repeated, "and I want you. I've wanted you for a very long time."

Hope's heart fluttered at his words. Her lips went soft and pliant, ready to meet and return his impending kiss, but she was unprepared for the searing intensity that flared between them at that first contact between hungry mouths.

His kiss was greedy, demanding a like response from her. Her lips parted under the onslaught. Raw need flooded through her, unlike anything she'd ever experienced. Passionate yearnings multiplied as the kiss deepened. Sensual awareness, dormant for so long within her, flowered with enormous blooms.

One small part of Hope's mind tried to protest, reminding her of all the reasons she should resist temptation, all the reasons she should push him away. She ignored the warnings.

At this moment, the only thing that mattered was the man holding her and caressing her. She craved more of the delicious sensations he was evoking. Her hands moved to his shoulders, exploring hard muscles through the soft fabric of his jacket.

She discarded her mittens. Her bared fingers twined upward again to tangle in his hair. His hands were just as busy, sliding steadily downward. At his first tentative, intimate touch, Hope arched toward him, too caught up in her own pleasure to deny him anything.

Coop was the one who broke the spell, stilling the stroking movements, then slowly separating his mouth from hers. She expected him to say something, but instead he just stared at her for a long, stunned moment, then silently set about freeing them from the snowbank.

When they were on their feet and at the top of the ridge again, he dusted snow off her clothes with swift, impersonal movements. Avoiding her eyes, he knelt to adjust the bindings on her snowshoes. He picked up her mittens, then located her earmuffs a few feet away and returned them to her. Deftly, he restored order to his own clothing and searched for his missing glove. And all the while he said nothing.

Hope watched in growing dismay. How had things suddenly become so awkward between them? He'd said he wanted her. Was he having second thoughts?

She rammed the earmuffs on her head and slipped cold hands into the mittens. Second thoughts. She was the one who should be having those. What did she think she was doing here? This was crazy.

"Ready to go back?" he asked.

"To what?"

"Silk sheets? Candlelight? Soft music?" He was looking directly at her now, but his expression was enigmatic. The passion in his eyes had been banked. She had no idea what he was really thinking. He might even be regretting what had just happened between them. Belatedly, her instinct for self-preservation kicked in.

"I'm not going to bed with you," she blurted.

"Can we talk about this when we're inside? We need to dry out before the windchill gets us."

"There's nothing to talk about. Neither of us wants to rush into anything based on, well, lust." As soon as she said the words, she knew they were true. He might desire her. In fact, there was pretty obvious evidence that he did. But they were both out of their depth here. They needed to put some space between them.

"Speak for yourself," Coop said gruffly, but he made no move to embrace her again, said nothing more to convince her to change her mind.

"You know I'm right. We got a little carried away just now, and it was . . . nice, but—"

"Nice?"

She smiled in spite of herself at his affronted tone. "Okay, it was more than nice. It was spectacular, enough to make me wish I was another type of woman, the kind who could treat sex casually and not have regrets, but I'm just not that sort of person, Coop."

She couldn't make love without becoming emotionally involved. With that kind of vulnerability, disillusionment and heartache would inevitably follow. She'd learned that lesson well, thanks to Elliot. Hope told herself she was grateful Coop had stopped before they'd ended up making love right there in that snowbank.

Coop looked toward the peaceful valley and the llamas. The air between them on the ridge thrummed with tension. "We'd be good together, Hope." Regret mixed in his voice with something she thought might be relief.

"We already have a good relationship, Coop. A wonderful friendship. Let's not risk spoiling that by trying for more."

Hope managed a brave smile, then took a step forward on the snowshoes, heading toward the house. Overbalancing, she would have fallen again if he hadn't been there to catch her.

Coop's touch jolted her, but she gripped his arm like a lifeline when he offered support. She swayed helplessly against him, suddenly afraid. Her eyes widened. Her heart raced. And those reactions had nothing to do with being held by a man she cared deeply for.

"Oh, no," she whispered. "Not a panic attack. Not now."

Hope closed her eyes tightly and swallowed hard, fighting to remain calm.

Coop might have set her upright again on her own.

He might have lost patience with her.

Instead he tugged her into the shelter of his arms. "It's okay. I'm here for you."

A warm wave of pleasure washed over Hope as Coop guided her head to a resting place over his heart. Eyes still closed, her hands found his waist.

She felt surrounded by him. His warmth. His strength. His scent. All were infinitely comforting. The momentary panic ebbed, then vanished. For a long moment there was no sound but their soft breathing. Neither moved. Neither spoke. Lethargic, Hope clung.

It felt good to be held there. Too good. The panic had passed, only to be replaced by renewed desire. His breath against her hair was a warm caress, as disturbingly intimate as a kiss. It evoked an impulse to tip her head back, lift her face and part her lips for him again. She knew she had to be strong, to break free of his spell before she forgot all her good intentions.

"I'm okay now," she said softly.

"Sure?"

"Yes."

He set her from him carefully and they started toward the house.

Coop set aside his completed paperwork and leaned back in his office chair to stare through the plate glass window at the ski slopes that generated all those balance sheets and bills and vouchers. Between being the boss and Maureen's father and spending a lot of time with Hope, he hadn't gotten much use out of his own trails. He had taken over the beginner class when one of his instructors had been down with the flu, and he'd made a couple of runs to test the south slope after a sudden thaw had forced them to resurface the entire thing with man-made snow, but that had been the sum total of his downhill skiing for more than two weeks.

He didn't miss it at all, even though, when he'd first decided to return to Norville, unlimited time on the slopes had been one of the things he'd most looked forward to. In spite of what he'd let people believe, he'd never actually earned a living as a ski bum. Even after the divorce from Julie, when he'd been sorely tempted to go back to his old, irresponsible ways, the work he'd found had been at the management level.

Socializing had been a bigger part of his last job than skiing. Coop knew he didn't miss that. Right this minute there were any number of luscious young ladies out there in the lounge, but none of them appealed. Neither did the idea of going out with Ginny Devereux, though she'd called him twice with invitations since the potluck supper.

A picture of himself, Julie and Maureen on a trip to Aspen sat on Coop's desk, a token gesture for Maureen's sake and a constant reminder to himself that appearances could be deceiving. Coop wondered again why there were no photographs of Elliot Rowan at Hope's house.

He'd left her at her door yesterday, reluctant to trust himself to be alone with her inside the house. She'd been absolutely right. That was the hell of it. They'd be crazy to risk ruining their renewed friendship, not to mention Hope's budding relationship with Maureen, for the sake of either a casual fling or a long-term affair.

Too bad his unruly body didn't want to listen.

Coop shifted uncomfortably, a rueful expression on his face. Just thinking about Hope could get his libido going. Face to face, what chance did he have?

Maybe he ought to consider sending Maureen out to visit Hope without him along. She had that exercise project to complete. He told himself he'd call Amie's mother and get them moving on that.

His relationship with Hope needed a cooling-off period. When he was sure he was back in control, then he'd try again to coax her into the van and get her off her own property for a few hours. They'd drive into Tardiff. Then he'd take her into Norville. Then into his condo and into his—

Coop realized he'd better stop thinking what he'd just been thinking because Hope was not the kind of girl a man took to bed unless he was prepared to marry her afterward.

The thought stunned him.

Marrying anyone was the last thing he wanted. Astonished that he'd even consider it, even with Hope, Coop tried to tell himself that he'd just come up with the best argument in the world not to get more involved with her.

Hearth, home and Hope.

They did go together somehow.

But not for him.

He'd been a fool for love once, yielding to the old-fashioned gentlemanly code of conduct that demanded an offer of marriage when a girl told her boyfriend she was pregnant. Julie had lied. She'd convinced one very gullible eighteen-year-old boy that she was carrying his child, and he'd believed her. He'd married her. Only afterward had she confessed that she'd have said anything to get away from her mother. She'd seen eloping with Coop as an easy escape route out of Norville and away from Penny Bellamy's elaborate plans for her future.

Coop picked up the silver-framed photograph of his ex-wife. She and Hope bore a superficial resemblance to each other, but there had always been a hard edge to Julie, a coldness. It hadn't taken him long to discover that once they were married. Still, committed, he'd been determined to stick it out. In his family there had been drunks and crooks, but there had never been a divorce.

In time, Julie had given him a child, and as far as Coop was concerned, Maureen was the only good thing to come out of his marriage. He'd decided long ago never to repeat the worst mistake of his life. He would never remarry.

"Quit while you're ahead," he muttered.

Still, he couldn't avoid Hope entirely, even if she didn't get out much. She was making so much progress, and he'd vowed to help her. Besides, Maureen enjoyed their visits to the farm, the time the three of them spent there together.

Coop frowned, wondering if Hope had been right about his daughter, too. Did Maureen have a crush on Barry Green? More to the point, how did the boy feel about Maureen? Hope's neighbor seemed to spend as much time at her place as Coop and Maureen did. Maybe more.

Coop didn't like the direction his thoughts were taking. Maureen was too young, even for puppy love. And Barry continued to remind him of himself at that age.

There was no help for it. He'd have to chaperon at least some of Maureen's visits to Hope's house.

Twenty miles away, Hope faced her aunt Penny across the teacups and struggled to hold on to her temper. The woman was concerned, not just nosy, Hope reminded herself. Penny Bellamy knew, from Maureen, that both Maureen and Coop had been spending a great deal of time at Hope's during the past two weeks, and that Coop had been by on at least one occasion without his daughter.

"Do you know what you're doing letting Cooper Sanford come around?" Penny demanded.

"He's an old friend, Aunt Penny. And Maureen is my cousin."

"Do you know how your old friend managed to afford the condominium he's living in?"

"He said it went with the job. I assume all the resort's employees get housing of some sort."

"Humph. A likely story. He's got way too much money, if you ask me. I think the mob is involved."

Hope choked on her tea. "Aunt Penny, that's absurd. He doesn't even own his car. He drives the resort van."

"And that's peculiar, too. What do we really know about how he's spent the past few years?"

Hope automatically discounted ninety percent of what her aunt said, though a small doubt niggled at her on this matter of Coop's job. It had seemed strange to her that he could take time off whenever he wanted to.

Angel chose that moment to fly through the living room, nearly upsetting the tea table.

"What ails that beast?" Penny demanded.

Glad of an excuse to change the subject, Hope stood. "I'll show you," she offered, and led the way to the small room at the back of the house that Elliot had used as his office.

Hope had cleaned all traces of her husband out after his death and turned it into an exercise room. The sliding glass doors opened onto a small deck, to give her something to look at while she worked out. So far, however, Angel was the only one who spent much time in front of those doors. Two large bird feeders were set up just outside and daily drew flocks of chickadees, a wide variety of other wild birds and a family of squirrels.

As Hope had expected, an immense calico cat was also out on the deck, ogling one of the feeders. "Angel's gentleman caller," she said.

Penny harrumphed. "He's after your birds, not your cat."

"Shh. She doesn't know that."

Angel dashed into the room, tail fluffed to twice its normal size, to take an ineffectual swipe at the glass.

The calico ignored her.

Angel growled, then tore out of the room again.

"This is the only exercise she gets," Hope said. "As for the Greens' calico, Theodore, he's too slow and fat to catch any of the birds, so I don't mind if he comes around.''

"Barry Green?'' Penny asked.

"Right. Maureen said she introduced the two of you at the potluck supper.''

"He seems like a nice boy. Are his parents respectable?''

"Yes, Aunt Penny. They both have jobs and everything.''

Her sarcasm went unremarked. "I'm worried about Maureen,'' Penny said.

"Why? She seems to be adjusting well to her new school. She's making lots of friends.''

"But are they the right sort? No public school is up to the standards of that private girls' boarding school she was enrolled in until Julie died.''

"She didn't live with her mother?''

"The best preparation for college can be found in a good boarding school,'' Penny said. "This one was in Connecticut. Julie worked in New York City, but she usually managed to visit Maureen on weekends.''

A note of doubt had crept into Penny's voice, but Hope suspected she'd never admit aloud that Julie might have been less than perfect as a parent. It sounded as if Maureen had seen as little of her mother after the divorce as she had of her father. All things considered, it was remarkable the girl had turned out to be as well-adjusted as she was.

"Coop didn't have to bring Maureen here,'' Hope reminded her aunt. "He might have taken her anywhere. Even farther from her grandmother than a school in Connecticut.''

When Penny made no comment, Hope was encouraged to go on. The role of peacemaker in the family suddenly felt right to her. She could do this, for Maureen's sake and for Coop's.

"You have to admit Coop is a good father," she said.

"I don't have to admit anything." Penny sniffed disdainfully, then grudgingly added, "Maureen is fond of him, but he was no good for poor Julie."

It was on the tip of Hope's tongue to ask what Maureen had felt for her mother, the mother she'd seen so seldom. It occurred to her that Maureen rarely mentioned Julie, nor did she appear to be grieving for her.

"Julie had to push herself too hard after he deserted her," Penny Bellamy grumbled. "Work. Work. Work. She didn't take proper care of herself. When she got that infection, she thought it was just the flu and ignored the symptoms. Two days later she was dead, and I blame Cooper Sanford. If he hadn't left her, forcing her to work so hard, she'd still be alive today."

Hope didn't bother to respond to that charge. Her aunt was clearly irrational in her conviction that Coop was at fault.

It was a tragedy Julie had died so young, especially from an infection that could have been cured if it had been caught early and treated properly, but Hope knew that it had not been anyone's fault but Julie's. Such unexpected deaths were nowhere near as uncommon as most people thought. Jim Henson, the man who'd created the Muppets, had succumbed to something similar. Julie had been moving up in the business world, fighting her way toward the top tooth and claw, if Hope was any judge of her late cousin's character. She'd been too busy to look after herself properly. Coop had not made her that way. If anyone had been responsible, besides Julie herself, then it had to be the woman now staring out at Hope's bird feeders with tears in her eyes and a bleak expression on her jowly face.

Hope's heart went out to her aunt. As a mother she'd had failings, but with other people's children, with Hope in particular, she'd had her moments. Whatever she'd been fifteen years ago when Julie ran away, now she was older, sadder and, if not wiser, then at least wise enough to fear losing her only grandchild's affection.

She was scared, Hope realized. She genuinely wanted what was best for Maureen but she was no longer certain she knew just what that was. She was terrified of making the same mistakes she'd made with Julie, but unable to take the emotional risk of admitting there had been mistakes.

Penny Bellamy took the easy route, blaming Coop, pretending to herself and everyone else that she'd never forgive him.

Hope understood such self-deception all too well. She wondered if she'd learned anything at all from her marriage to Elliot, because all too often lately, she'd caught herself wishing there *could* be more than friendship between herself and Coop.

She was dangerously close to falling in love.

Chapter Seven

Hope gritted her teeth.

As Saturday morning sunlight poured through the sliding glass doors, she tried in vain to steady her right leg, which was suspended two feet off the floor in front of her. A overly cheerful taped voice chanted, "Hold, two, three, and down."

Released, her foot plunged to the carpeted floor with all the grace of a falling rock.

Hope winced. What on earth had possessed her to participate with Maureen and her friend Amie on their gym project? She could have let them work out to her collection of exercise tapes without making this ridiculous attempt to keep up with them.

The answer wasn't hard to find. It had something to do with not having seen either Coop or Maureen for six whole days. Hope had suffered disconcerting bouts of loneliness all week long, and a spurt of bad weather at midweek had made matters worse. She'd planned on making a daily trek on skis to the treeline and back and had only managed to do so on Monday, Tuesday and Friday. On Friday she'd come very close to a panic attack when she was halfway back to the house. She didn't look forward to the next attempt. She was afraid of failure. She didn't want to go back to her old way of coping with the phobia.

She'd told Coop once that she didn't suffer from cabin fever. Now she wasn't so sure. In addition, for some reason, she was overcompensating today. Without meaning to, she'd started playing a twisted version of supermom.

Sweat made her hair hang in damp clumps that stuck to her neck and face. Now that she'd stopped holding everything in and up, Hope felt as if each little-used muscle was sagging, producing unflattering rolls of fat around her middle. She knew she wasn't really out of shape. And the loose fit of her sea green jogging suit would have hidden a multitude of sins in any case. Just now, however, believing it was difficult.

It was being here next to these two kids, kids with perfectly flat tummies and backsides. Hope admitted to jealousy, plain and simple. She could still remember how, at their age, she'd longed for a woman's figure. Now she wished she could be as young and energetic as they were again.

And as innocent.

The voice on the audiocassette drew breath and pushed relentlessly ahead. "Exercise number five is the same motion backward. Ready? With the music."

"Not ready!" Hope jabbed the Stop button. "Enough is enough!"

Maureen and Amie looked puzzled. Neither one of them was the least bit winded, even after working their way through parts of four videos and two audio work-outs, each led by a different fitness guru.

"These people are sadistic torturers," Hope gasped. "We have to take a break."

Running in place had left her breathless, and the two dozen squat thrusts had come close to spraining both wrists and both ankles. Hope knew she was in great shape when it came to skiing and skating and snowshoeing, but after the past couple of routines, she had to have a breather.

She sank to the floor in a cross-legged position, one that in no way resembled the lotus. Slowly lowering her head until her sweat-covered brow could rest on one upturned knee, she curled herself forward into a ball.

"Hope, you can't quit now," Maureen said.

"Slave driver," Hope muttered.

Maureen and Amie both laughed. Obviously, they had no concept of what she was going through.

"Thin as rails, both of you," Hope grumbled under her breath. "Don't you realize that neither of you has any need to exercise this hard?"

It was barely ten o'clock in the morning and they'd already been at it more than an hour. Hope wiped the perspiration away with her sleeve and looked at Maureen. She was ready to beg.

Coop's daughter was a lithe figure in skintight royal blue dancer's leotard and tights. Not only hadn't she worked up a sweat, she hadn't even begun to glow.

How far did a role model have to go? Hope wondered. Did she really need to bond *this* thoroughly with her young cousin?

"Come on, Hope," Maureen teased her. "You can do it. We've only got three more exercise programs to get through. Amie and I are going to try out all the routines, so you might as well join us. Right?''

''Wrong.''

Amie, a serious, bespectacled sprite who had said little since her arrival, finally decided to put in her two cents' worth. ''You should think about your health, Mrs. Rowan,'' she told Hope. ''Once you get past thirty, you have to start worrying about strokes and heart attacks. If you don't get enough exercise, you could go just like that.'' She tried to snap her fingers but didn't quite manage it.

''Thank you so much for sharing that with me,'' Hope said. ''You're a dear child to remind me how old and decrepit I am.''

Amie missed the sarcasm. ''Besides, my mother says you can't start too young to stay slender and sleek and supple.''

''You mean there's no such thing as being too rich or too thin?'' Hope meant the words as a joke, but Amie beamed at her and Maureen was nodding in agreement.

''That's right,'' Amie told her. ''My mother says that being petite is the best way to attract the man of your dreams.'' She executed a few more deep knee bends without music and then added, in a singsong voice, ''Maureen's in love with Barry!''

Maureen pretended intense interest in the activity at one of the bird feeders, where two chickadees were disputing the same source of sunflower seeds. She was too still, Hope decided. Undoubtedly, she was waiting to hear what her designated role model would say before she responded to her best friend's teasing.

How easy it would be to blurt out the wrong remark, especially since Hope was not sure exactly what her place was in Maureen's life. It wasn't mother. She chided herself for even imagining for a moment that it was. Big sister or aunt didn't seem much easier parts to play. Role model? What on earth did that entail?

Penny wasn't the only one who could make mistakes, Hope thought, beginning to panic. What if she unintentionally misled Maureen? What if something she said or did ended up ruining her young cousin's life?

"Do you think Barry would like me better if I was thinner?" Maureen finally asked, impatient with Hope's silence.

"I think he likes you fine just the way you are," Hope assured her, but she was still in a quandary, uncertain just how much Coop wanted her to be involved in giving Maureen advice.

Hope did not agree with Amie's mother, but it was all too likely that Maureen's peers did. That shouldn't matter, Hope told herself. She could not evade this issue. Visions of anorexic teenagers would haunt her if she tried.

"I have to be honest," she said. "I think that meeting anyone else's idea of how you should look is a lousy reason to do anything. If you go on a diet or start an exercise program, shouldn't it be because that makes *you* feel better about yourself?"

An awkward silence followed her question, and Hope wondered if she'd blown it. Being Maureen's friend had just gotten trickier than she'd ever anticipated it could. Hope tried to tell herself that she was making too much of the situation, but it seemed to her that a generation gap had suddenly materialized out of nowhere.

"It's okay for me to like Barry, isn't it?" Maureen was staring at the bird feeders again. A woodpecker was assaulting the suet ball that hung between them.

"Of course it is. You two are friends."

"Just the way you were with my father when you were my age?" She glanced over her shoulder at Hope.

"Amazingly like that."

"Grandmother Bellamy says she doesn't know Barry's parents. She says I'm too young for a boyfriend, anyway, and that she'll see to it that I meet the right sort of boy when I'm old enough."

Hope barely held in a heartfelt groan. Maybe Aunt Penny hadn't learned from her mistakes. "Your grandmother wants what's best for you," she said carefully.

"She makes a lot of rules," Maureen complained. She seemed about to say more when Amie, tired of turning somersaults and cartwheels all by herself, interrupted.

"Are we going to finish the exercises, or what?" she asked.

Hope winked at Maureen and mouthed, "We'll talk more about this later." Then she reached out and hit the Play button. The music started up at once.

"Continue, ladies, if you please," Hope said as she heaved herself to her feet, "but I do believe that this aged crone is going to retire for the day."

The two girls resumed the routine, bouncing happily as they kicked their legs back and held them, effortlessly, impossibly high off the floor, for the count of three.

Shaking her head at her own earlier foolishness in thinking she could keep up with them, Hope reached for the towel she'd thrown into the seat of the armchair. Her hand struck not terry cloth but fur—Angel had curled up on top of the towel. From that vantage point she had an excellent view of the deck.

Hope lifted the cat, extracted the towel and slung it around her neck. She glanced at the girls as she left the room, relieved to realize that their discussion of boys had been abandoned.

Thank goodness the subject did not yet have sufficient importance in their lives to hold their attention for long. They were easily distracted by jumping jacks, which they were now executing with so much enthusiasm that they made the floor shake.

Limping slightly, Hope headed upstairs toward the bathroom and a much-needed shower. She wasn't out of shape, she reminded herself. In fact, she'd been too thin when she married Elliot. Nervous tension had kept her downright skinny during their marriage. She'd actually been relieved when, after he died, she managed to put on a few pounds.

Coop seemed to think they'd all been added in the right places, too.

Hope frowned, remembering that she did not want Coop to be attracted to her. Maybe, she thought with a grim smile, she ought to embrace Amie's mother's theory in reverse. There might be a definite advantage to being...what? Stout? No, not at her height. Stout conjured up the image of a Victorian matriarch with a cameo pinned to her shelflike bosom. Hope knew that she'd never develop one of those, no matter how much weight she gained.

Catching a glimpse of herself in the mirror on the back of the bathroom door, Hope decided that plump sounded more like it. Pleasantly plump. Why, if she'd been plump five years ago, a man like Elliot Rowan would never have noticed her. She would have been spared no end of heartache.

She turned sideways and studied her profile. Would adding, say, twenty pounds convince Coop she wasn't for him? Somehow she doubted it. Coop wasn't the sort of man who judged a person only be physical appearance. Not like Elliot.

Struck by that thought, Hope peeled off her sweat-soaked clothing and stepped into the shower stall. The pulsing water quickly finished clearing the cobwebs from her brain. Hope paused in the act of squeezing a dollop of shampoo into her hand. No, Coop wasn't like Elliot, but she could not allow herself to become dependent upon him for her happiness. She'd offered friendship. That was just going to have to be enough for him. For both of them.

More was just too dangerous.

Coop turned up on Hope's doorstep early the next afternoon, too late for lunch and too early for supper. "I'm only here to talk," he said when she opened the door.

He wondered if that was really a flash of disappointment he saw in her sapphire eyes. It was gone in a moment, and she stepped aside to let him come into the house.

"Talking is good." Hope led him into the kitchen. He wondered how baggy sweats could look so damned appealing on a woman. Unaware he was ogling her, she quickly poured coffee for them both and sat down across from him at the table.

For a moment Coop continued to drink her in instead. His thoughts had gotten as hot and steamy as the contents of the mug in front of him.

"Talk?" she prompted softly.

He jerked his eyes away from the gentle swell of her bosom and picked up the ceramic mug. When he'd drained half the scalding brew he cleared his throat and confessed, "I'm really here because of Mother Bellamy."

Hope looked startled. "What's Aunt Penny done now?"

"For one thing, when I dropped Maureen off just now, she made some stupid remark about my spending too much time over here. I'm afraid it brought out the worst in me. I hadn't really intended to come by today, but just to be perverse I told her I was on my way to see you. I can leave again if you want."

"I'm glad you're here," Hope said. "In fact, there's something I want to say to you. I want you to know that you don't need to feel any obligation to keep coming here to coax me out of the house. I've made a good start now. I can keep going on my own."

He held up a hand to stop her. "If my only motive for stopping by was to get you to go out, I'd have bought the dog."

"What dog?"

He found her bewilderment endearing and smiled at her. "I was going to get a mutt from the shelter and con you into taking care of it for Maureen because there aren't any pets allowed at our place."

"Ah," she said, nodding her understanding of the plot. "Bad idea."

"Yeah, I figured that out about five seconds after I thought of it. I'm only telling you now to convince you that I'm not completely underhanded."

"Why am I not reassured?"

"I also thought about contacting some of your old friends from high school and getting them to badger you into going out more. Dennis would do it in an instant."

"Dennis Long?"

Coop nodded. "He says he hit on you."

Hope laughed aloud, and any tension that remained between them vanished at last. "If he did, I must have missed it. I didn't know you'd renewed your old friendship with Dennis." She grinned. "Who'd have thought he'd end up on the right side of the law?"

"Who'd have thought he'd try to protect you from me by not telling me why you didn't get out much?" That had hurt when Coop first realized what had happened. For all he'd seemed to accept Coop's reformation, Dennis had put Hope's privacy ahead of his old friend's need to know. "I gave him hell for keeping secrets from me," he added.

"That's sweet," Hope said. "Who else have you seen since you've been back? You were ahead of me in school, but let's face it, it was a small school. I knew all of your classmates and you knew all of mine."

"I haven't gone out of my way to renew all my old acquaintances," he admitted. "A lot of the guys I hung out with didn't turn out as well as Dennis did."

"But you must have run into some of the girls," she teased. "I remember you had a whole string of girlfriends before you started dating Julie. I was insanely jealous of every one of them." She made a face and added, "I know Ginny's still around. Have you seen her yet?"

"Ginny Devereux? She was at the potluck supper, but other than that . . ."

He let his voice trail off and wondered if he looked as guilty as he felt for trying to avoid the subject of Ginny Devereux. Casting a wary glance in Hope's direction, he saw that she was momentarily absorbed in her thoughts. She didn't seem to have noticed how ill at ease her question made him.

"How about you?" he asked, suddenly suspicious. "Have you seen Ginny lately?"

"As a matter of fact, yes. She stopped by in the middle of last week. Wednesday."

Another wave of guilt washed over Coop. "Why?"

"To make me an offer on this place."

"She wants to buy the farm?"

"Apparently. It's nothing new. She approached me about selling once before, right after Elliot died. She was her usual pushy self, and I wasn't very polite about turning her down. Come to think of it, I wasn't all that polite this time, either."

Coop picked up his coffee and drank the rest of it down. It had gone stone cold, but he hardly noticed. "I need to get back to work," he mumbled.

"There's a change." Hope was smiling with wry amusement. "I won't try to talk you out of going, but at least let me send you off with a fresh cup of coffee. You'll need it to ward off the chill."

Coop watched her bustle about the kitchen and concluded that she couldn't know about Elliot's affair with Ginny and still speak that lightly of the other woman. With any luck, she'd never discover that Coop had taken Ginny out to dinner on Tuesday night, either.

He'd told himself when he called Ginny that his "friend" Hope would have no business questioning his social life, but even then he'd known deep down that she'd be hurt if she heard about his date. Ironically, he'd ended up spending the entire evening trying to get Ginny to talk to him about Elliot Rowan. If he'd had other things in mind to start with—some half-baked idea about using Ginny to help him get over his craving for Hope—he'd quickly discovered that the solution to that particular problem was not so simple.

Taking Ginny to bed had been the last thing he'd wanted within five minutes of picking her up. By the end of the evening, he resorted to using his daughter as an excuse to escape her amorous clutches.

All in all, it had not been an evening to be proud of.

He took the travel mug of coffee from Hope and dropped another one of his patented brotherly kisses on her brow, but the words hearth, home and Hope flickered through his mind as he left her.

Well, Hope thought as she watched him go. That didn't go too badly. Their friendship was firmly reestablished.

Now if she could just stop daydreaming about kissing him, she was sure she'd soon be back to normal.

It was three days before Coop saw Hope again.

Obligations at work had picked up. The resort was in the middle of its best ski season in years.

Coop met Maureen after school and drove to Hope's farm, but this time he did not get out of the van. He sent Maureen in to fetch Hope out.

She came willingly enough, but he read the wariness in her eyes.

"Get in," he ordered.

"Now, Coop—"

"We're not going far."

"Let's go to Barry's house," Maureen suggested. "That's only a half mile."

Coop saw Hope's hesitation and was aware that it took courage for her to open the passenger side door, but he was here to encourage her, not to remind her of her fears. Without any fuss he reached across the seat and gave her a hand in. As soon as she was settled and her seat belt fastened, he put the van in reverse and backed in a wide arc to turn around in her dooryard.

Hope lost color in her face, and the hands resting in her lap clenched tightly, but she didn't say a word.

"Which way?" he asked when they reached the bottom of the driveway.

"Right," Maureen said.

"The rooftop you can see from your office?" Coop asked.

"Right," Hope echoed.

He smiled to himself.

They reached their destination before there was time to shift gears. The Greens had a smaller, newer house than Hope did, and a much shorter driveway. A small barn and a detached garage had been built nearby.

"Looks like nobody's home," he remarked. The only sign of life was an overweight calico cat sauntering across the snow-covered front yard.

"Barry must be here," Maureen said. She was already letting herself out of the back of the van. "I'll go look in the barn. He told me he's got a workshop there. He makes models and things."

Silence settled between Hope and Coop in the front seat when his daughter left. Coop studied the woman beside him, noting with satisfaction that her cheeks were a healthy pink once more. "You told me once that Barry has a younger brother and an older one in college. Are there any other siblings?"

"That's it. Both parents work. Maureen's probably right, though, that Barry's in the barn. Maybe his brother is, too, although Jason might not be home yet. Barry's little brother takes gymnastics classes twice a week after school."

"And Barry plays basketball."

"Yes. I suppose he could be at a practice. Or even have a game."

Coop kept her talking. It didn't matter what they said to each other, as long as he kept her mind off the fact that she'd left home. After a while, though, he realized that Maureen had been gone for quite some time.

Hope seemed to realize it, too. "I'll be fine here if you want to go after her." Her lips curved into a sad smile. "If she's anything like I was when I had a huge crush on the boy next door, she's forgotten all about you and me."

"She's too young," Coop muttered under his breath as he got out of the van and stalked toward the barn. He told himself he was worried over nothing, that Barry had to think Maureen was too young, too. He'd simply ignore her.

But Coop also remembered how he'd felt about Hope. Three years hadn't been all that great a gap between them. Still, Hope had at least been a teenager, not twelve, and even wild as he'd been as a kid, he'd had sense enough to know she was too young and innocent for the likes of him.

He wasn't sure Barry was that sensible. The boy was sixteen, Coop kept telling himself. Maureen was only twelve. She couldn't possibly interest him. Then he opened the door to the workshop.

Maureen had both arms clasped around Barry Green's neck and was kissing him enthusiastically on the mouth. Coop didn't take time to analyze whether Barry was kissing her back. He exploded into the room, ripped his daughter out of the boy's arms and dragged her to the van.

Maureen was in tears by the time they reached it. Hope's sympathy for her was obvious, and that served to make Coop even more furious. "Don't say a word," he warned. "Either of you." He slammed into the van and drove Hope home.

It took him four days to calm down.

Hope was relieved when Coop turned up at her place on Sunday, even if he was still in a rotten mood. "Are you coming in or are we going out?" she asked.

"Do you have a car?"

She swallowed the sudden lump in her throat and nodded. "In the barn."

"Will it start?"

"It should. I have . . . someone exercise it for me regularly."

Coop had the good grace to look sheepish. "It's okay to say Barry's name, Hope. I won't bite your head off."

"That's a relief."

She was tempted to bring the entire situation out into the open and discuss it, but a closer look at Coop's closed expression discouraged her. His temper might have cooled, but he wasn't yet ready to talk about his reaction to seeing his little girl kissing a boy.

Maureen had tried repeatedly in the van that day to explain that she'd kissed Barry, not the other way around. Coop had been too incensed to listen, let alone answer her.

"Barry takes my car out at least once a week," Hope explained, "even though he usually prefers to use his mother's station wagon to pick up groceries for me or deliver packages to the post office or whatever. I've always told myself I'd need to have a car again someday."

"Someday just got here. We don't have to go far, but you're driving."

Without another word, Hope got her coat and a hat and gloves. It was the twelfth of February and somewhere around twenty degrees Fahrenheit. Maybe she'd get lucky and the car wouldn't start. Then she chided herself for cowardice. There was no reason to be timid about this. She'd already been out with Coop. And in the past she'd had plenty of experience with winter driving.

She tried not to think about the fact that Elliot had been killed on an icy winter road. She was trying to put everything about that night behind her.

"They say riding a bike or a horse or driving a car comes back to you, no matter how long it's been," he said as they got in and she turned the key in the ignition. "I've been thinking that with all the progress you've made so far, driving again should increase your rate of recovery even more. Before long, you should be able to come visit Maureen at our place. And take her places without waiting for me to be free to come along."

Hope didn't answer. She was too busy concentrating on what she was doing. She wondered if the old rule about not letting a loved one teach you to drive applied when you were relearning the skill. Coop had never been known for his patience.

She was more scared than she wanted to admit at first, and a quick glance toward the passenger seat told her that Coop didn't look particularly understanding. Did he secretly resent all the time her desensitization was taking? To her relief, though, he'd been right. She hadn't forgotten how to drive.

Turning left at the foot of the drive, they set out along Columbia Hill Road at a sedate twenty miles an hour. There was no other traffic and gradually Hope began to feel more confident. Her optimism increased when she turned onto Route 2. Before she knew it, she was five miles from home, then six, and she was feeling not at all threatened.

Almost as soon as she had that thought, her hands started to tremble. Coop's soft voice was barely audible through the rushing sound in her ears.

"We'll go back now," he said. He reached across her and flipped the left turn signal on. "Pull in at the market. Get yourself turned around."

Mike's Market. Just under seven miles from the house and the place where it had all begun, a country store at a

four corners, a convenience for those who didn't want to
drive all the way to Tardiff or Norville for their milk and
eggs and cat food. For a second, Hope stopped breathing.

Coop said her name. Sharply.

She snapped out of her trance and managed to obey his
command. As soon as she was headed for home again, her
respiration slowed to normal. The sense of accomplish-
ment returned.

"I'm doing okay," she said aloud.

"Yes, you are."

"I'll do even better the next time."

"Damn straight," he said.

Back at her house, they took steaming cups of coffee
into the living room and shared the sofa. Hope was still
buoyant with her recent success, and delighted to find that
she felt comfortable around Coop again.

"How's Maureen?" she asked.

"Still peeved at me," Coop admitted. "She'll get over
it."

"You did go a little overboard. As you keep saying,
she's only twelve. Even if she does have a crush on Barry,
he can't possibly be interested in her."

"Want to bet? I was plenty interested in you when you
weren't much older than Maureen."

At first Hope thought he was joking. Then she got a
good look at his brooding expression. "How old?"

He shrugged. "Well before you got your nerve up and
asked me out."

"How old?"

"Fourteen." He sounded irritable.

"I didn't even have a bosom yet. How could you have
been interested . . . that way?"

"I didn't say I could explain it. I'm just telling you what was. Don't you think I agonized over it? I was having hot dreams about a little kid." He managed a weak grin as he ran agitated fingers through his hair. One lock ended up falling across his forehead.

"I loved that lock of hair," she said, reaching over to push it into place. "It was always sliding down over your eyes. And that mustache you used to have! That was the stuff of teenage fantasy."

"I could grow it back."

She retreated into her coffee cup and realized the liquid was tepid. She started to stand, reaching for his cup. "Want me to heat that up for you?"

"What we need here is ice water."

Hope pursed her lips as she sat down again. "Maybe we don't need to talk about Maureen and Barry as much as we need to talk about this...thing between us." She set both cups on the coffee table and folded her arms in front of her chest.

He lifted one brow. "Thing?"

"It just doesn't make sense that we're so attracted to each other."

"Makes perfect sense to me. There's something you should know, Hope. I wanted you when we were next-door neighbors. I kept my hands off you then because it wouldn't have been right. I intend to do the same thing now, unless you change your mind, but it's not because I don't want you. Never that."

She took a deep breath. "Sexual attraction is something we ought to be mature enough to ignore. After all, we've both got histories of letting chemistry rush us into unwise romantic decisions. We've both lived to regret hasty marriages."

Coop opened his mouth, then shut it again.

"What?"

"I can think of entirely too many things I could say in response to that remark, which means I probably shouldn't say any of them."

"If we really are friends, Coop, you can say anything you want."

"Does that mean I can also ask anything I want?"

"As long as it works both ways."

"Fair enough. You're right, up to a point. I was young and stupid when I eloped with Julie. I was obsessed with her and I mistook good sex for love."

"You stayed together a long time."

"For Maureen's sake."

He seemed reluctant to say more, and Hope wasn't at all sure she wanted to know the details. She remembered her cousin well enough to be certain that it had been Julie who'd wrecked the marriage, no matter what Aunt Penny claimed.

"What about you, Hope? Why did you marry Elliot Rowan?"

Waves of shame washed over her. She'd never told anyone what her marriage had been like. It was harder to start than she'd anticipated. She dared a glance at Coop. His expression was guarded, almost dispassionate, but his eyes were sympathetic as they searched her face.

This was it, she decided. The true test of friendship. If she told Coop everything now, they could get on with an honest relationship. There would no longer be barriers between them.

"He controlled me with sex," she blurted. "We got married because we literally couldn't keep our hands off each other. At the end there was nothing else left. Nothing to base a life together on. Maybe there never had been."

The compassion in Coop's eyes did not dim, nor was it sullied by pity. If he felt any revulsion at her words, he did not allow it to show. Instead he said, "Sometimes it's scary how much we have in common."

Hope took a deep, steadying breath. "You had the strength to leave a bad marriage." All she'd ever done was quarrel with Elliot that last night, and send him to his death on icy winter roads. That was one confession she couldn't quite bring herself to make, not even to Coop.

"It took me twelve years to do it," Coop reminded her. "And to be honest, Julie was the one who demanded a divorce. I'd have stuck it out."

"At least you had a good reason to stay together. You had Maureen. I look back now on the three years I was married to Elliot and I can hardly believe I was such a fool. Three wasted years. And do you know the most terrifying part? If he hadn't died, I'd probably still be married to him, still letting him—" She broke off, suddenly too choked up to go on.

Coop reached for her hand, then drew back. "Hope?" She didn't answer.

"Hope, did he... abuse you?"

Her head jerked up. She started to deny it, then hesitated. "Not in the way you mean. Not physically."

"Can you talk about it?" He did take her hands then. His grip was gentle, comforting.

The words came more easily after that. "Elliot Rowan was a very charismatic man. Ask anyone. He could talk people into going along with things they'd never think of doing ordinarily. And he could take anything you said that went against what he thought and twist it until you felt like a fool, until you believed everything he said, even when you knew it was a lie."

Coop used one fingertip to wipe away tears Hope hadn't been aware she'd shed. She shied away from his touch, wary of his kindness. Elliot had seemed kind once, too.

"He used you," Coop said.

"I allowed myself to be used."

"It wasn't your fault."

Now she was gripping his hands, willing him to understand. "But it was. Don't you see? I gave him power over me." She couldn't bring herself to describe what it had been like, the way she'd been seduced, time and time again, going to bed with a man she'd started to hate because she'd been too weak-willed to resist the sensual lure.

He looked almost angry, but it did not come through in his voice. "Explain to me," he urged gently. "Help me to understand."

"I don't know that I can. I only know that I will never again turn over that much control over my life to anyone else."

"You're letting what one man did dictate how you live the rest of your life." Coop's voice altered slightly as he added, "And since we started this conversation talking about the sexual attraction between us, you'd better not be comparing me to Elliot Rowan. I'm nothing like that piece of scum."

She managed a weak smile. "I know that."

Neither of them spoke for a few moments. Then Hope shook herself free of memories. She released her grip on Coop's hands.

"I never meant to unload on you like this."

"That's what friends are for."

"It was my own fault that Elliot was able to make me over, to turn me into nothing more than an extension of himself."

"You were vulnerable." He gave her a thoughtful look. "Your parents had died recently, hadn't they?"

She nodded. "And my grandparents, too. I suppose I was feeling very alone in the world."

"You were taken in by a con man," Coop said bluntly.

Twisting her hands together in her lap, Hope reached for words. She'd gone this far. She might as well tell him everything. "What I feel for you when you kiss me is more powerful than anything I ever had with Elliot. That makes me feel vulnerable, weak. I can't risk getting involved with you, Coop. If things didn't work out between us, I don't know what I'd do, and frankly that scares the hell out of me." Coop had the power to hurt her far more than Elliot ever did. He'd already hurt her badly once, when he'd eloped with Julie.

"You're not making sense, Hope. And I have to tell you that you've got this weakness thing all wrong. You're one of the strongest women I know."

"You mean that, don't you? In spite of knowing about my phobia."

"Do you think that's why you stopped going out?" he asked abruptly. "To avoid temptation? To avoid meeting men like Elliot?"

Hope stared at him, startled and dismayed by the suggestion. She could understand how he might think that, but he was wrong. He had to be. "Whatever triggered the onset of my little problem, it was more than a desire to avoid men."

In her own mind Hope felt sure she could distinguish between what she thought of as her weakness, which was her fear of involvement, of getting her heart broken again, and her phobia, which had been something completely beyond her control. She wasn't at all sure that she could make the difference clear to Coop, though. She didn't know if she wanted to try when her thoughts were in such turmoil.

What he said next confused her even more.

"If Elliot Rowan wasn't already dead," Coop muttered under his breath, "I'd be tempted to kill him."

"Don't say that." Hope's voice shook. She knew, as Coop did not, that the one time she'd overcome her weakness and stood up to Elliot, the result had been horrifying.

In her darkest moments, she felt the guilt like an unbearable weight, pushing her down. She'd never meant to, but in the heat of anger that last night she had sent her husband to his death.

Chapter Eight

Several hours after Coop left, Hope heard frantic knocking at her front door. She turned off the computer and hurried downstairs, and when she saw who was there she quickly unlocked the door.

"Maureen! I didn't expect a visit from you today." There was no sign of the Pleasant Prospect van in the dooryard, or of any other car. "How did you get here?"

"Hitchhiked." Maureen stepped past her into the house, and her tone of voice dared Hope to criticize.

After considering all the various reactions she ought to have as a concerned relative, Hope settled for asking who had given Maureen a ride. The girl was obviously unhurt and healthy. Dangerous as what she'd done was, she'd survived unscathed. There would be time for lectures later.

Maureen discarded her coat and swooped down on Angel, who'd come to investigate the sound of a new arrival. Her voice was muffled by the cat's thick fur. "Barry's parents picked me up."

"Well, that's good, then." Hope followed Maureen and Angel toward the kitchen. Maureen helped herself to water and a packet of hot chocolate and fired up the microwave.

"Barry was in the back seat," she said in a small voice. Hope heard incipient tears. "He wouldn't speak to me the whole way from Norville."

"But that wasn't why you wanted to come here," Hope prompted, "or why you were hitchhiking. It's a long way from your grandmother's house to mine, and very cold out. I'm sure Aunt Penny would have driven you here if you'd asked her to."

"I wouldn't ask her for the time of day."

Hope blinked in surprise as Maureen turned to face her. The girl's eyes, eyes so like her father's, were shards of green ice. "I don't want to spend another minute with Grandmother Bellamy. Not ever. I knew I could get here on my own."

"Oh, Maureen," Hope murmured in dismay. "Don't you realize the risks you took? It's so dangerous to hitch a ride from anyone, even someone who isn't a stranger, and it's well below freezing outside. The idea of you trying to walk fifteen or twenty miles—"

"I'd have called you to come get me," Maureen interrupted, her tone defensive, "but I didn't think you could drive that far."

Hope blanched, never more painfully aware of how inadequate her problem made her as mother material. Even as a role model, she was sadly lacking. Before she could think of any reply, the phone rang. With a mute apology, she left Maureen in the kitchen and went into the living room to answer it. She wasn't at all surprised to hear Coop's voice on the other end of the telephone line.

"Barry just called me," he said without preamble. "I'd already heard from Mother Bellamy. I take it she's running away from home."

"Looks that way," Hope agreed. Coop sounded calm. She tried to match him.

"Talk to her, Hope. I don't know exactly what's going on here, but she needs somebody to straighten her out. You're—"

"I'm not her mother, Coop."

"Who said you were supposed to be?" The facade cracked. He was as upset by Maureen's precipitous actions as she was.

"Here's the deal, Coop," Hope told him. "Right now, first and foremost, I'm Maureen's friend. That may be a far cry from the role model you had in mind, but it's the best I can promise."

"I'll be over as soon as I can get away," he said, and hung up.

"Was that Dad?" Maureen asked from the doorway.

"Yes. Do you want to come in and sit down? It will be a while before he arrives." Hope indicated the other half of the sofa.

"I don't want to go back to the condo, either. Can I live here with you?" Maureen put her cocoa on the end table and reached for Angel again.

"I wouldn't be any easier to get along with than any other adult in your life," Hope warned as girl and cat settled in beside her. "And you were right. I'm not much good at coming through with rides."

"My life could not get any worse," Maureen declared with the overdramatic passion only a young girl could manage.

"Why don't you tell me about it," Hope suggested.

"You were there. You saw how mad Dad was about Barry. Ever since, things have just gotten worse and worse. Amie blabbed. I confided in her and she told everybody in the school."

Hope remembered well how painful it was to think the whole world knew something embarrassing about you. "Is that why Barry isn't speaking to you?"

"I guess." Maureen had her face buried in Angel's fur again. "I thought Grandmother Bellamy would understand. I told her everything."

Noting the aggrieved tone, Hope waited.

"She said Amie isn't really my friend and I shouldn't have anything to do with her from now on. And then she said Barry isn't good enough for me, so I shouldn't care what he thinks. And then she said Dad couldn't possibly know what was best for me. She said I ought to go back to my old school."

"Did you like it there?"

"No. I hated it. I don't want to leave here. Living with Dad is so much better than..." She broke off, looking guilty.

"Boarding school?"

"And living with my mother. And better than living with both of them before the divorce, too. They yelled at each other all the time. And I don't think my mother liked me very much. She sent me away just as soon as Dad moved out."

"Your father won't do that, Maureen. You know he won't."

Looking doubtful, Maureen fought tears. "But when I called Dad to come for me, he said I had to stay with Grandmother Bellamy because he was too busy to get away. That's when I left on my own." She sighed deeply and released the cat. "And now Dad is mad at me again, too. Are you sure I can't stay here with you? This has been one of the worst days of my life."

Hope tugged the girl into her arms. "Things will get better, Maureen. I think I can promise you that."

"When?"

"Well, that's the trouble, isn't it? Nobody can predict how long anything will take, especially when you have to bring other people around to your point of view."

"Grandmother Bellamy hates my father, and she's just mean enough to trick him into sending me away again. She's an awful old witch."

Hope felt the trembling in the thin shoulders, but with disconcerting maturity, Maureen refused to cry. The legacy of that boarding school? Aunt Penny had a lot to answer for, but Hope knew she was misguided, not evil, and believed that Maureen needed to understand the difference.

"Let me tell you a story," she said, stroking the girl's tangled hair from her face.

"About you and my father?" Maureen asked.

"No. About me and your grandmother and about one of the worst days in my life. You see, once I thought of her as an old witch, too, until I discovered that under all her strict rules there is a softer side."

Maureen looked doubtful, but Hope settled herself more comfortably on the sofa, with one arm around Maureen's shoulders, and used her free hand to point to the corner knickknack shelf.

"See the figurine of the lady in the ballgown? The one with the fan? That used to belong to your grandmother. She gave it to me."

"It's broken," Maureen said after a moment. The crack at the wrist, just below the opened fan, had been carefully mended, but to someone with Maureen's sharp eyes the damage was easy to spot.

"That's right. I broke it. When I was about eight years old, I was staying at Aunt Penny's house for the weekend, and I thought that little lady was the most beautiful thing I'd ever seen. It was kept up on a high wall shelf and even though I'd been told not to touch anything in the parlor, I couldn't resist climbing up on the piano bench and taking it down to look at more closely."

"You dropped it?"

"I dropped it. And the hand with the fan broke right off. I was absolutely terrified. Aunt Penny was just as scary then as she can be now. She hardly ever smiles, and she's very strict."

"She's an ugly old witch," Maureen said again. Hope didn't contradict her. That was exactly how Aunt Penny had struck Hope at age eight.

"I thought about getting rid of the evidence, but I couldn't bring myself to destroy something that was still so pretty."

Hope hesitated, wondering how much editing to do as she told the rest of the story. It had been Julie who'd suggested smashing the figurine to dust. Even after all this time, Hope wondered if her older cousin would have ratted on her afterward. That seemed likely. Either that or Julie would have held the threat of telling over Hope's head for years thereafter. Grimacing, she decided to leave Julie's role out of her rendition entirely.

"It took all my courage," Hope continued, "but I finally faced up to what I'd done. I wrapped the two pieces in tissues so they wouldn't get damaged any more than they already were, and I showed them to Aunt Penny."

"Did she yell?"

Hope shook her head. "She was upset. I could see that. But then she took a good look at me and realized just how scared I was. The next thing I knew, she got right down on her knees next to me and she said, 'You broke it, so you'll have to fix it.' Then she showed me how to glue the two pieces back together, and she convinced me that the figurine was almost as good as new."

"Did she give it to you then?"

"No, she didn't. Which is why I know she meant what she said. She kept that mended figurine in its regular place, where everyone could see it, for years afterward. I was thirteen when she finally made me a present of it. She said she thought I was probably safely through my clumsy stage by then. I bought other bisque figures after that, ones I particularly liked when I saw them in stores, but none of them ever meant as much to me as the lady with the fan."

Neither one of them had heard Coop come in. Hope had no idea how much of the story he'd listened to. His face was carefully blank. Hope held her breath, praying he'd figured out for himself that being angry at Maureen right now wouldn't help anything.

"Ready to go home?" he asked.

Maureen flung herself into his arms.

When they left together, Hope was happy for them, but she couldn't remember when she'd felt more alone.

"Yoohoo! Coop!" Ginny Devereux's loud voice echoed across the bunny slope.

Coop ignored her and continued giving advice to a six-year-old novice skier. He'd taken over the class while his regular instructor got a tooth filled, and had enjoyed every minute of it.

Ginny waited until the children had started to disperse before she came closer. "You're good with the little rug rats." She sounded surprised.

Maureen could take credit for that, he thought, and he felt once again the sense of relief that his relationship with his daughter was less shaky than it had been on Sunday. For first time, after leaving Hope's house together, they'd talked about the school in Connecticut and about Julie's death. Coop had given Maureen his solemn promise that he'd never send her away when he'd realized that she'd done her grieving for her mother almost three years before Julie actually died. Maureen had felt she'd lost both parents for good when they divorced.

To Ginny he said only, "Part of the job. Those kids have parents with deep pockets."

She lifted one finely drawn eyebrow. "You could do better than this, Coop. Ever think about getting into real estate?"

"Thanks, but no thanks, Ginny."

He was tempted to tell her what his real job was. He'd begun to wonder lately if it was worth the effort to keep his ownership of the resort a secret.

"Tell me, Coop—what do you charge for private lessons?"

"More than you can afford," he answered, well aware that in Ginny's mind ski instructor equaled gigolo, a misconception that was probably his own fault. He knew she'd discounted getting home to Maureen as a reason for him to cut short their one evening together. Trust Ginny to have put her own interpretation on an invitation to dinner and the subsequent refusal to take her to bed.

She answered this second rejection with a pout. "Don't be so sure what I can and can't afford. I do all right for myself." The sun caught her bright red hair and the gold hoops in her ears.

"I'm sure you do. What brings you to Pleasant Prospect, Ginny?"

"I wanted to give you a little Valentine's Day gift." Before Coop could guess what she intended, let alone stop her, Ginny was embracing him. She was almost as tall as he was, and had no trouble finding his mouth. Her hands were just as busy, unzipping his ski jacket and sliding an envelope into the inner pocket. "Give me a call when you have a chance to think about it," she whispered wetly into his ear. With one last nibble, she released him.

Scattered giggles told Coop that the stragglers from his beginner class had witnessed the entire spectacle.

Coop had to put up with some good-natured ribbing from his employees after that, but once Ginny left he got on with the rest of the day. It turned out to be a busy one. At first he ignored the Valentine's Day card Ginny had slipped into his pocket. Eventually he forgot all about it. He didn't think of it again until he removed his ski jacket in the hallway at home.

No sooner had Coop withdrawn the bright pink envelope from his pocket than Maureen appeared on the upper floor, leaning over the balustrade to greet him. "Hey, Dad!" she exclaimed. "You got a valentine. Is it from Hope?"

"No, it isn't." He tossed it, with what he hoped was a casual air, onto the hall table where Maureen had left the mail. He turned his back on his daughter while he hung up his jacket. "You know Hope and I aren't sweethearts."

"You don't have to be in love to send a valentine," she informed him. "You just have to like someone."

Too late, Coop heard the sound of an envelope being ripped open. Maureen had snaked a hand down through the railing to filch Ginny's card off the table. Before he could stop her, she'd read it.

From this distance it looked innocuous. Typical hearts and flowers. He could only hope Ginny hadn't written anything obscene inside. "Give me that, Maureen. I don't read your mail."

"Mama used to." She passed him the card and envelope but held onto the single sheet of thin paper that had been enclosed.

Coop took the stairs two at a time but he was too late to stop Maureen from unfolding it and reading the contents.

"Wow, Dad." Her eyes were wide as she looked at him over the top. "And you were upset about one little kiss."

Coop held out his hand and waited. She giggled as she handed it over. He sent her a quelling glare, then dropped his gaze to the sheet of paper.

His first reaction was appalled disbelief. His second was a strangled chuckle.

There was no name on the document he held. It had been neatly blacked out. But these were obviously Ginny's test results, and it was equally obvious that this was her idea of an invitation to begin an affair. She'd given him the report on a very recent blood test.

Coop wondered if he was now supposed to provide one in return. The irony of it was that he actually could. He'd had himself tested right after the divorce, when he'd entertained the gravest suspicions about what Julie had been up to during the last year of their marriage. He'd thought she might have been cheating on him. It had turned out he did have a rival, but it had been her career, not another man.

"Uh, Dad? Is there something you want to tell me?"

Reluctantly, Coop met his twelve-year-old daughter's knowing expression. He kept trying to believe she was an innocent, but there were few taboos these days. Between school and television, she'd already learned the basic facts about sex and most of its risks. He was less sure how much she knew about love.

"For the past three years," he said carefully, "I've had sense enough to be careful, not only with my health but with my heart."

He couldn't tell Maureen that Ginny was too much like Julie to hold his interest, and that wasn't the main issue now, anyway. Maureen was clearly expecting him to tell her how he felt about casual affairs. It was up to him to make sure she knew that he was too particular these days to settle for simple physical release.

Taking his daughter by the hand, he led her over to the comfortable blue and white striped sofa that faced the television and sank down on the cushions to stare at the blank screen. His mind felt equally blank.

"The lady who gave me this card," he finally began, "is interested in me, but I'm not interested in her. When two people decide to start an, er, intimate relationship, there should be more than physical attraction between them. There should also be respect and love."

"How do you know when you're in love?" Maureen asked.

"That's the tricky part," Coop admitted. "And another good reason to be cautious. If you make a mistake, it can affect your whole life. These days, it can even cost you your life."

"Oh, Daddy," Maureen said. "I know that." She looked at him, her expression serious, and added, "That's why you should always wear a condom."

Maureen didn't seem particularly embarrassed, but Coop felt heat creep up his face and into the roots of his hair. "Er, right," he said.

She leaned over and kissed his cheek. "I'm glad you aren't going to go out with that Ginny person again," she said. While he sat there, thunderstruck, she bounced up off the sofa. "She signed the card," Maureen explained. "I've got homework to finish. See ya."

Coop stayed where he was, mentally reviewing the conversation that had just taken place. He didn't think he'd handled things too badly, considering that he'd completely lost control of the discussion.

With a sigh that was half relief and half exasperation, he rested his head against the back of the sofa and closed his eyes. For the first time in months, he deliberately thought about the past and Julie's part in it. There had been some good times, he admitted. At first.

They'd been a couple of mixed-up kids who'd decided they were in love. Mostly they'd been out to have a good time. He hadn't even been too angry when she'd confessed to lying about being pregnant. And then she really had gotten pregnant, with Maureen. Suddenly everything had been different. Better. More stable.

The birth of his daughter had changed Coop's life. The moment he'd looked into that tiny face and seen his own eyes looking back at him, he'd known that the time had come to shape up. He'd been elated when Julie agreed with him, and together they'd worked out a master plan. First he'd put her through college. Then she'd work while he got his degree.

Everything had appeared to be falling into place right on schedule. He'd worked nights and taken care of Maureen during the day while Julie got her education. When she'd accepted her first job, a good one in middle management, she'd moved up fast. He'd continued to be Maureen's primary care giver even while he was taking a full course load.

By the time Coop had his degree in business, Julie was CEO of a small company. Everything should have been perfect, but by then they'd no longer had much in common except their eight-year-old daughter. That was when Julie had tried to turn him into an ornament.

"Stand by my side at cocktail parties and look good," she'd said. "I'll do the rest."

"What about Maureen?" he'd asked. "You don't spend much time with her."

"We'll send her away to some nice boarding school. It will be good for her. She'll meet the right sort of girls."

That was when he'd known the marriage was over. He hadn't filed for divorce only because he'd thought that staying together would be better for Maureen. So much for what he'd wanted! Julie had divorced him, put Maureen in school and continued to pursue her career. The court hadn't even considered letting him raise his daughter. He hadn't had a job then, and he hadn't had any savings.

When Julie had been given full custody, Coop had tried to give her the benefit of the doubt, to assume she actually did think she was doing what was best for Maureen, but he couldn't be sorry he had their daughter now. He knew Maureen was far happier at Norville Junior-Senior High and living with him than she'd ever been in that posh Connecticut girl's school.

She was also turning out to be more of a handful than he'd anticipated. She was growing up, approaching womanhood . . . and beginning to remind him that she was Julie's daughter, too. There were times lately when he wished he could just lock her in her room till she turned thirty.

He'd been right to think she needed a woman's influence in her life, a good role model. She'd had three years in that school to reinforce Julie's twisted view of family life. Somehow, he had to counteract that.

The image of Hope crept into his mind. Coop still did not understand why he was drawn to Hope so strongly or why, after all these years, he still found himself wanting to protect her. The impulses were decidedly contradictory, especially since he was the one she was most likely to need protection from.

His fists clenched involuntarily and the crinkle of paper brought him abruptly back to the present. He'd crumpled the results of Ginny's blood test in his hand. A grim smile twisted Coop's lips as he looked at it. Ginny had been having an affair with Elliot Rowan. If she was healthy, then Hope was, too. Considering how promiscuous Rowan had apparently been, Coop tried to tell himself he was glad of it, for his friend's sake.

Only he wasn't thinking about friendship. He was thinking that what he had just told Maureen was true. Sex without love was empty.

And love was the greatest risk of all.

As the evening wore on, Coop found he couldn't stop thinking of Maureen's words of wisdom. "You don't have to be in love to send a valentine," she said. "You just have to like someone."

For a twelve-year-old, she was one smart cookie.

Coop considered and discarded several ideas. He couldn't do anything that night anyway. He didn't want to leave Maureen alone at the condo and he didn't want her along on this particular visit to Hope's house.

The next morning he made one stop, at the resort gift shop, then headed for Tardiff.

"Happy Belated Valentine's Day," he said as Hope opened her door.

She looked at the heart-shaped box he was holding out to her with suspicion.

"Relax, no jack-in-the-box snakes are going to spring out at you when you open it."

"That's not what's worrying me." She stood back and let him into the house, but she continued to watch him with a wary expression on her face. "I thought we were just friends."

"According to my intelligent daughter, valentine presents are a gift of like as well as a gift of love. I did consider sending this over with a delivery boy and signing the card 'your secret admirer' but I decided I wanted to see you. Besides, this way you have to share."

He was following her toward the living room and would have missed her change in expression if the light hadn't illuminated her face at just that moment. Coop frowned. "Hope? What have I said wrong now?"

"It's not you. Just a stray memory."

"Not a good one by the look of you."

"Something silly."

She sat on the sofa and began to open the box of chocolates. He sank down beside her and waited, hoping she'd share both her thought and the candy. After a moment, she met his questioning gaze.

"When I was a freshman in college, before my parents moved to Texas, I got a valentine, mailed from home, signed 'your secret admirer' in bright red ink. I didn't know who it was from, but there was someone in Norville I'd hoped would remember me."

To Coop's surprise, he felt a brief flash of jealousy toward this unknown suitor.

"I convinced myself it was from him, and I wrote him a note to thank him. Then, when I called home the next weekend, I found out the terrible truth. My mother had sent the card. As a joke."

"Ouch."

"I never felt quite the same about Valentine's Day after that."

"He *should* have sent you a card. Whoever he was."

Hope plucked a chocolate-covered cherry from the box and held it toward his mouth. "Open up."

Coop savored the taste, and watched enviously as she lifted a cream-filled confection to her own lips. Awareness crackled between them, building as they consumed the candy. Without a word, they turned toward each other on the sofa, the box on Hope's lap forgotten. Their lips were only an inch apart when she spoke.

"What are we doing?"

"Giving in to temptation?"

"This isn't smart."

"I know." Coop also knew he ought to be fighting the urge a lot harder, if only to protect his own peace of mind. He ought to be thinking about protecting her, too, from the risk of getting too deeply involved with him.

Neither of them seemed to have the willpower to pull back. Slowly, inevitably, they both leaned closer. One stolen kiss. What harm could that do?

Lips touched lightly, then with more assurance. Hope sighed her pleasure.

It was all Coop could do not to haul her into his arms and keep on kissing her until they were both sated. The taste of chocolate on her lips was proving an unexpected aphrodisiac. Instead, he let her go.

"Would it be so bad?"

"No. Just . . . complicated."

He waited for an explanation, but none came. Only another sigh.

"Maybe . . . someday . . . if I can only be sure."

"Of me?"

"Of myself." Hope saw the question in his eyes but couldn't give him any better answers. She was still struggling to understand what she felt herself. "I need time. And I can't talk about this now."

"I'll try to be patient, Hope, but you know that's not my strong suit."

Elliot would have pushed, right into bed. Hope's awareness of that fact was as great as her sense of Coop's restraint. That meant Coop cared about her as a person, and that meant that maybe, just maybe, they did have a chance for something more than friendship. If only she wasn't such a coward.

Insecurity plagued her, and self-doubt. What if it was only wishful thinking on her part that made her believe Coop was different? How could she take the risk that she might be wrong about him? Coop already meant far more to her than Elliot ever had. The attraction between them went beyond chemistry. Even now, losing just his friendship would devastate her. She didn't dare contemplate how she would feel if they became lovers before he left her.

"If it helps any," Coop said, "I probably have some of the same concerns you do, and for similar reasons. And I've got one more. If we start an affair it affects more than just our relationship. Maureen would probably start to think of us as a couple. Then, if we eventually split up, she'd take it almost as hard as she took my divorce from her mother."

"A sobering thought, and I guess that means we don't really have any choice." Hope wondered why she didn't feel more relieved by what seemed to be a mutual decision. "Maureen has been hurt enough. She needs all the stability she can get in her life. An affair could threaten that, but our continued friendship doesn't."

"So, we stick with friendship?"

Just as she'd been urging all along. "We know we can succeed at it. Look at all the practice we've had." They shook hands solemnly, and Coop filched another chocolate.

By the time he left to return to work, they'd planned the next week's worth of outings, occasions when they'd work on Hope's desensitization.

All three of them.

Hope didn't know where Coop was taking her on the last Saturday in February, but she was certain she'd enjoy herself. Ever since she'd started driving again, nearly two weeks earlier, one success had followed another. She hadn't experienced even the whisper of a panic attack. She hadn't tried to over-extend herself, either, but she couldn't help but feel optimistic.

He parked in the lot next to the Norville fire station. The faint sound of music drifted out from the upper level. Visions of being held tight in Coop's arms as they danced flashed into Hope's mind. The interior of the van suddenly seemed overly warm.

Coop cleared his throat. "I guess you can tell there's a dance tonight. I thought we might try socializing a little."

"Why do I suddenly feel like a teenager on her first date?" Could he tell she was blushing? Did he remember the agreement they'd reached ten days earlier, after their Valentine's Day kiss?

"Not to worry," Coop assured her in a gruff voice that betrayed he was a little nervous, too. "I'm not going to put any moves on you. And neither is anyone else. This is billed as nostalgia night. Nothing but sixties rock and roll. We'll be dancing a good two feet apart all evening."

"That's a relief."

"Yeah."

As she got out of the car and took Coop's arm, Hope felt certain neither one of them was relieved that there would be no touching. What they were both enduring, and would have to continue to endure for the sake of their friendship, was frustration.

One week later, little had changed, including Mike's Market. Hope's first impression was that Mike hadn't altered so much as a floor display since the last time she'd been in his store. That shopping trip, nearly two years earlier, was still vivid in her mind. It had been one of the worst experiences of her life and she dreaded the possibility of a repetition, but it was too late to back out now. She took a deep breath and squeezed Coop's hand to let him know she was still okay.

Maureen plucked a cart from the row at the entrance and pushed it past the baked goods display. "Oh, finger rolls," she said. "They make great snacks."

"Did you ever make bread sticks?" Hope asked.

"Like the ones they give you in restaurants, the ones that taste like long, fat, cardboard pretzels?"

"No, I mean the kind you create yourself from plain old white bread. You roll it up and squash it together in your fist and once it holds its shape you can nibble it down from end to end."

"Yuck," said Maureen.

"Is there no end to your depravity?" Coop's teasing voice cheered her. In the week since the dance at the fire station, in spite of the continual sensual awareness that hummed between them, they'd managed to relax in each other's company.

They went up and down the aisles, picking up odds and ends Hope was out of while they searched for the special ingredients they needed for their dinner tonight. It was going to be a group effort and had been Maureen's idea. Hope suspected that Coop's daughter might also be trying her hand at matchmaking, but she was sure she and Coop could handle that. They'd done all right so far, and Maureen's presence always made it easier to keep things under control.

One or two other shoppers recognized Hope and stopped to say hello. No one remarked on how long it had been since they'd last seen her in Mike's Market. Quite possibly they didn't realize. Hope smiled to herself. Amazing how self-centered a person could become. Of course they hadn't noticed. Other people's worlds didn't revolve around Hope Rowan's comings and goings.

"What's so funny?" Coop asked.

"I am," Hope told him, but she didn't explain. It had been the same at the dance. Old acquaintances had just assumed their paths hadn't crossed in a while. No one thought her long absence from their lives at all odd.

Maureen went off on her own after the eggs, and Hope and Coop rounded the next corner side by side. Coop's sudden stillness alerted her that something was wrong. She looked down the aisle, unsure what to expect. The only person in sight hardly seemed to merit such a strong reaction.

"Well," Ginny Devereux drawled as she sauntered toward them. "Fancy meeting you two here."

"Small world," Coop said.

Ginny sidled closer and Hope noticed she had neither cart nor basket. As usual, she was stylishly dressed in clothes that emphasized her generous proportions. She was the kind of woman who made other women feel inadequate, and it didn't improve Hope's mood when Ginny lifted one hand and ran her brightly painted fingernails along one side of Coop's face. "I thought you'd have called me by now, big boy."

Hope got it then. Ginny had been one of Coop's old girlfriends. She obviously thought he was worth getting to know again. Hope could hardly fault her for that.

"I've been busy, Ginny," he said in a strangely flat voice.

"So I see." Her disdainful gaze swept over Hope, then fixed on the grocery cart. "Eating in, Hope? At least he took me out to dinner."

Hope ignored the barb, though she felt its prick as a sharp, deep pain. She was determined not to let the other woman see that she'd been hurt. So Coop had taken out an old flame. No big deal. Hope had no claim on him. They were just friends.

And as a friend, Hope was aware of Coop's discomfort. He was not acting like a man who wanted to impress a woman. He didn't even seem to like Ginny much at the moment. That made Hope wonder exactly what had happened on their dinner date, and then she wondered if Ginny had come into Mike's Market only because she'd recognized the Pleasant Prospect van in the parking lot. Was she actually so hard up that she had to chase a man? The idea cheered up Hope considerably.

"What brings you to this neck of the woods?" she asked sweetly. "Slumming?"

Ginny's throaty voice was very nearly a purr. "Why, my dear, you know I'm always looking for land to buy."

"I wasn't aware any of my neighbors were interested in selling."

Ginny's glance flicked to Coop and then away. That he was glowering at her didn't seem to faze her in the least. "It's only too obvious that you don't know a lot of what goes on."

Coop stepped between them, interrupting before Ginny could say anything more. "We're running late, Hope. Let's collect Maureen and get going."

"You collect Maureen," Hope suggested. "I'd like to have a word with our old friend Ginny. Alone."

Reluctantly, he left them together. They watched his retreat, and Hope was willing to bet that Ginny and she were, at least momentarily, sharing a similar frustration as they stared appreciatively at that magnificent back view.

She sighed and shifted her focus to the other woman. "All right, Ginny. Spit it out. You were itching to tell me something the other day when you came to the house. What is it?" She suspected now that Ginny's visit had really been about Coop, but she kept up the fiction that Ginny only wanted Hope's land. "Is there gold on my property? Oil wells, maybe? A tourmaline mine? Just what is it that prompted your sudden interest?"

"You think I'm going to share my secrets? I'm in the real estate business to make money for myself."

"It doesn't matter, you know. I have no intention of giving up anything that's mine."

"Pity your husband died," Ginny snapped. "He knew there were advantages to doing business with me."

With that enigmatic statement, she turned and stalked away, leaving Hope to stare after her in confusion. She'd expected the other woman to make some remark about Coop, since it was obvious they'd seen each other since he'd been back. Instead she'd brought up Elliot, which made no sense to Hope at all.

Still puzzled, Hope headed for the checkout line, where Coop immediately began to argue that he should pay for the groceries.

"We're eating two-thirds of them," he pointed out.

"So next time you cook. I pay for my own groceries."

"Okay. I'll cook. At my place."

Coop's place was twenty miles from her house. But that was only six miles beyond the fire station. Hope's self-confidence soared as she sent a radiant smile in Coop's direction.

"Why not?"

He grinned at her. "Good. What about Friday?"

"What about it?" she teased. "It's a day of the week. It's almost a week away from today. It's not the thirteenth. Is it?"

"No, it isn't. I'll pick you up at five."

"Fine. Okay with you, kiddo?" she asked Maureen, who had been listening to their conversation with undisguised interest.

Maureen's face was wreathed in smiles. "You're a nut, Dad," she said. "You, too, Hope."

"Why, thank you. I think. Does that mean I can come over?"

Maureen giggled. "Of course it does."

"Good." Hope dug her wallet out of her ten-pound purse and paid for the groceries.

They were out of the store and loading the bags into Coop's van before she remembered that another small milestone had just been passed. Her last shopping expedition to Mike's had been a disaster, but the onset of her agoraphobia seemed like a nightmare to her now, something remote and ready to be forgotten.

Dinner that night became a celebration.

It lacked nothing but a congratulatory kiss.

Chapter Nine

Maureen shifted her weight from one foot to the other and kept her eyes on the pale lavender wall-to-wall carpet that decorated her bedroom. If ever a kid personified guilt, Coop thought with reluctant amusement, Maureen did at this moment.

"You have to stop embarrassing the boy," he said gently.

Maureen remained silent, standing halfway between a poster of the latest bare-chested teen heartthrob and the shelf where she kept the teddy bear she'd had as a baby and a Barbie doll and a framed photograph of her mother.

"Barry and I had a long heart-to-heart talk earlier today—"

"Da-a-ad! How could you?"

The wail came from the heart, but he couldn't apologize. "He told Hope and she thought I should know. Then, when I talked to Barry myself, he confirmed that you're being such a pest that some of the boys in his class are getting on his case about it. Believe me, the last thing you want for either of you is to have all the other kids gossiping about you."

She looked as if she might cry, and Coop wondered if he should have waited until he could talk to her with Hope present. But as he watched, his daughter straightened her shoulders and lifted her head and glared at him.

"I bet my mother had a boyfriend when she was my age," Maureen said defiantly.

"That's not much of a recommendation." As soon as the words were out, Coop regretted them. Somehow, he had to deal with this without bad-mouthing Julie. Maureen and her mother might not have been close when Julie was alive, but she ought to be left with whatever good memories there were.

Coop raked his fingers through his hair and lowered himself to sit at the foot of Maureen's bed. The whole room reflected a disconcerting mixture of little girl and budding woman. He scowled at the collection of makeup and jewelry on the dresser. Penny Bellamy considered all that suitable. Come to think of it, Julie had encouraged Maureen to get her ears pierced when she was only eight. Was he the one out of step here?

Maureen stood with her arms crossed in front of her flat chest, and she was still glaring at him. This was easier to deal with than tears, he told himself, and patted the mattress beside him, inviting her to sit. She ignored the gesture. He warned himself to be patient.

"This isn't about anyone else but you and Barry," he said slowly, "and you're right that I shouldn't interfere, and after today I won't say another word on the subject, but just this once you'll have to put up with me pontificating."

Maureen gave a long, drawn-out sigh.

"Very theatrical, but not very convincing," Coop told her. "I give it a five."

He took heart from the twitch of her lips. She was having to fight to hold on to her irritation.

"Okay. Here are the words of wisdom. There's no getting around the fact that Barry is four years older than you are. He's got different interests. I'm sure he doesn't mind being your friend, but to him you're still a little girl. When it comes to this kissing business and you asking him to take you to the movies, what it boils down to is that you're just too young for him."

At last, Maureen came over and sat down beside him. "But, Daddy," she protested, "it isn't really four years at all. I'm nearly thirteen and Barry's just barely sixteen. His birthday was in November. That's only three years. Just like you and Hope."

"Three years, or four, or even more, don't mean much when you're older, but right now, at least from a boy's point of view, even three years seems like a century."

"But you and Hope—"

"Trust me on this one, Maureen. When I was sixteen I never for a minute considered taking Hope out to the movies or to a dance. I'd have been just as shocked and upset as Barry is if she'd up and kissed me the way you kissed him. And I'd have been embarrassed. In fact, I'd probably have retaliated, and I'd have been a whole lot nastier than Barry's been to you."

"Nasty? How?"

"The truth?"

She nodded.

"I'd probably have played some kind of practical joke on her, to try to embarrass her right back. Maybe I'd have stuck a piece of notebook paper on her back with tape. I'd have written something rude on it first, of course.''

Maureen's stifled giggle told him that old trick was still in use. "What would the note have said?"

Coop decided shock tactics were called for. "I'd have written: Kiss me. I'm easy.''

"You wouldn't!"

"I might have. I was a rotten kid. Ask anyone. The point here is that when I was sixteen, I'd never have been interested in a girl so much younger than I was." A year later, things had changed drastically, but Coop didn't think Maureen needed to know that.

Maureen mulled over what he'd said. "So, you liked Hope then, but not as a girlfriend?"

"Right. I'd started dating at sixteen, but I only went out with girls my own age, or maybe one year younger.''

"What about now?"

"What about now, what?"

"What about now with Hope? You took her to a dance. Does that mean you're dating her?"

There was a spark of something Coop didn't like in his daughter's eyes. Had this whole discussion of age differences and dating been set up just to get an answer to that question?

"Dad? Aren't you going to tell me?" She was looking at him warily, as though she thought he might think she had no right to know.

He shook his head to clear it. Maureen didn't have to come up with plots to find out how he felt about Hope. All she had to do was ask. And she had. Now all he had to do was be honest with her.

"This isn't as easy as you might think," he confided. "I'm not always sure myself just what my relationship with Hope is."

"You don't know if you're dating?" Maureen sounded incredulous.

"We go places together as friends. We did that in high school, too."

"Oh." This time her voice betrayed her disappointment.

"I like Hope now even more than I did when I was younger," he mused aloud, trying to sort things out as much for himself as for Maureen. "The three-year difference doesn't matter anymore, but we've both had unhappy relationships with other people, so we're both a little gun-shy." Looking at his daughter, he met her intense gaze head-on. The one thing that was more important to him than anything else was maintaining a good relationship with Maureen. "We aren't ready to get serious about each other. Not yet, anyway. We just like to spend time together, especially if that time is also spent with you."

Maureen's face crinkled into a frown. His rambling explanation didn't seem to have had the effect he'd wanted. "Do you like her more than she likes you?"

"Maybe."

"Is that why you let her think I'd be here on Friday?"

For a moment Coop just stared at her, torn between exasperation and laughter. "How old are you again?" he finally asked, and reached over to ruffle her hair. She'd done it to him again, neatly turning the conversation topsy-turvy.

"Da-a-ad!" she squealed as she jumped up and went to grab a comb. She stood in front of the mirror, carefully repairing the damage. "Face it, Dad. You have a date with Hope on Friday night while I'm away."

"Okay. Okay. I'm guilty. I set Hope up. I want to spend some time alone with her and I wasn't sure she'd accept the invitation if she knew you were going to be in Boston that night. She's even more reluctant to, uh, date than I am."

"You're hoping she'll stay overnight," Maureen said smugly, meeting his eyes in the mirror. Once again he had the uncanny impression that she was twelve going on thirty. "I think you're in love with Hope. Are you going to ask her to marry you?"

He couldn't come right out and deny either the accusation or the possibility, not if he intended to be truthful with his daughter. He hedged instead. "Neither Hope nor I intends to rush into anything. It was probably a stupid idea of mine to try and trick her. Tell you what, Maureen, I'll confess all, let Hope know you won't be home that night, if you want me to." He had to set a good example, he supposed. Maybe he'd get lucky and Hope wouldn't be angry at his deceit.

"That's okay. I think you two should spend more time together. Besides, she'll probably find out about the trip anyway. There's going to be an article in the paper."

"Figures."

The *Norville Journal* was little more than a twice-weekly gossip column. If there was no crisis over zoning ordinances or school funding, the new books at the library were likely to be a lead story. It had been a minor miracle that no one had noticed his name in the real estate transfers when he'd taken over Pleasant Prospect. That Maureen's class was going to Boston to spend Friday night on a camp out inside one of its museums was newsworthy of the entire front page and would be impossible for Hope to miss.

"I can ask Barry to steal her paper as soon as it's delivered," Maureen suggested. "Then she'll never know until it's too late."

He didn't know whether to be amused or dismayed. Now Maureen seemed to be casting him in the role of practiced seducer. And the ease with which she mentioned Barry made him suspicious of that relationship all over again.

"Let me get this straight," he said as he stood. "Are you telling me that you wouldn't be upset if I ended up married again?"

Maureen's brilliant smile was undoubtedly genuine. "Not if you married Hope."

"Then listen closely, Maureen. If, and that's a big if, there's any chance of that happening, that's for Hope and me to figure out. Hope's a very independent lady, and she's not as slow on the pickup as I am. She'd resent anyone playing Cupid." As an afterthought he added, "She's capable of going out and buying her own paper these days, too, as you well know."

Maureen attempted to look innocent, but her eyes were twinkling. "You sure are defensive, Dad. You know what they say about protesting too much."

"She'll see right through any heavy-handed matchmaking schemes," he said bluntly. "No tricks, Maureen. I mean it."

"I promise, Dad. But..."

"What?"

She looked very serious. "If you *need* my help, you've got to promise you'll ask for it."

Resigned, Coop stopped trying to convince her that he hadn't been hoping for a romantic weekend. "I promise, Maureen, as long as you remember that you can't arrange my life, or Hope's, to suit yourself."

It occurred to him, after he left Maureen to do her homework, that lately he'd been the one trying to rearrange Hope's life. She didn't seem to mind, which was a good thing. He had a feeling that it was far too late for him to stop now. It was too late, too, to stop trying to protect Hope, or to stop trying to cure her.

Or even to stop himself from falling in love with her.

Hope contemplated the nearly empty carton, then glanced out the kitchen window. It was an overcast Wednesday afternoon. Snow was predicted by evening, but for the moment the roads were clear and no precipitation was falling. If she left at once, she could drive to the store, pick up more milk and be back well before the storm hit.

She saw no reason not to do so.

She'd been to Mike's Market twice since she'd gone there with Coop and Maureen. She didn't expect to encounter a bit of difficulty this time, either.

It was just starting to spit snow when Hope came into the parking lot with the milk and a few other items she'd added to her list at the last moment. She put the grocery bag in the trunk and turned up the collar on her coat. It was getting windy, too. The storm was early.

Hope didn't worry too much about driving home. She'd had years of experience on winter roads, even if none of it was very recent. All it took, she reminded herself firmly, was a little common sense and caution and an awareness that in conditions like these snow could turn without warning to sleet. She reduced her speed accordingly.

The road was slick under her tires. She could feel it. Tightening her grip on the steering wheel, Hope peered through the windshield. She had to squint a bit to see—the flakes were coming down faster and faster, creating a disconcerting tunnel effect.

It took Hope much longer than usual to reach Columbia Hill Road, and by then she suspected that the surface of the road had turned to black ice. When she felt her car begin to slide as she made the turn off Route 2, she pumped the brakes, but it did no good. An instant later they locked on her. A sense of profound helplessness engulfed Hope as the car began to spin. Matters were out of her control, and everything seemed to be happening in slow motion.

At the same time events were going much too fast to stop. The car slid on, into the ditch and out again, scraping along a stand of pine until it finally bounced to a stop. The hood came to rest against a sturdy evergreen tree.

The impact wasn't hard, but it left Hope momentarily breathless. When the first shock passed, she took stock. A hasty check revealed no bumps or bruises. Nary a scrape. She hadn't really expected to find anything wrong. It was difficult to be seriously hurt when you were only traveling at five miles an hour.

The car didn't seem to be severely damaged, either. However, contact with the tree had caused the engine to stall. Hope turned the key and removed it from the ignition, which shut down the windshield wipers and the heater at the same time. In the sudden silence, she realized just how stormy the afternoon had become.

It was not snow but sleet that obscured her view through the car windows. The interior of her car was dry, but a chill was already starting to seep in. The temperature outside was right around freezing. She shivered at the thought of how much colder she'd be if she had to stay put for long.

Physically, she was unhurt. She told herself that there was no reason to panic. In fact, she was close enough to the house to walk the rest of the way home. Resolved to try, she pulled up the hood on her heavy wool coat, grabbed her purse off the passenger seat and started to open the driver's side door.

It moved a scant two inches and stopped.

"Great," Hope muttered, peering through the crack. Her car had come to rest right next to a low stone wall. She wouldn't be getting out on that side.

Undaunted, Hope slid across the front seat to the passenger side and pulled on that door handle. She checked the lock button and tried again, but it was no use. Nothing happened. That door wasn't going to open, either.

Calmly, Hope assessed the situation. The impact with the tree had obviously jammed the door, but there had been no real damage to her car. A cautious sniff revealed no odor of gasoline, so it was unlikely the car would explode.

She simply had to be patient and sit tight until someone came along and rescued her. She had a blanket in the back seat to help her keep warm if she needed it. There should be no problem. Columbia Hill Road wasn't a major thoroughfare, but at the least there would be a sand truck coming along soon.

Tugging her coat closer about her, Hope contemplated the side window. She could climb out if she rolled it down. She suited action to thought, got on her knees on the seat and stuck her head and shoulders through the opening, thinking that this was one day when she should have stayed at home. She really didn't want to go out there. And, as quick as that, the panic came upon her.

Hope was aware, in a dazed sort of way, that Dennis Long had been calling her name for some time. It took a mighty effort to turn her head and look at him.

His face was distorted by the frost on the window. If she hadn't known his voice, hadn't seen the brown of his uniform, she wasn't sure she'd have recognized him.

"Hope," he repeated. "Snap out of it. Are you hurt? Can you move?"

Her words sounded distant even in her own ears. "I'm okay," she said. She squinted at Dennis, to see if he'd been able to hear her.

"Good. Now try to relax. The wrecker is here. He'll haul you back far enough for me to get the door open."

She was dimly aware that her car had been hooked up to a tow truck. The back end was lifted, and she felt a bump as the car began to move.

Another wave of panic threatened, making her heart beat too fast and her breath thready. Her hands locked on the wheel in front of her.

Dennis opened the door and reached in. He had to loosen her fingers one at a time before he could get her out. When he set her on her feet, her knees refused to hold her upright.

Arms cradled her. Strong, comforting arms.

"Coop," she murmured.

"I'll get hold of him," Dennis promised.

His words momentarily snapped her out of her trance. "No. Don't. He misses too much work already. I don't want him to lose his job."

She thought Dennis stifled a laugh. "Whatever you say, Hope."

"There's a bag of groceries in the trunk."

"I'll go back for it." Dennis kept hold of her, steering her toward the dark brown police cruiser waiting at the edge of the road. Blue lights strobed in the eerie white of the storm. "Do you want the car towed anywhere in particular? It looks like it's going to need some work before you can drive it again."

She gave him the name of the dealership in East Tardiff where she'd bought it and let him bundle her into his vehicle. It was warm and dry inside, but much too noisy. Blinking lights and distorted voices came from pieces of equipment she couldn't begin to identify.

Dennis got in beside her a few minutes later and handed her the paper sack from Mike's Market. Then he got on the police radio. Even what he said into it confused her.

"Can't you guys speak English?" she grumbled.

He grinned at her as he finger-combed the ice out of his mustache. "Gotta use the codes. Even if we didn't, we'd want to, in order to confuse all you folks out there with police-band scanners."

"I must be in worse shape than I thought. That actually made sense to me." She peered into the bag she held on her lap. "Looks like all my groceries survived, too."

"Not even a drop of milk spilled."

"Amazing."

"Do you want to go to the hospital, Hope? Get checked over?"

"No. Just take me home, Dennis. I'll be fine."

Right then she just felt foolish. Why had she reacted as she had? She could have gotten out of the car through the window and been home by now. Instead she'd apparently rolled the window up and gone into a full-blown panic. Her irrational behavior bothered Hope more than the fact that she'd been in a minor car accident.

Dennis drove slowly along Columbia Hill Road. "You didn't look so fine back there. You looked dazed. Sure you didn't hit your head?"

"I'm sure. I had a small setback, that's all. A panic attack snuck up on me."

Dennis nodded, but he looked puzzled.

"You knew I had a little problem with agoraphobia," she reminded him as he pulled into her dooryard and cut the engine on the cruiser.

"Well, sure. But last time I talked to Coop he seemed to think you were just about over it."

"You two sure have dull lives these days if I'm the best subject you can come up with for conversation." She breathed an audible sigh of relief as she unlocked her front door and entered the safe haven of her house. "Coffee?" she offered. "Before you go looking for the next car off the road?"

"Thanks, I'd appreciate a cup. Mind if I use your phone?"

She waved him into the living room, hoping he didn't notice that she still had the shakes. It took three tries to measure ground coffee beans into the basket on her drip pot, and she nearly dropped the milk getting it from the grocery bag to the refrigerator.

When Dennis joined her in the kitchen and took a seat at the table, worry had deepened his frown lines and creased his broad brow. Hope didn't ask what was troubling him. She suspected being a deputy on a night like this one was unpleasant enough without having to talk about it. Instead, she busied herself arranging cookies on a plate and setting out cream and sugar, glad of something to do to keep busy.

Her hands were steadier. She was getting better by the minute. By the time the coffee had brewed, she was able to fill two cups and carry them to the table without spilling a single drop.

Dennis gave her a hard look as she served it and sat down across from him. "How are you really doing, Hope?"

"Better. Which is why Coop does not need to hear about this little fender bender."

She wanted time to regroup before she faced him again. Time to figure out if her progress had suffered as much of a setback as she feared. Right now the thought of going outside again for any reason sent chills running all through her.

"Sorry," Dennis mumbled, though he didn't look particularly contrite.

"What do you mean, sorry?" Hope's grip tightened on the handle of the coffee cup.

"Coop is the one I just phoned. He's already on his way over."

Twenty miles away, at Pleasant Prospect Ski Resort, the precipitation was coming down as soft, puffy snowflakes, but Coop didn't have any trouble believing the weather was worse where Hope was. Winter storms in this part of the world were like that. It was what made driving in them so hazardous.

Dennis had said she was unhurt, just frightened.

He hoped his old friend was right, but he knew he had to see for himself.

Coop met Maureen's school bus when it stopped in front of their condominium and motioned for her to get into the van. "I'm taking you to your grandmother's for the night," he told her. Then he explained about Hope's accident.

Maureen shot a speculative look in his direction. "Does this mean you're going to stay over at Hope's house?"

"Maybe." His hands flexed on the steering wheel as he forced himself, in order to keep Maureen from worrying, to sound unconcerned. "Don't start planning a wedding, Maureen. This is about friendship. From what Dennis told me on the phone, Hope could use someone to keep her company right now.''

He wasn't sure himself why he felt so strongly that she shouldn't be left alone, or why he didn't just take Maureen along with him. Maybe it had something to do with the fact that Elliot Rowan had died in a traffic accident on a stormy night much like this one. He'd always suspected that Hope's phobia had more to do with her husband's death than she was willing to admit.

The drive to Tardiff seemed endless, but at last Coop arrived. Dennis had left shortly before he got there, responding to a call about another accident.

''I don't envy him the night's work ahead,'' Coop said as he stamped his feet to get the snow off and unzipped his jacket. Beneath it he wore his usual uniform of comfortable jeans and a sweater. ''I've got the feeling there are going to be cars off the road all over the county by morning.''

''My thoughts exactly,'' Hope agreed. ''That's part of the reason I didn't want him to bother you.''

''No bother. And the roads aren't all that bad. I've got four-wheel drive in the van.''

Hope seemed to be her normal self, except that she was fiddling nervously with the fringe on the collar of her sweater. She let him into the foyer with obvious reluctance.

''Honestly, Coop, you can't just keep taking time off like this. You didn't need to come over, and you really should go back to work.''

''Not a chance.'' He shrugged out of his jacket and handed it to her. She handed it right back.

''I don't need a baby-sitter.'' Hope appeared unscathed by her experience, but something was making her edgy. He could hear it in her voice.

Coop took his coat with him as he moved past Hope toward the living room. "I had to see for myself that you were okay. What happens to you is important to me."

Left with no option, she followed him. "I need some time to myself. You might as well go back to work."

"Why?" He made himself comfortable on the sofa. She stopped in the doorway.

"You might get fired if you keep taking time off like this."

"I mean, why do you want to be alone? You had a panic attack, right? That's no reason to send me away. I've already seen the aftermath of one of those. You don't need to be embarrassed."

"This was worse than the time you found me in that snowbank." Hope's admission came so softly that Coop almost missed the words.

"We got past that. We'll overcome this," he promised. "Come here and sit down with me."

She stayed where she was. Everything he said just seemed to make her more determined to resist. "What is this 'we' business? This is my problem, Coop. I really want you to go. I don't want you to lose your job."

"Will you stop worrying about the damn job!" He came to his feet in a rush and strode to the window, pushing back the draperies to look out at the storm. A ski resort could always use more snow, and he didn't need to be there to supervise the way it fell.

She sounded as testy as he felt. "I mean it, Coop. Go back to work. I'm just fine. I don't need you here, taking over my life for me."

He wasn't so sure about that, and this preoccupation she had with his job grated on his nerves. He hadn't thought she was one of those people, like Julie, like

Ginny, who believed that a job was worth more than the man or woman who held it, but he'd been wrong before.

"I have nothing but contempt for anyone who thinks a person isn't important unless he has an important job," he muttered into the windowpane.

"Where did that come from?"

He turned to find Hope staring at him from the center of the room. She looked as if she thought he'd lost his marbles.

Coop wondered if he had. He raked his fingers through his hair and groped for an apology. "This isn't much of an excuse, but it's worry about you that made me lash out that way. And for a minute there, you reminded me of Julie."

"I think you'd better go," she said stiffly.

He supposed he'd insulted her. At the moment he was too irritated to care. "Fine," he snapped. He was still holding his jacket. He slipped it on, suddenly impatient to be gone.

"I just need to be alone now," she said softly. "Later, I can talk about this, but not yet."

"Oh, we'll talk about it, all right. We're going to talk about a lot of things real soon. On Friday, in fact. At my place." He was so busy fighting the balky zipper on his jacket that he missed seeing her reaction to that statement, but he sensed the sudden increase in the tension between them.

"I don't think Friday at your place is such a good idea," Hope said.

"I suppose that means you found out. Maureen said you would. I should have told you up front that she wasn't going to be there. Assuming this weather clears up, she'll be on that school trip to Boston."

After a short, strained silence, Hope said, "Maybe we should wait until she can join us."

"Maybe we need some time alone." He gave up on getting the zipper to catch and looked at her.

She avoided his eyes. "You could be right, but I can't come to your place on Friday. I'm sorry, Coop, but I just can't."

Impatient, already frustrated, Coop wondered if he'd been closer to the truth than he'd supposed. She did sound like Julie, changing her mind at the last minute, letting him down, and he wasn't going to let her get away with it. "You agreed to come to my place and I mean to hold you to your promise."

"We agreed to friendship, Coop. Friends cut each other a little slack."

"There has always been more than friendship between us, Hope, and I think you know it."

She pressed her fingers to her temples, as if she might be trying to ward off a killer headache. "Yes, I do know that. We need to talk about that, too."

"Damn straight. Friday. My place."

"No!"

"What the hell's the matter with you, Hope?"

"I can't go out. I can't! Don't you understand? I don't think I could stand to go through that again. Not yet. I'm going to have to start over. Start slow. Please, Coop. If you are a friend, you'll understand."

"I understand, all right. I understand that you're using this phobia of yours as an excuse. You'd be over it by now if you wanted to be cured badly enough."

There were tears in her eyes, but he didn't believe in them. Julie had always been able to cry on cue.

Anger overwhelmed him. He'd almost fallen into the same trap again.

If she loved him, she'd do as he asked. It was that simple.

Without giving Hope a chance to say anything more, he stalked out of the house. His last glimpse of her as he roared off into the fury of the storm was as a small, slender silhouette frozen in the door frame.

She'd no sooner reached the door than the panic started. Blackness edged closer. Hope nearly doubled over with fear, dreading the onslaught of nausea and pain. She watched Coop drive away with a sense of despair deeper than anything she'd ever known. It wouldn't have taken more than a few steps into the dooryard to bring him back. She was certain of it. And she was equally certain that she couldn't manage even that much.

She felt better the moment she stepped inside the foyer and shut the door. By the time she returned to the living room and curled up on the sofa, she was completely recovered physically, but her emotional state continued to deteriorate.

Hope tried to convince herself that, in the past, she'd simply liked staying at home. She could learn to like it again.

"Liar," she whispered. She knew in her heart that everything had changed the moment Cooper Sanford first set foot in her dooryard.

There was no denying that she was still prone to panic attacks. Her experience when she'd tried to get out of the car had proved that. The attacks were still debilitating. And frightening. But there was also some truth in Coop's charge. She had been using her phobia as an excuse not to get on with her life. The symptoms were real enough, but she'd let her fears take control of her life.

Just as she'd let Elliot control her when they'd been married.

Contemplating her own weaknesses was not something Hope wanted to do, but now she forced herself to look back on the darkest days of her marriage. Then she deliberately recalled the most severe of her panic attacks. Finally, as rationally as possible, she faced the worst fear of all, the fear that she would lose Coop forever if she did not act.

She had survived the trauma before. There was no reason she couldn't endure it again, and overcome it, too, if she had to. But did she have to? Was it possible to have it all?

One thing she did know. She wanted Coop more than she wanted the security and safety of staying at home. The more she considered all he had come to mean to her, the more she thought she might even be able to force herself to go out there in pursuit of him. She realized, with a liberating sense of certainty, that she *was* willing to make the effort, to take the risk.

She was on her feet before she remembered that she no longer had a car. For the moment she was trapped at home by something far more tangible than any phobia.

Hope went to the window and looked toward the road, and for the first time the wild intensity of the storm fully penetrated her consciousness. She'd given its dangers lip service all along, but in reality it was snowing much harder than she'd thought. The wind was howling. She couldn't see more than a yard from the house in the ever-deepening twilight.

Hope's hand went to her throat. A new kind of panic assaulted her. She'd quarreled with Coop and driven him out onto treacherous roads in bad weather.

The same way she'd sent Elliot to his death.

Mind-numbing fear swept through Hope, momentarily paralyzing her. It couldn't happen again, she told herself. History would not repeat itself. That would be too cruel.

She didn't know how long it had been since Coop left but she went to the phone and tried his number at the condo. It rang twenty times before she hung up.

She tried the number again at ten-minute intervals for the next half hour, her anxiety increasing with each unanswered ring. Where was he? Where was Maureen?

In an effort to distract herself, she went upstairs and changed into a soft, warm velour robe. Comfort clothing. She used the extension in the bedroom in yet another futile attempt to reach Coop at his condo.

Belatedly, it occurred to her to try Penny Bellamy's number. That was the logical alternative. Coop had undoubtedly left Maureen there. With the storm this bad, he might decide not to risk his daughter's safety by driving from downtown Norville out to the ski area and their condo. For her sake he might even be willing to endure his ex-mother-in-law's company for the night.

Hope had dialed the first three digits when the lights went out. By the time she extracted a flashlight from the bed table drawer and was ready to start again, the phone had gone dead, too.

Chapter Ten

Coop got as far as the Norville town line before he realized he was acting like an idiot. Not only had he left Hope alone just when they most needed to be together, he was also risking life and limb out here on the highway.

He understood his behavior, but that did little to make it more acceptable. This had all been a last-ditch effort to avoid confessing that he was in love. In fact, he had been in love for some time, and he would continue to love Hope for the rest of her life, even if she never left her house again.

He'd known she didn't have complete control over her fears. Not yet. He *knew* that. There was no excuse for his impatience and less for telling her she reminded him of Julie. If he'd hurt her with that comment half as much as it hurt him to be compared to Elliot Rowan, he deserved to be horsewhipped.

The roads had been terrible and got worse after he turned back. The plows and sand trucks had been through but the tarmac was still greasy under his tires. According to the local radio station, they might be in for a line storm. He smiled grimly at the use of the old term. He remembered one of his teachers, years ago, explaining that a line storm was a blizzard that occurred at the line between winter and spring. Technically that date was a week and a half away yet, but there was no doubt a big one was brewing. Snow squalls buffeted his car as he drove slowly and steadily toward Hope's house. At times there were brief whiteouts when visibility dropped to zero, but he kept on.

The harrowing journey was worth every tense second when he stepped onto Hope's front porch and she burst through the door to fling herself into his arms.

"Thank God you're safe!"

Coop held her tight, reveling in the knowledge that she did care. Her lips met his, ending an agony of doubt. She had been as worried about his safety as he'd been about her.

"Let's go inside," he suggested when they finally separated long enough for him to speak. "In case you hadn't noticed, it's cold outside."

She looked appalled by her shortcomings as a hostess. "You're frozen. I'll make coff— Oh. I forgot. We'll have to start a fire in the fireplace before I can heat the water."

The presence of an oil lamp on the foyer table confirmed Coop's suspicions. "How long has the power been out?"

"Not long. The phone lines are down, too." She picked up the lamp, which looked like something left over from her great-grandmother's day, and started toward the living room. "It hasn't had time to get all that cold in here yet, but you'd probably like something to warm you up."

"I've got something to warm me up." Overtaking her, he tugged her into his arms. "This time I don't mean to let you go."

"And I don't want you to." She moved only enough to set the lamp down on an end table, then snuggled closer.

She was wearing something incredibly soft, a long, concealing robe, but beneath it he was almost certain there was nothing but bare skin. "You do realize I'm staying the night."

"Oh, yes." She began to unzip his jacket. It was on the floor a moment later. Her eyes were luminous in the softly glowing lamplight.

Coop looked down at her and spoke from the heart. "I love you, Hope. Let me show you how much."

"I've been so afraid of losing myself again," she whispered, "so afraid of letting myself love you, but I never really had a choice. I've loved you forever, Cooper Sanford."

Coop gathered her close, dropping feather-light kisses on her face. What Elliot Rowan had done was a crime. He'd made this lovely, passionate woman afraid of her own sensuality. Coop prayed he could be gentle enough, patient enough, to teach her that love didn't have to be that way. For them, there would only be joy.

"I know you're still afraid," he murmured. "Afraid I'll try to use you the way Elliot did once we become lovers. It won't happen, Hope. You are your own person again, strong and self-confident. And I'm nothing like Elliot. Tell me you believe that."

She couldn't look away from him. His gaze burned with intensity and his words scorched her. "I do believe it."

"Prove it."

Their gazes still locked, she saw the passion intensify until his eyes were nearly black. Trembling only slightly, Hope took him by the hand. "Bring the lamp," she said as she led him toward the stairs.

When he set the light down again, it was on the small table next to Hope's high oak sleigh bed. She was suddenly very glad that Elliot had disliked Victorian furnishings, that they'd used a modern bedroom set during their marriage. She'd given it away after he died and replaced it with these beautiful old pieces that had been in storage in the attic. Her grandparents had shared this bed throughout their long, happy marriage. And her great-grandparents before that.

Coop's eyes were on the bed, too. With one swift movement he scooped her up and brought them both down on the soft, down-filled quilt she used as a bedspread. His arms encircled her. His lips slid invitingly over hers, brushing butterfly kisses everywhere they touched.

Hope welcomed the long-suppressed sensual excitement that bubbled through her veins. When Coop tugged at her gently, fitting her body to his, she made a sound of deep contentment. For a long, delightful moment she let pleasurable sensations wash over her. Surrender had never felt so right.

Coop drew her ever closer, adjusting and caressing until every pleasure point on both their bodies was perfectly aligned. "If I'm rushing you, tell me now."

Low and raspy with passion, his whisper excited her every bit as much as the feel of his long, lean frame pressing against her. "You aren't rushing me." For once she considered his impatience a virtue.

The skin beneath his sweater was hot, she discovered. Fascinated, she inched her hands up his back, her palms absorbing that wonderful warmth. Lovingly, she grazed each masculine contour with her fingertips, then brought both hands around to the front of him and ran them through the soft mat of hair on his chest.

"I love the way you feel," he murmured as he brushed aside the fabric of her robe.

Hope trembled at the first touch of one fingertip on the sensitive underside of her breast. Instinctively, she moved against him, flexing one leg to caress his thigh.

"I've been wanting to be with you like this for so long," Coop whispered in a husky, passion-deepened voice.

She had been longing for it, too, Hope realized. Desire had lingered just at the edge of her conscious thoughts for weeks.

His lips slid along the line of her jaw and teased her collarbone. Both warm, hard hands had delved inside her clothing to cup her breasts. She whimpered in sweet torment when languid thumbs brushed against her nipples.

"You are so perfect," he breathed.

Still feather light, Coop's lips brushed her cheek, then moved to caress her neck. When they again sought her mouth, he lifted his head and their eyes met.

He teased her with the tip of his tongue. Hope responded by nibbling on his sensual lower lip. She wanted to taste him, needed to kiss him deeply and have him return the favor until they were tangled in a passionate duel. Hope's every rational thought fled as he divined her wishes and complied.

The taste of him in her mouth was heaven. With a sigh of pleasure, she slid her hands up his arms to his shoulders, then further, into the thick, curling hair. Coop broke off the kiss, as if it had sent him past reason, and his groan was caught against the pulse point in her neck. He slid one hand down to the small of her back and drew her closer, pressing her body to his in a way that left no doubt of the strength of his desire for her.

Suddenly bold, Hope's hands left the upper regions to dip low and explore more fully the promises he was making. Eagerly she sought and cupped that most intimate part of him and was rewarded with a swift intake of breath. One of his hands splayed across her backside, warm and hard, then swept downward over the curves and valleys to invade the sensitive territory between her thighs.

The pleasure was almost unbearable, and Hope twisted and writhed against his palm, but when he began to tug at her robe, easing it off entirely, it caught beneath the weight of their tangled limbs and reality returned with a jolt as jarring as an electric shock.

Hope stiffened, turning her head away from his kisses, suddenly desperate to break the spell that his intense green gaze and his intimate caresses had woven around her.

"It's okay, Hope. It's going to be okay. It's going to be wonderful. Trust me."

The lips that again took hers were softly demanding, and she felt herself weakening under the onslaught, but the consequences of losing herself in his embrace were more terrifying than ever. Her common sense had reappeared, somewhat belatedly, and demanded that she point out the last barrier to their lovemaking.

"Coop. Wait a second. There's something—"

"Damn." Reluctantly, he released her and started to move away. "I knew I was rushing you."

"No, Coop, I . . . that's not it." She reached for him, desperate to dispel the hurt she saw in his eyes. He thought she'd changed her mind, but in fact it was her one last vestige of self-protection surfacing through the layers of sensation. "We have to . . . take precautions."

They lay, face to face, bodies throbbing, struggling for a few moments of clear thought. There was so much she wanted to tell him, but she couldn't seem to find the right words.

Hope had nothing against babies. It had been Elliot who'd decided that they didn't want a family. In spite of that, she couldn't allow herself to be irresponsible about creating another life. Until she was sure she was cured, that she'd be able to care for a child, to take it to the doctor or to school without fear of a panic attack that would leave them both helpless, she didn't dare take the risk of getting pregnant.

That was too much to try to explain to Coop now. She abandoned the effort and instead looked hopefully at him. She tried to sound lighthearted. "Please tell me you carry a condom or two around in your wallet."

Coop closed his eyes for a moment. When he opened them, his expression was bleak. "There's something I guess I should tell you before this goes any further."

Hope had a feeling she was not going to like what he said next. "What is it?"

"You don't have to worry about any unwanted consequences from making love with me. Not only am I certifiably healthy, but I had a vasectomy years ago so that Julie wouldn't have to keep taking the pill. I couldn't get you pregnant if I wanted to."

Caught off guard by his announcement, Hope couldn't hide her surprise or her distress at Julie's sudden presence between them in bed. And he could not mask his vulnerability. Her reaction plainly bothered him. He started to pull away from her.

"Don't you dare change your mind!" She threw her arms around him again, holding him tight. She wasn't put off. In fact, she could think of much worse confessions he might have made. Her predominant feeling was one of relief that they didn't have to stop what they'd begun. "You promised to make love to me," Hope reminded him and kissed him soundly.

Coop surrendered without a fight.

Desire rekindled, blazing rapidly into wildfire, raging out of control. He nipped at her earlobe. She explored the textures of his neck with her tongue.

Coop groaned, reaching between them to struggle with the lower edge of his sweater. Hope had other ideas. She found his zipper and jerked it down with one hand even as the other slipped inside to cradle him.

"Hope!"

The raspy voice was barely recognizable. Frantic, he separated from her only long enough to strip off the sweater and fling it away from him, heedless of where it landed. She took a quick look, enough to assure her that it hadn't knocked over the lamp. Then she forgot everything but their consuming need for each other. They removed the rest of their clothing in record time.

His mouth dipped low over her breasts, suckling, arousing, as she peeled away his jeans and briefs and freed him at last for their mutual enjoyment. One hand found its way back to her core, intensifying her pleasure with a single touch. Incapable of coherent thought, Hope gave herself into his keeping.

His breath caught as he lifted himself and his eyes traveled over the full, bare length of her for the first time. His admiration was fiercely apparent. Hope had never felt so alive, so beautiful, so female as she did reflected in his glittering gaze.

With a rough sound of desire he reached for her. She did not need assurances that he would be gentle, that he would bring her only delight. At the next intimate touch of his fingers, Hope exploded in his arms. A gasp of pleasure burst from her throat. Then, as demanding as he, she twisted, straining against him, grinding her lips against his. Her senses were spinning out of control and she didn't care. She writhed against his long, lean body, boldly caressing his aroused flesh.

Patience was beyond her. Hope arched against him as his hands swept under the curves of her derriere, squeezing, caressing. By the time he positioned himself at the cradle of her thighs, she was desperate to fill the great emptiness inside her. She tugged at his hips, trying to pull him closer, and ended up nearly tumbling them both off the bed.

A wild hunger surged through her when he finally moved over her. At last she felt his manhood probe the damp warmth between her legs. He had regained a little control, but only enough to keep from hurting her. She was more than ready to take him inside her, even if it had been a long time since she'd last made love.

Coop went slowly, letting all her tight muscles stretch to accommodate him. It was exquisite torture until at last, irrevocably, they were fully joined.

Lovemaking had always brought Hope pleasure, but this went beyond simple satisfaction. Never before had she been so attuned to the ancient rhythms. She wrapped her legs around his waist and lifted herself to meet each thrust. She was as wild as he, his equal in every way as the delicious sensations built. She knew he was aware when the rippling began for her, that he felt the gentle squeezing of muscles contracting, clenching around him. She reveled in the knowledge that they were together in this, and welcomed the pulsations that heralded the inevitable climax.

He opened his eyes. She met his gaze, letting him see her pleasure even as he felt it, even as he heard her shattered cry. Then they were both hurtling headlong, out of control, exploding into near-violent ecstasy.

She returned to reality slowly. He was watching her, searching her face for any sign of regret. She smiled.

"That was wonderful," she whispered.

"Wonderful," he echoed.

Their lovemaking had awakened a hunger in her that she'd long kept buried. It had been only temporarily quenched. Hope felt desire renew itself as she lay curled against his nakedness. Her oversensitized skin was tingling in anticipation. She squirmed a little, trying to get closer.

He misunderstood at first. "This doesn't have to get awkward," he whispered. "It was perfect. Beautiful. A whole new plateau. And best of all, we're still friends. We're just more than that now, too."

"I'm not feeling awkward, Coop. I'm feeling... needy. I want to do it all over again. Right now." A self-conscious little laugh escaped her. "Crazy, huh? I mean, what kind of person—"

"My kind." His laugh was one of unbridled delight as he pulled her against him. "Feel that? You and I are obviously on the same wavelength. Two of a kind." He began to kiss the back of her neck, little erotic touches of lips and tongue that made her imagination run wild.

More than an hour passed before either of them thought about talking again.

"It's getting cold," Hope whispered.

"I've been trying my best to keep you warm."

"You've been doing a grand job, but if the power's going to stay off for much longer, we'd better go down and start a fire in the fireplace."

"How about one in front of the fireplace," he suggested.

"That, too," she agreed.

A few minutes later Coop was attempting to comply with her wishes. Hope did her best to hold back a smile. She had no doubt he could kindle her desire again, but he was not doing as well with the wood.

It was obvious Coop had never attempted this feat before, for all that he was familiar with ski lodges and winter sports. One crumpled wad of newspaper after another went up in flames without igniting the pieces of kindling he'd tossed on top. The logs he'd selected weren't even singed.

"Would you like some advice?" Hope asked. "Or is fire starting one of those sacred male rituals?"

"I'd be delighted to find a lovely lady at my side, full of helpful suggestions."

Laughter bubbled up and spilled over as she hastened to join him. He sat cross-legged on the floor, staring disconsolately into the hearth. Kneeling behind him, her elbows resting on his shoulders, Hope surveyed the charred remains.

"Pathetic, isn't it? I never knew there was a trick to getting wood to burn, at least not when you had matches and everything. A child ought to be able to do it."

Snaking his arm around, he caught her waist and gently tugged her forward until she sat next to him on the floor in front of the fireplace. The other hand crept up to cup her chin. Coop's mouth was almost covering hers before she slipped out of his grasp.

"One fire at a time," she whispered. "Atmosphere, you know."

"As my lady wishes, only the fire is not cooperating."

Hope deftly plucked the sooty pieces of kindling apart and once more added crumpled paper. Then she arranged the kindling on top, layering it at right angles and leaving plenty of airspace. "We need smaller pieces of wood."

"These are the ones that were in your wood rack. Besides, I'd think the big ones would last longer."

"Not if you can't get them to burn."

With a disgruntled look in her direction, Coop stood. "Okay. Where's your woodpile?"

"Go through the exercise room and out onto the deck where the bird feeders are. The wood is stacked against the far railing under a tarp."

Coop gave a dramatic shudder at the thought of going outside. "Maybe we could just—"

"Go get some?"

"You're a hard woman, Hope Rowan." Chuckling, he planted a smacking kiss on the top of her head, then found his jacket where she'd left it on the floor hours earlier. "I'll be right back with the wood. Tonight, whatever the lady wants, the lady gets."

A few minutes later he deposited the wood at her feet, then stripped down to jeans and sweater again. He was distracting, and Hope was hard put to ignore him long enough to finish fixing the fire. She fumbled repeatedly, but at last the kindling caught and the small pieces of wood were blackening nicely. Angel appeared, as if by magic, to soak up the warmth of the little blaze.

"The lady now wants something with which to wipe soot off her hands," Hope announced as she rocked back to sit on her heels. She was glad she'd rolled up the long

sleeves of her robe. She'd forgotten, since she rarely used
the fireplace, just how messy heating with wood could be.

Coop had been standing a little apart, watching her.
Now he was quick to oblige, fetching a damp cloth from
the kitchen. Instead of handing it to her, he knelt facing
her in front of the fireplace, catching and holding her eyes
as he began, with gentle, arousing strokes, to wash each
individual finger.

More than the warmth of the flickering fire brought
heat to Hope's cheeks. She stared at the top of his dark
head when he bent over her hands and felt her whole body
throb with longing. When the damp cloth was replaced by
moist lips, soft and warm, it was all she could do to keep
from collapsing against him.

Never before had she realized how sensitive the tips of
her fingers were, or the insides of her wrists, or the center
of her palm. Coop's lips and tongue explored and teased,
until Hope's limbs lost their strength and she swayed toward him.

Coop caught her, his hands strong and firm as he adjusted his body to fit hers, sliding his hands from her
shoulders to her back and then down to clasp her bottom
and pull her tight against the cradle of his thighs.

Once more his hands drifted up to cup her face, tilting
her head for his kiss. The tongue that nudged her lips
apart was bold and hungry, and his heart was slamming
against his ribs even as hers was. Gently, he lowered them
both until they were lying side by side on the deep pile
carpet. He bent close for a kiss and—

A loud, raucous buzzing filled the room, bringing them
both abruptly upright. Angel let out a howl of protest and
fled.

"What the—" Coop came to his feet, pulling Hope
after him.

She dissolved into helpless laughter. "The smoke alarm," she sputtered, pointing.

High above them, out of reach, on the ceiling, a small circular alarm continued to blare. The smell of wood smoke teased Coop's nostrils. He swung around, staring in consternation at the thin spiral curling out from the hearth. The wood was smoldering, already half extinguished.

Hope was still laughing.

"This isn't funny," he muttered. "What if the fire had spread?"

"Kind of hard to burn without a draft. We forgot to open the damper."

"The what?"

They had to shout at each other to be heard over the alarm. Coop put his hands over his ears and watched as Hope adjusted the damper. As soon as the chimney flue was opened, the smoke changed direction. Their fire perked up.

Disgusted with himself for forgetting that a fire needed air to burn, Coop started opening windows, even though that let the snow in. He glared at the hearth, and then scowled at the offensively loud smoke alarm. Without a ladder, there was no way he could reach it and shut it off.

"And I thought a fire in the fireplace was going to be romantic," he grumbled.

"Just be grateful that thing isn't connected directly to the fire department," Hope said as she glided toward him, her face radiant and loving. She giggled as she snuggled into the hollow of his arm. She was warm and solid and already doing incredible things to his willing body. "It will stop soon," she promised, "and it could have been worse. We could have been—"

He cut short her speculations with an incendiary kiss. His fingers tangled in her long, luxuriant hair. He felt her smile against his lips. If anyone had ever tried to tell him that laughter could be so arousing, he'd have been certain they lied.

"Just as soon as that damned buzzing shuts off," he whispered, "I'm going to—"

As if by magic, the sound stopped. They could hear the howling of the blizzard beyond the windows again. The room had aired out, all right. Now it was at least ten degrees colder inside.

Working swiftly, Coop closed and locked the windows and drew the drapes again. Then he turned to Hope, his desire as plain as if he'd spoken.

"I want to make love again, too," she whispered. "Don't you know that thinking about it has been keeping me awake nights for weeks? We haven't even begun to make up for all that lost sleep."

"Tell me about it. Your fantasies cannot possibly equal mine."

Her soft hair tickled his chin as she returned to the circle of his arms. "Not even this one?" She whispered an explicit suggestion in his ear.

Coop felt his blood heat. His body hardened in a rush. "You probably shouldn't have shared that with me."

"Why ever not?" she teased.

"I'd planned to take it slow this time. Then again, I'd planned to wait until at least Friday at my place to make love to you for the first time. I was going to have wine cooling, and the makings of a late supper set out."

"There's a lot to be said for spontaneity."

"So there is." His voice dropped even lower. "Brace yourself, Hope. Your wildest dreams are about to come true."

* * *

A long while later, Coop got up to add another log to the fire. Angel had returned to curl up next to the hearth. Hope slept on the floor nearby, exhausted. The afghan they'd filched from the sofa to cover themselves had slipped off one shoulder, leaving it enticingly bare.

Coop shifted his hungry gaze away from her to stare at the flames. He still felt stunned by the almost savage passion that had accompanied this last round of lovemaking. He was finally beginning to understand why Hope had said that her own sensuality frightened her. She went totally out of control when she made love.

So did he.

And then he realized what he was really feeling was an intense satisfaction. So they both went a little crazy. That was not such a bad thing, not now that they'd finally found each other. He glanced over his shoulder at Hope. If this hadn't been quite the romantic seduction he'd planned, it certainly ranked as the most memorable night of his life.

That was the difference being in love made.

Coop gave the fire one last poke and returned to Hope's side, crawling beneath the afghan with her and rearranging it over them both.

There was no longer any doubt in his mind that he loved Hope Rowan. Nothing less could account for the fact that for an instant, upstairs, when she'd reluctantly warned him that she wasn't protected, he'd found himself imagining her in an advanced stage of pregnancy. He'd not only seen the vision clearly, he'd known it was his child she was carrying. And he'd liked the idea.

He still liked it, which was probably why he was remembering the case of a co-worker several years back, a man who'd remarried and decided to have his vasectomy reversed so that she could have his child. At the time,

Coop remembered, he'd thought his friend was taking a foolish risk, since there were no guarantees and the process could end up being very painful.

Now he looked at the possibilities in a whole new light. If Hope did want children, he'd do anything he could to see that she had them. Of course, she would have to agree to marry him first.

The idea had definite appeal. He realized now that subconsciously he'd been contemplating marriage ever since that day in his office when he'd strung the words hearth, home and Hope together in his mind.

Coop rolled toward her and gathered her close.

Hope opened sleepy eyes and smiled at him.

"Again?" she murmured.

"Not just yet," he whispered. "I have a favor to ask first."

"Anything."

"Marry me, Hope. I want you to be my wife."

To his dismay, she sat bolt upright, her shock and denial clearly reflected on her face even before she spoke. Her words only confirmed what he saw there. In a strangled voice, she whispered, "But I don't want to get married."

Chapter Eleven

Hope stared at him, desperately trying to sort out the conflicting emotions his unexpected proposal had aroused in her.

Marry Coop?

She wanted to shout an acceptance. At the same time, she was terrified by the very idea.

"Don't you think we're rushing this a little? I mean, the sex was good but—"

"Good? Hope, trust me, the sex was great."

"That isn't the point. Just because we're, uh, physically compatible doesn't mean we should rush into marriage. I thought we agreed we'd both made mistakes in that area before."

"This wouldn't be a mistake."

"How can you be so sure?"

"Because I love you, and you love me, and you and Maureen get along just fine."

"There's a big difference between being Maureen's cousin and being her stepmother, Coop."

"You're saying you won't marry me because I've got a daughter?"

"No, of course not."

"Good. Then there's no reason not to get—"

"Coop! You aren't listening to me! I don't want to marry you."

He rolled onto his back and stared at the ceiling. One arm, bent at the elbow, rested against his forehead. She couldn't see his eyes.

"What are you afraid of, Hope? Really? It wouldn't be showing weakness to let me take care of you for the rest of our lives. It would be a partnership. You ought to know me well enough by now to believe that."

"In some ways I don't know you at all."

"Name one."

She blurted out the first thing that came to mind. "I didn't know you'd had a vasectomy."

Stupid answer, she thought. That was hardly an issue here.

She could feel his eyes on her, but she avoided looking his way. Instead she stared at the flames of the fire they'd built with so much laughter. Was everything going to burn away, like the logs in the hearth, leaving only smoky memories behind?

"I've heard it can be reversed. If that's the only reason you don't want to marry me, if you want kids of our own, I'm willing to give it a try."

Confused, Hope turned her head and stared at him. "Give what a try?"

"The vasectomy. I can try to get it reversed. If you want children. After we're married."

"Do you want more children?"

"I didn't think I did. Then I started thinking about marrying you, and it suddenly seemed like a pretty good idea."

She didn't know what to say to that. It was too soon to be thinking about marriage, let alone a family. "We're just getting to know each other again," she murmured.

A gusty sigh answered her. "Well, that's progress."

"What?"

"You didn't say no."

Hope risked a glance in his direction. Coop was sitting up and watching her, but he no longer seemed so upset. When he extended one hand in her direction, she grasped it.

"I need time to think," she told him honestly as he pulled her to her feet. "I'm not even sure I can be a good mother to Maureen, let alone manage other children. I'm not sure I can be the kind of wife you want, either."

"But you *do* love me?"

"Yes, damn it, I love you!"

Unsettled, she jerked her hand free, found her robe and put it on, tugging it tightly closed. She moved to the window and pulled back the drapes. Dawn was just breaking, showing her a glistening world, newborn, renewed.

Until the plows came through and tossed up all the dirty old snow underneath.

The past always seemed to come back to taint the present, no matter how bright that present might look.

Hope shook her head, bemused by her thoughts. No sense writing poetry about it. The plain fact was that she was afraid to rush into a new commitment when so much in her old life was still unsettled. She was beginning to think she could trust Coop not to let her down, but the doubts about herself, about her ability to deal with the future, were still powerful.

"I need time," she said again when he came up behind her and gently began to massage her shoulders.

"I've never been known for my patience," he reminded her, "but for you I'll make the effort." He bent his head and kissed her cheek. "Besides, I don't think my ego can take it if I keep asking and you keep turning me down."

She could see his face reflected in the windowpane, and once again Hope also saw the vulnerability Coop was usually so careful to hide. In spite of his teasing words, he was just as afraid of being hurt as she was. Julie had left him with as many insecurities as Elliot had bequeathed Hope.

"We're a pair, aren't we?" She turned in his arms and lifted her face.

"So I keep trying to tell you."

They did not kiss. In searching silence they simply stared into one another's eyes, tentatively opening the windows to their souls.

Outside, a snowplow went past.

Coop slowly released her.

"I've got to go pick up Maureen," he said. "She's at her grandmother's. Do you have a snowblower in the barn?"

Hope nodded, reluctantly returning to reality.

He kissed her lightly on the forehead and began to dress.

Coop was at Pleasant Prospect by nine that morning but his thoughts were still on Hope. Too late he'd remembered how worried she'd been by the possibility of a simple affair between them. She'd been afraid of becoming too dependent on him, of being hurt.

For Hope, in the past, marriage had offered no guarantees. The same burning resentment against Elliot

Rowan that Coop had managed to suppress earlier returned with a vengeance. He knew he wasn't going to leave her. He wasn't going to try to control her life. But he didn't know how to convince Hope of those two simple facts, not after the number Rowan had done on her.

Unable to come up with any answers, Coop concentrated on work. By ten, the worst of the accumulated paperwork had been dealt with. Fifteen minutes later, he was suspended forty feet over the ski slopes, sharing a triple chair lift with his daughter for the ride to the summit.

School was closed for the day, since the roads had been deemed treacherous at the time the buses usually ran. Now, only a few hours later, the sun was shining brightly and the ground cover was a sparkling and inviting white. By tomorrow, when Maureen's trip to Boston was scheduled, the roads would be bare, as safe to travel as if it was summer. Coming the other way on the turnpike would be a host of skiers, anxious to take advantage of a deep packed powder base and ten inches of new snow.

"Are you planning to ski all day?" Coop asked his daughter.

"Probably. Amie's mother is bringing her out later."

"You've made up with Amie, then?"

Maureen nodded.

"And your grandmother?"

"Sure. She's okay. I'm glad I live with you, though."

They watched a skier clad in brilliant fuchsia glide down the pristine surface far below. This was near perfection, Coop thought. Beautiful day. Exceptional company. If only that empty third seat in the chair lift had Hope in it, he'd be in heaven.

He hadn't expected her to be able to come with him today. Still, they'd both hoped for better than this morning's debacle. While Coop had used the snowblower to clear snow out of Hope's dooryard and driveway, she'd decided to sweep off what had accumulated on the porch. Succeeding at that small task, she'd gone inside, put on her warmest clothing and returned with shovel in hand to tackle the sidewalk.

One step off the porch had been enough to turn her complexion dead white and stop her in her tracks. As much as she'd wanted to continue, she'd been unable to stop the panic from welling up inside her. Still, she'd forced herself to walk as far as the edge of the dooryard, where he'd been waiting, and tell him, with a voice that trembled, that she thought she ought to go inside again. More than ever before, Coop had been aware of the sheer courage it took for her to make each attempt. Failure meant enduring not only mental anguish but physical pain.

But she'd made it to the porch on her own. She'd conquer this thing. Eventually.

Meanwhile, he had to find a way to conquer his impatience. If he couldn't, he'd soon become more of a hindrance to Hope than a help.

"Can I go on Windy Woods?" Maureen asked, naming one of the most advanced trails.

"Not by yourself. Wait for Amie."

"She's not good enough to ski it. Could you go down with me?"

He glanced at his watch. "Sure. One run. Then you stick to the easy stuff, okay?"

"Okay."

The men Coop employed as snowmakers had been able to take the night off, but the groomers had been hard at work ever since the worst of the storm passed at around four in the morning. They'd smoothed and packed the surfaces of the lower slopes with the help of specialized heavy equipment. They left the expert terrain alone, except for checking the trails on snow cats to make sure there were no tree limbs down or any other potential dangers blocking the way. The few hazards that had been deposited by the storm's high winds had been removed.

Pleasant Prospect was anticipating a boom weekend. Coop was looking forward to the chance to ski with Maureen, something he rarely had the time to do. He knew he ought to feel on top of the world.

He caught himself grinding his teeth. What he wanted more than anything else was to be with Hope. Might as well wish for the moon, he chided himself. Even if everything went smoothly at Pleasant Prospect today, he knew he'd be dealing with one minor crisis after another. For once he couldn't delegate jobs to others, not with a clear conscience.

During the power outage, emergency generators had been used but phone service had been lost entirely, including the ability to send faxes. Coop hadn't been available to deal with the complaints, and his staff was unhappy about that. He'd be spending a good deal of time today reassuring irate guests and smoothing ruffled feathers.

There had also been one totally unexpected emergency this morning. His switchboard operator had gone into labor three weeks early. He'd had to hire a replacement without checking her references. All he knew about the young woman was that she was a local, for he'd decided shortly after the first time he'd been out to Hope's and heard her voice her opinion of Pleasant Prospect's management that whenever it was feasible new hiring would be done from the local labor pool. This had been the first time he'd been able to put the new policy into practice.

Coop supposed he had to give Hope credit for his personal attention to today's operations, too. She'd succeeded in making him feel guilty about neglecting the job that kept his future, and Maureen's, secure. This was not the time to be unavailable. In fact, he ought to plan to stay right at the resort all weekend long.

But that was too much to ask.

He could not get back to Hope tonight. He had Maureen to think of. But as soon as he could manage to leave work tomorrow, Friday, Coop fully intended to head for Tardiff and the woman he was going to marry.

The chair lift jerked a little as it stopped at the top of the mountain. As Coop and Maureen got off, she looked at it assessingly. "Did you ever ride a rope tow, Dad?"

"Years ago. What made you think of that?"

"Just something one of the kids said. That Pleasant Prospect didn't get real fancy, with triple chair lifts and quads and snow machines, until the owner before last."

"That's true. Lucky for me, he did the hard part, renovating and upgrading the place."

"Why don't you want anyone to know you're the boss?"

Coop bent to check the bindings on his boots. It was beginning to be hard to remember the answer to that. "To tell you the truth, Maureen, I don't plan to keep that secret much longer." He straightened and met her eyes. "In fact, after you come back from Boston, you can be the one to tell your grandmother."

"You'd better tell Hope first," she said.

"I intend to." They had a lot to talk about tomorrow evening, not the least of which was the true nature of his employment at Pleasant Prospect.

They'd spent a glorious night together. It couldn't be more obvious to him that they ought to make the arrangement a permanent one. Except that Hope didn't yet see it that way.

He knew all her fears were real, not just the ones connected to her phobia.

He knew he needed to be patient. The wait would be worthwhile when she finally agreed to marry him.

But, damn, it was hard.

"Let's go," he said to Maureen. "This way to Windy Woods."

When he got back to his office, Coop phoned Hope, just so he could hear her voice again. He used the excuse that he wanted to make sure her power and phone lines had been restored.

After they said goodbye, Coop relegated the photograph of Julie in the bottom drawer of his desk. Maureen was due to have her class pictures taken soon. He'd put one of those in the silver frame instead.

At home that evening, Hope called to wish Maureen well on her field trip. To Coop's surprise, his daughter had shown little curiosity about the night he'd spent at Hope's house. He'd just decided that she was too excited about her own plans to grill him, when she looked at him and smiled knowingly, apparently convinced that she could predict what the future held for the three of them.

"You definitely ought to ask Hope to marry you, Dad."

"I have. She said no."

"She'll change her mind."

Coop wished he could share Maureen's certainty. He had the nagging feeling that there was something he hadn't taken into account.

He called Hope again after Maureen went to bed. She was just about to turn in, she told him. He wished her pleasant dreams and hung up. He had the feeling his night was going to be extremely restless, and filled with frustrating dreams.

Twenty miles away, Hope drifted off with a smile on her face and slept deeply for several hours.

Then the nightmare started.

She knew she was dreaming because she was seeing everything from a bird's-eye view, as if she was high above the road. It stretched like a soiled white velvet ribbon clear to the horizon, empty of traffic, bounded by small trees on either side. There was one exception, at the end of the road, where there stood a giant maple with bloodred leaves.

Great billowing snowflakes were falling—the wet, sticky kind that would turn to ice at the moment of contact with the ground. She heard the noise first, the sickening sound of tires skidding. Then the car, Elliot's old car, appeared. It was spinning slowly, so slowly, but she knew no power in heaven or on earth could stop it from smashing into that enormous tree.

For an instant the car seemed to grip the side of the road, clinging desperately, but then it went flying sideways, aimed directly at an unyielding expanse of bark. It crushed together like an accordion when it hit.

The nightmare had come like this before. Hope thrashed, trying to fight her way awake. And then, without warning, the pattern of the dream changed.

She was still caught in that peculiar state where running is impossible, either away from danger or toward it. She was fated to watch, without control, the unfolding of dire events. This time the car did not strike the giant tree. This time it began to roll over and over, until front, side, top and back were all caved in from the impact.

Pieces began to come off the car—bits of metal, shards of glass, one wheel. That wheel spun slowly, off center, with a hypnotic, cycling, dancelike rhythm. What was left of the vehicle plunged through a layer of ice and came to rest, undercarriage up, in a shallow stream.

With infinite slowness, as the automobile settled to the bottom, the color of the water began to change. Pink froth seeped hesitantly around the crushed doorposts

from the interior of the mangled wreck. The froth mixed
with the oily residue of the upside-down engine to form an
obscenely colored film just under the surface of the surrounding ice.

Through the cracked and mangled windshield, Hope
saw a face. At first it was Elliot's face, staring back at her,
accusing, hateful. Then, abruptly, it changed. It became
Coop's face, eyes closed, all life vanished.

Hope started to scream.

In the last moment before she came awake, sitting bolt
upright in her lonely bed, the identity of the body in the
wrecked car changed again.

This time it was her own face staring back at her.

Shivering uncontrollably, her first instinct was to call
Coop and make sure he was all right. She reached with
one trembling hand for the phone, then pulled back when
she saw the illuminated dial of her clock. Of course he was
all right. It had only been a dream. She couldn't wake him
up at two in the morning just because she'd had a nightmare.

But, oh, she wished he was beside her in the bed, to take
her in his arms and comfort her, to make her feel as if she
belonged to him.

She had to settle for Angel, who had slept through
Hope's nightmare curled up at the foot of her bed. Hope
hauled the protesting feline into her arms, tucked her under the covers and held her close. After a moment, the cat
began to purr.

It helped, but not enough. A small, furry mound could
not compare to the feel of a man. A man—at least one
particular man—was what she really wanted. Hope slept
only fitfully from then on, and woke at first light.

Friday turned out to be another cold and bright late
winter day, perfect for beginning ski vacations and field

trips. As Hope sipped her first cup of coffee and stared out at the snow-covered fields, she was still thinking about her nightmare.

She drank more coffee, too much, as she struggled to find a reason she was in such emotional turmoil. Her thought processes seemed hopelessly tangled. The dream made no sense. She didn't understand why she'd reacted so strongly to Coop's proposal, either. She loved him. He loved her. Why shouldn't she marry him?

The only answer Hope could come up with disturbed her greatly. She still didn't trust herself. She'd been terribly wrong before. There was no guarantee she was right about Coop, just as there was no guarantee that her little problem would ever get any better. What if more setbacks followed this one? What if she never did reach the point where she could lead a normal life? Would Coop still love her if she put that kind of restriction on him and, more importantly, on Maureen? Coop wouldn't come into a marriage alone. He'd bring to his wife all the complex responsibilities of instant motherhood.

Abruptly, Hope left the kitchen. She wasn't quite ready to contemplate what that would mean, or to think about the suggestion Coop had made that they have children together. She had to do something first, something that might just clear the way for her to have a future with Coop.

She had to exorcise Elliot Rowan's ghost.

When he died, Hope had packed up all his belongings and put them in storage in a locked closet, unable to face dealing with so many reminders of their life together. She'd extracted the papers she needed when it came time to pay her taxes, but except for that she'd ignored the things Elliot had left behind.

All that should have been sorted through, and for the most part thrown away, long ago. Hope had kept putting the job off, in a futile attempt to forget him, forget her own mistakes, forget that last awful night together. Now, she realized, she had to face up to the distasteful task. She couldn't really begin anew until it was done.

Maybe then he'd stop coming back to haunt her dreams. Maybe then she'd have a shot at happiness.

They were just boxes, she told herself when she unlocked the upstairs closet and stared at the stacks and stacks of cardboard containers. She'd forgotten how many of them there were.

She had the rest of the day ahead of her. Coop had said it would be at least six or seven in the evening before he could get over to her place. With hands that shook a little, Hope reached for the top carton.

Soon she had two piles, one of things to take to the dump and one of items to donate to charity. The latter consisted mainly of clothes. Elliot had liked to look good. He'd never stinted on quality when it came to his suits and shirts and silk ties.

The dump pile included photographs. Hope wanted no mementos of her marriage. She couldn't seem to stop herself, however, from taking one last look at the few snapshots of the two of them together, and of Elliot alone. For the first time she realized that, superficially, Elliot had borne a certain resemblance to Cooper Sanford.

Was that what had drawn her to him in the first place?

Shaken by that possibility, Hope threw the other photos on the pile without looking at them. A little later, she went down to the kitchen for a plastic garbage bag and raked everything inside. A pity the landfill had insisted on going to clear bags, she thought. A couple of years ago they'd all been a nice, dark green, which had served to hide whatever unsightly trash they'd contained. Now Elliot's eyes seemed to stare up at her in disapproval from the other side of the plastic.

She took the bag downstairs and put it on the porch. Maybe out of sight, out of mind had not been such a bad idea, after all. Then she transported the cartons of clothing and put them outside, too. She could call Barry to come over and haul everything out to the barn. Unfortunately, she'd have to wait until tomorrow to have him take a load to the dump. Tardiff's politically correct landfill was only open on Tuesdays, Wednesdays, Saturdays and Sundays.

There wasn't much left to go through. Hope treated herself to a soda, then tackled the one cardboard box that remained. It had been on the bottom and she knew that it contained the clothing Elliot had been wearing that last afternoon, the garments he'd changed out of just before he'd left the house for the last time.

Hope was almost certain there was nothing she wanted to keep in that box, but she'd gone through everything else. She intended to do a thorough job, now that she'd finally gotten to it. She pulled out the pieces of the expensive business suit and accessories that had been strewn around the bedroom for her to pick up. Beneath them was the wallet Dennis had returned to her. She hadn't even bothered to remove the cash it contained.

She did so now, and inspected the remaining contents. There were no surprises. A few dollars. A few credit cards. Some business cards. A condom.

"Just like a good Boy Scout," she muttered, dropping it in distaste as the memories swamped her. It seemed to symbolize what they'd quarreled about that last night.

She'd accused him of cheating on her.

She didn't know who the other woman was. She didn't want to know. But he'd come home from "business lunches" with a self-satisfied smirk on his face once too often for her to ignore it any longer.

Elliot had lied at first. Then he'd deftly attempted to shift the blame. Hope's expression was grim as she remembered his efforts to convince her that she was inadequate, both as a wife and as a woman. For the first time, she'd fought back, defending her self-worth and telling him to get out of her life if he wasn't satisfied with her.

He certainly had done that.

Hope was shaking as she stuffed the clothing back into the box. She wanted to get rid of it quickly and never think about Elliot again, but the crinkle of paper caught her attention. There was something in a pocket of the dress slacks she held in her hand.

She'd never been particularly good at predicting the future, but as she extracted this single, crumpled page Hope felt a distinct chill run up her spine. She was certain she wasn't going to like what she saw when she smoothed the paper out and looked at it, and she was right.

Hope read the note three times before the contents sank in. The shock of its revelation rocked her back on her heels.

Still dazed, she got up and went downstairs, into the room that had been Elliot's office. She sat in the chair that faced the back deck. Absently, she stroked Angel, who was perched on its arm, her feline gaze glued to the feeding frenzy just outside.

Elliot had always said it was a waste of money to feed wild birds. Hope had put up the bird feeders a week after he died.

Even on the most difficult days of coping with her little problem, she'd managed to go through those sliding glass doors and replenish the supplies of sunflower seeds and suet. Her sense that she was making a small contribution to preserving wildlife through the bitter-cold winter months had made the effort worthwhile.

This was a banner day for birdwatching. The chickadees had been joined by purple finches, goldfinches, grosbeaks and nuthatches. A few morning doves were around, too, picking up seeds that fell from the feeder to the ground.

Soon the juncos would be back, Hope thought, and perhaps that solitary indigo bunting she'd spotted the previous spring.

Hope heaved a deep sigh. It was no good. She was going to have to face up to the contents of the note. She forced herself to look away from the window and read it again. Nothing had changed.

It hadn't been her fault Elliot went out that night.

Their quarrel hadn't driven him from the house into the storm. He'd already had an assignation planned, at ten, near the place where his car had gone off the road.

He'd arranged to meet Ginny Devereux there.

That he'd been unfaithful to her Hope had already known. She didn't understand why this proof of it should hurt so much. And then she realized that it wasn't just confirmation of his affair that was eating at her. There were other matters hinted at in the paper she held clutched in her hand.

Did she understand it correctly? Had Elliot really been planning to sell the farm, Hope's land, right out from under her?

She read the words one more time, and they made a horrible kind of sense. Elliot and Ginny had been scheming to swindle the Greens and the Hendersons and some of their other neighbors out of their property, as well. They had a developer lined up.

That Ginny Devereux had been Elliot's lover disturbed Hope deeply, but that the two of them had been engaged in a shady business deal bothered her even more.

Her first impulse was to phone Coop, but she resisted it. She had a little more to work out on her own before she talked to him.

She'd known for a long time that the two men were nothing alike, but this was certainly the proof of it. Elliot had lied to her, used her. Whatever else Coop might be, he'd never deliberately deceived her in any way. On occasion he'd been almost too honest, painfully so.

Humming, Hope fetched the last box and put it out on the porch, then set about getting herself cleaned up. She took special care in selecting an outfit and fixing her hair. And then, hours too early, she was ready to greet the man she loved.

And she'd come to a decision.

If he was willing to take her on, irrational fears and all, she would marry him. Feeling as if a great burden had been lifted from her heart, Hope went into the living room, curled up on the sofa, reached for the phone and dialed the number of the ski resort. Maybe she'd be lucky. Maybe he'd be able to come over earlier than they'd planned.

"Cooper Sanford, please," she said when the switchboard operator answered. It was late afternoon and she had no idea what Coop's work schedule was like, but he had told her to call him anytime if she needed him. She definitely needed him now.

"Just a minute, ma'am." The cheerful voice on the other end of the line was only slightly muffled, by the effect of a hand held over her mouthpiece as the operator addressed someone at the resort. "Hey, Johnny!" she called. "Is the boss in his office?"

Boss? Hope's grip on the phone tightened. Her breath caught and a lump began to form in her throat. She was getting another one of those awful premonitions.

"Should be," she heard a baritone voice reply.

"I can't find his extension number on this list," the operator complained.

The male voice was louder, as if he'd come closer to the switchboard. "Coop likes to keep a low profile," he said. "Here it is under CEO."

"Oh. What's that mean?"

"Chief executive officer. That's Cooper Sanford's title around here, since he owns the place."

Hope heard a scraping noise. Then, directly in her ear, the chirpy voice apologized for the delay. "I'm new here," she cheerfully explained. "I'll put you through to Mr. Sanford right away."

"Wait a minute."

"Yes, ma'am?"

"I may have misunderstood." She hoped she had. "Could you tell me, please, just what Mr. Sanford's position is there at the resort?"

"Well, sure. He owns the place." A buzzing sound told Hope the call was going through.

A wave of hurt and confusion washed over her, followed by a rapid swell of anger. She'd been wrong again about a man she thought she loved.

Coop *had* lied to her.

Chapter Twelve

Coop's fingers froze on the keyboard at the sound of Hope's strained voice. She wasn't making much sense. He punched a series of keys to save the budget figures he'd been entering and exited the program. Something was wrong. Something that demanded his full attention.

"Slow down, Hope," he said into the phone. "What's the matter? Are you okay?"

"No, I'm not okay." He heard her take a deep, shuddering breath. "I just found out the man I love has been lying to me. Why didn't you tell me that the real reason you don't need to worry about losing your job is that you own the place?"

She slammed the phone down before he could answer, so hard that for a moment his ear ached. Very slowly, Coop hung up, pushed himself away from the desk and stood. This was his own damn fault, he reasoned. He had no excuse for not telling Hope the truth weeks ago. On the other hand, there had to be more behind this emotional reaction than one little oversight on his part.

His first impulse was to rush over there and demand an explanation. He controlled his impatience. He didn't break any speed limits getting to Hope's house when he did leave the resort, either. She needed time to calm down. And, he reminded himself a little grimly, she would be there whenever he arrived. He wished he could be as certain that she would let him in.

"I'll camp on her porch all weekend if I have to," he muttered as he turned into her driveway.

The resort would just have to get along without his constant supervision a little longer, he decided. Hope had been right. He did have to start spending more time tending to business, but first he had to make sure she understood that she was more important to him than any job.

She answered the door, but only after he'd pounded on it so long and hard that his knuckles were bruised. There was no welcome in her expression. She glared at him, her eyes shooting fire. "How nice. You could get away early."

"Okay, so I'm not just a ski instructor. I'm the boss. I own Pleasant Prospect. Most people would think that was a plus, that I'd finally done something right with my life."

"Most people object to being lied to, Coop."

"Did you ever stop and consider why I chose to...mislead everyone?" He was impatient again, and she was blocking the doorway. He took a good look at her, and his breath caught.

She might be mad at him, but she was wearing that sinfully clingy black jumpsuit, the one she knew he liked. That fact gave Coop a much needed jolt of self-confidence. He wasn't the only one here with mixed feelings.

Abruptly, he reached for her, taking her by the shoulders and lifting her bodily. The feel of the soft, sensual fabric beneath his hands and of the even softer woman it concealed urged him to haul her into his arms and kiss away her anger and mistrust. Instead, he set her aside and slipped past her into the house. He had no intention of leaving again until they'd talked and she'd forgiven him.

"We both have some explaining to do," he announced.

Hope closed the front door and followed him into the living room, reluctantly taking his coat when he handed it to her. She tossed it into the chair, then realized her mistake. He was sure she'd meant to imply that he would be leaving too soon to bother hanging it up in the closet, but now the two of them were left with only the sofa to sit upon.

Coop sat, stretching his long, blue-jean-clad legs out in front of him. "I'd like a chance to explain, Hope," he said. "And to apologize. I know it sounds like a poor excuse, but I was planning to tell you everything when I saw you tonight."

"I don't see why you had to lie to me, to everyone in town, in the first place." Tossing her long, loose hair away from her face, she went to stand by the fireplace. That, too, held memories. Coop saw the play of emotions across her expressive face, and his optimism begin to return.

"Long before I came back here to live," he said slowly, "I made up my mind not to tell anyone about my good fortune. I didn't want to be welcomed home as some sort of prodigal son just because I'd had a lucky break. I wanted to win a place in the community by showing people that I'd changed."

Hope had moved to the window and stood with her back to him, her forehead resting against the cool surface of the glass. She was listening. That was all he asked...for now.

"You can tell people they ought to respect you because of the job you hold," he continued, "and some of them will actually do it if they see an advantage to themselves, but I wanted to show them I was worthy, earn their respect." He ran agitated fingers through his hair. "I suppose it was a stupid thing to do, but I wanted to be valued for myself, not for the fact that I own a business."

Still she said nothing, but she'd turned slightly. Her beautiful, heart-shaped face no longer radiated suspicion. Instead she looked thoughtful.

"I didn't come right out and lie. I just didn't volunteer anything. Until I hired a new instructor in January, I was teaching. I still do, in a pinch."

"Is that the only secret you've been keeping?" Hope asked.

Unable to sit still any longer, Coop stood and moved slowly toward her, until he was close enough to see what effect his words would have. "There is one other thing. The way I acquired ownership of the resort in the first place. It wasn't all that respectable. I won it in a card game."

The corners of Hope's mouth twitched. She refused to smile, but he knew the worst was over now. She understood.

Coop was the one whose face was overspread with a rueful grin. "Can you just see the reception I'd have gotten if that bit of information had come out the wrong way? It would have been the last nail in the bad-boy coffin."

"Aunt Penny thinks you have connections to the mob."

"Oh, great. That's all I need."

"I wouldn't worry about it too much," Hope said. "As soon as you tell her the truth, she'll change her tune. At least by local standards, you are now among the rich and important in this community. She'll be bragging about your successes before you know it.''

He stared hard at her, searching her face, trying to discover what she really felt about that, about him. Her words sounded casual, but her eyes were alight with a familiar gleam.

Frowning, Coop put a little distance between them. "That's exactly the kind of thing I wanted to avoid.''

"Does it really matter what people like Penny Bellamy and her friends think of you? You know your own worth. So does Maureen.'' Her voice dropped to a lower register, imbuing her next words with an unspoken promise for the future. "And so do I,'' she said.

Coop went perfectly still, his eyes locked on hers. "Does that mean I'm forgiven?'' He felt as if he was waiting for a judge to pass sentence on him. Would she condemn him to a life without her in it or grant him the chance to make things up to her, to prove he was worthy of her trust, her respect, and most of all, her love?

Hope reached for his hand.

"You don't need to worry about your reputation any longer, Coop. You impressed everyone who counted just by bringing Maureen back home. Even Aunt Penny has to admit that you're a good father.''

She walked past him to the sofa, pulling him along with her. When they were seated side by side, she leaned closer, planting one soft kiss on his chin. "I'm sorry I got so angry with you without hearing your explanation. I was upset by something else, and I overreacted.''

He'd lied, yes, but it was not the same kind of lie Elliot had told. Hope understood how much becoming respectable had meant to Coop. She understood why he'd kept his success a secret.

One hand came up to frame her face, brushing lightly over her cheek and pushing a stray wisp of hair behind her ear. His touch soothed and aroused at the same time. In Coop's jade green eyes, Hope saw the intensity of his love for her, undiminished by her fleeting loss of faith.

It was too soon to tell him that she'd decided to accept his marriage proposal, she thought, but past time to feel his arms around her again and to hold him tightly in her own. She snuggled closer and rested her head against the nubby wool of his cable knit sweater. She breathed in the mingled scents that were uniquely his. A contented sigh escaped her. Her hands itched to touch him and inched around his waist, heading for the well-remembered heat and enticing textures of his bare torso.

Coop put his hands on her shoulders and held her away from him. "Not so fast," he said in a husky whisper. "You're trying to distract me."

"Guilty," she whispered.

"Why did you call me, Hope? What was so important that it couldn't wait until I got here? You knew I was coming over later this evening."

Hope drew in a deep breath. He deserved an explanation. Indeed, she'd meant to tell him everything. She just wished they could postpone this particular discussion until morning.

The look in his eyes warned her not to procrastinate any longer, and told her that any attempts at seduction, designed to delay the inevitable, would not succeed. It was clear to her that he wanted her, but even more obvious that he wanted answers.

Haltingly at first, but then with growing assurance, Hope told him about the quarrel she'd had with her husband on the night Elliot died. She confided her feelings of guilt, something she'd never before confessed to anyone.

"I realized from the start that I shouldn't blame myself," she said when he started to object, "but logic didn't help much. Subconsciously I felt I'd been responsible. It was only after you and I spent so much time together that I began to gain a little perspective."

In a rush she told him about her nightmare, then added, "Today I decided it was time to face the past."

"How?" Coop's arm was around her shoulders. He held her hands in his. Spongelike, she absorbed the unspoken encouragement and comfort he offered.

"I went through Elliot's things." Hope extricated one hand and reached across Coop to the end table to pick up the crumpled piece of paper she'd found in Elliot's pocket. "He was going to meet Ginny," she said as she handed it over. "So you see, no matter what might have happened before he left home, he'd still have gone out that night. He'd still have been in a fatal accident. It wasn't my fault at all."

Coop barely glanced at the note. "Good old Ginny." At her frown, he took her face between his hands and met her eyes. "No more lies, Hope. Dennis told me a long time ago that your husband had been having an affair with Ginny at the time of his death. Everyone was protecting your feelings. None of us had any idea that it would be better for you to know the truth."

Hope sagged against him. It didn't matter. Not really. Not as long as she and Coop were honest with each other from now on. "I suppose that means the whole county knew he was unfaithful to me," she said with a sigh.

Coop stroked her hair, and she cared even less about what Elliot had done or who knew of it.

"I'm beginning to wonder if gossip is as powerful as we thought it was when we were younger," he mused. "A few people knew Ginny and Elliot were spending time together. So what?"

Blinking rapidly, Hope sat up. Coop had let the piece of paper drift to the floor in front of the sofa. She retrieved it. "Read it," she said, placing it in his hand. "I think it may have been much more than a love affair."

She watched his face as he scanned the contents of the note. "The entrepreneur at work," he muttered.

"Did Dennis tell you anything else about Elliot?"

"Enough to indicate that his business ethics were non-existent. I guess I'd better make another confession while I'm at it." He met her gaze head-on, no apologies, no hesitation. "I asked Dennis to find out all he could about your husband and his business dealings, and I took Ginny out to dinner, mostly because of what Dennis told me about her and Elliot."

"Mostly?"

He looked sheepish and shrugged. "Jealous?"

"No."

He grinned at her. "Now, what did we just agree about lying?"

Hope smiled, secure in the strength of their love. "Okay. Maybe just a little jealous, but you have better sense than to get involved with her."

"What? You aren't going to ask me if I slept with her to get information?"

"You aren't Elliot," she said simply.

Coop kissed her soundly. "About time you realized that."

Hope kissed him back. "I don't want to talk any-more."

"I'm not quite through confessing," he whispered. "The minute I sat down to dinner with Ginny, I knew I wasn't interested. I realized that you were the only woman for me."

"Are you telling me that I owe Ginny Devereux a debt of gratitude for making you admit that to yourself?"

He nibbled at her ear, sending chills up her spine. "I guess I am."

When his fingers edged toward the ring at the neck of her jumpsuit, Hope knew that if he reached his goal he wasn't going to stop until they were in her bed and naked. She caught his hand, postponing the pleasure just a little longer.

"I need to find out more about this plan Ginny refers to in the note. I have the uneasy feeling she hasn't given up on it."

"Dennis didn't come up with anything." The fingers were moving again. Heat prickled along her skin every place they skimmed.

"You asked him to check on Elliot, not Ginny."

The zipper began to slide down her bosom. "Do you want me to call Dennis now and invite him to join us?"

Hope inhaled sharply as his mouth found her nipple. "Later," she gasped.

"Good."

But she made one last stab at finishing their discussion, in spite of the incredibly erotic things Coop was doing to her. "There's something else we should check. There was one box I couldn't fit into the closet. Oh, Coop!"

"A box?" There was laughter in his voice as his fingers made new and exciting demands.

Panting, Hope broke free. On her knees at one end of the sofa, she faced him and began to wriggle out of her jumpsuit, revealing the sheer silk teddy beneath the clinging black fabric. "It was filled with Elliot's business papers," she said in a rush. "I weeded through them to take out what I needed for that year's income taxes, but I barely looked at the rest. There are folders I never even opened."

As she disrobed, Coop followed every movement with eyes that sizzled, but he seemed to be getting as much of a charge out of the challenge of carrying on their conversation as she was. They both knew that their joining would be the sweeter for this constant hinting at postponement.

"How come you didn't check this box today when you were going through the rest of it?"

For a split second the sensual haze thinned. "I didn't remember it until just now."

"And?" Coop's eyes narrowed as he caught her hesitation. He'd banked the fires within, but there was no loss of heat.

"It's stored out in the barn," Hope confessed.

"Good."

"Good?"

"Yes. That means we can leave it there until morning." He was tired of the game. Hope smiled. So was she. "We'll kill two birds with one stone. We'll check the contents of the carton and we'll get you started on the desensitizing again. Okay?"

Even her last vulnerability would not be allowed to keep them apart. "Okay," she breathed as she melted into the warmth of his embrace.

If their fiery lovemaking did not set off the smoke alarm this time, it would not be for lack of trying.

The morning light woke her, streaming in through the drapes to pick out Coop's big body sprawled next to her in the sleigh bed.

He looked right there.

As she watched him, he opened his eyes. When he saw that she was staring at him, admiring him, he smiled.

"I begin to see the lure." His voice was gravelly with sleep, and Hope thought it was the sexiest sound she'd ever heard.

"What lure?"

"The one that baits the Rapunzel trap. The overwhelming desire to stay inside, specifically in this room, particularly in this bed. Right at this minute, I can't think of a single reason ever to leave. There is nothing at all appealing beyond that fancy footboard."

She was taken aback by his teasing, but only for a moment. This was good. This was healthy. She loved him more than ever for what he was trying to do.

"What about food?" she asked. "Breakfast?"

"We'll live on love."

"Tempting thought, but I have a hankering for bacon and eggs. Besides, you promised me a trip to the barn today."

"Only if you were very, very good."

"And I was. You said so several times during the night."

They both grinned, delighted with each other and completely at ease.

Coop had been in Hope's barn before, but only far enough to pick up a shovel or get out the snowblower. He saw now that it was old and in poor condition, though the box they were looking for was stored in a section that seemed solid enough. Hope had put it in a small separate room in the loft.

"The hired man used to sleep here, back when the place was built," she explained. "I figured this was the driest spot to leave papers, not that I was all that concerned about them at the time."

He slit the tape holding the flaps together and wrinkled his nose. The contents had mildewed in the two years they'd been out here. They looked perfectly readable, however.

"Take this inside or look through it here?"

"Let's not stink up the house. It isn't that cold today, and there's light enough here."

He divided the contents between them and began to read.

"Find anything?" she asked some twenty minutes later.

"I'm not sure. What do you make of these?"

Hope took the papers he'd unearthed and scanned their contents. "These are results of testing water samples."

"Yes. One for your well. The others seem to be your neighbors'."

"But this doesn't make any sense. We had the well water tested shortly before Elliot died, but it came back just fine. A little heavy on iron, but no bacteria problems and certainly not this." She jabbed a finger at the line that had caught Coop's attention.

High levels of arsenic.

"I don't get it, Hope. Arsenic is a poison. What is it doing in well water?"

Her brow furrowed in thought, she began to pace. "A couple of years ago there was a problem with the well water in a town south of here. Arsenic occurs naturally, you know. For some reason the levels were too high for safety in that area. There was a fair amount of publicity. A lot of sales of water purifiers. The very expensive kind. We had our well tested as a matter of course. It came up clean. I've got the report in the house somewhere."

"And this one?"

"This is going to sound farfetched, but Elliot was ready to sell my farm and he wanted the adjoining lots. Maybe he hoped to scare the neighbors into selling with a rumor of arsenic in the water supply."

"To what end? A developer wouldn't buy the place with a problem like that."

"That's just it. There is no problem. Once Ginny had the deeds in her greedy little hands, she could produce documentation to prove the water was safe."

Coop heaved himself to his feet, moving around in the loft to stretch his legs and ease the stiffness from squatting in the cold. What Hope said made a convoluted kind of sense, and con men were known for their elaborate money-making schemes. "We may never know," he warned.

"Ginny hasn't given up on trying to acquire the land."

"Let's turn these over to Dennis and let him handle it."

Hope murmured her agreement, but she seemed distracted. Coop glanced at her, realizing that he'd wandered farther than he'd thought.

"What really bothers me," she said, "is that I've been using the money Elliot left me to live on. I hate to think I might have been profiting from other underhanded swindles like this one."

At the unhappiness in Hope's voice, Coop started across the loft, taking the most direct route. He'd find a way to cheer her up again, maybe suggest that she donate the rest of Elliot's estate to charity. He'd support her from now on. They'd put the past behind them once and for all. Together.

He'd almost reached her side when a sharp crack rent the air. He recognized the sound as splintering wood too late to do anything about it. Beneath his feet, the century-old floor had abruptly given way.

Hope's scream of sheer terror followed Coop through the rotting timber. He tried to go limp, tried to pretend he was on skis and taking a fall, but on the way down his arm struck the manger pole. Unlike the floor of the loft, it was a very solid piece of wood. A moment later the packed, frozen dirt floor came up to meet him. Coop landed hard, in what had once been the stall for a horse or a cow. The impact knocked the wind out of him and his head bounced on the unforgiving surface.

Stars danced in front of his eyes. Slowly, he opened them. He was staring up at the hole he'd fallen through. Hope's white face appeared in the opening. He wanted to tell her he was okay but the only sound he could manage was a groan.

He wasn't sure if he lost consciousness or not, but the next time he opened his eyes, Hope was kneeling beside him. Tears streamed down her cheeks and she had clamped her teeth down so hard on her lower lip that she'd left a mark.

"I'm okay," he gasped. "Just winded."

Then she touched his elbow and he nearly screamed in agony. Pain lanced through his arm, bad enough that he forgot about the throbbing in his head.

Hope gave a little sob, then got her emotions under control. She wouldn't go to pieces now. Coop was depending on her. "I don't think it's broken," she said in a choked voice, "but you may have a hairline fracture."

"I can't tell you how happy that makes me." He closed his eyes again, clearly hurting.

With gentle hands, she examined the bump on the back of his head, wishing she could absorb his pain and spare him this agony. "Dizzy?" she asked.

"Oh, yeah."

"Open your eyes. Tell me how many fingers I'm holding up." She stuck three in front of his face and wiggled them. Coop managed to lift his undamaged arm and catch them in his hand. "Three," he said.

Hope stared deep into his dazed green eyes. He sounded stronger already. He didn't seem to be severely injured, but she was no doctor. She didn't even know much about basic first aid. Coop needed to get to the hospital, where he could be checked out properly, and he needed to get there as soon as possible.

It didn't even occur to Hope to call the paramedics. The hospital was only a few miles away and the quickest way to get Coop there was by taking the Pleasant Prospect van.

"Come on," she urged, sliding her hands underneath his shoulders and lifting. "Upsy daisy."

To her relief, he was able to struggle to his feet with her help and walk under his own power as long as he could lean on her.

"I can't drive with this arm." He winced as he tried to gesture with it.

"You shouldn't anyway," she chided him, "not after a knock on the head." With swift efficiency, Hope settled him on the floor in the back of the van and relieved him of his keys.

The trip to the hospital took less than twenty minutes, and the emergency room staff had hustled Coop off into an examining room within seconds after he walked in from the parking lot. Hope sank down on an uncomfortable plastic chair in the waiting room and breathed a sigh of relief.

And then, for the first time, she realized the enormity of what she'd just done.

She hadn't had time for irrational fears.

Her love and concern for Coop had outweighed any subconscious terrors.

Scarcely daring to believe, Hope stared at the stark white tiles on the wall in front of her. She'd read about this phenomenon. She'd even mentioned it to Coop, way back when she'd first told him about her agoraphobia.

Her elation increased. There was a good chance that she'd just, without even thinking about it, managed to break the pattern of the phobia. Hadn't she read of numerous cases where agoraphobics resumed normal lives following incidents similar to this one?

Hope tried to be realistic. She reviewed all she knew of her condition, but what she kept remembering was that, just as the causes of agoraphobia were shrouded in mystery, so were the reasons for abrupt recovery. Hope was aware that her belief that she was cured could, in fact, be enough to cure her.

A slow smile overspread her features. At the least, she had reason to be optimistic.

When Coop was released a short time later, Hope was still in the waiting room. She didn't tell him her news at once. He was in no condition to appreciate it.

"Steady," she told him as she helped him out of the building and into the passenger seat of the van.

"I'm still a little woozy," he admitted, settling in and closing his eyes against the glare of the sun, "but I'm not in such bad shape. No broken bones, and the doctor says my head's too hard to be seriously damaged."

Hope started the engine.

At the hospital exit onto Route 2 she had a choice. If she turned right, the road would take her to Tardiff and her own house, to the safe, secure haven she knew. If she went left, the road passed through Norville and eventually reached the turnoff for Pleasant Prospect Ski Resort and Coop's condo. She could take him up, somewhat belatedly, on his invitation to dinner.

One glance at Coop made Hope's heart swell with love. There was no room left for any other emotion, and her decision was very easy to make.

A short while later, she parked the car. Coop opened his eyes for the first time since they'd left the hospital and blinked in surprise.

"How'd we get to my place?"

"You gave me the directions more than a week ago," she answered. "Remember?"

Slowly, Coop turned his head. The short nap had gone a long way toward restoring him but her action had done even more to speed up the cure. Jade eyes fixed on sapphire with an intensity beyond anything Hope had seen before.

"Does this mean what I hope it does?" he asked.

Hope leaned across the seat and kissed him lightly on the lips. She moved back only inches and held his gaze as she answered him. All the love she had for him was in her voice.

"It means that Rapunzel has finally left her tower," she said, "and that she is ready, willing and able to marry her handsome prince and ride off with him into the sunset."

* * * * *

Get Ready to be Swept Away by
Silhouette's Spring Collection

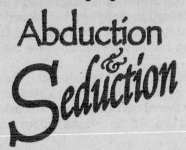

Abduction & Seduction

These passion-filled stories explore both the dangerous
desires of men and the seductive powers of women.
Written by three of our most celebrated authors, they are
sure to capture your hearts.

Diana Palmer
Brings us a spin-off of her Long, Tall Texans series

Joan Johnston
Crafts a beguiling Western romance

Rebecca Brandewyne
New York Times bestselling author
makes a smashing contemporary debut

Available in March at your favorite retail outlet.

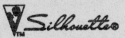

The Loop™

Is the future what it's cracked up to be?

This February, find out if Emily's marriage
can be saved in

GETTING OUT: EMILY
by ArLynn Presser

When Emily said "I do," she had vowed to love Marsh
forever. And she still loved him, but marriage wasn't
as easy as her parents made it look! Getting married
so young had been hard enough, but now that she
was going back to school, things were getting even
worse. She wanted to meet new people and try
different things, but all Marsh wanted to do was
cocoon! Suddenly the decisions that had seemed so
right just a few years ago seemed totally wrong.

The ups and downs of life as you know it continue with

GETTING AWAY WITH IT: JOJO
by Liz Ireland (March)

GETTING A CLUE: TAMMY
by Wendy Mass (April)

Get smart. Get into "The Loop!"

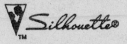

Silhouette

SPECIAL EDITION
™

That
Woman!
SPECIAL

THE SULTAN'S WIVES
Tracy Sinclair
(SE #943, March)

When a story in an exotic locale beckoned, nothing could
keep Pippa Bennington from scooping the
competition. But this time, her eager journalist's heart landed
her squarely in, of all things, a harem!
Pippa was falling for the seductive charms of
Mikolar al-Rasheed—but what exactly *were* the
sultan's true intentions?

Don't miss
THE SULTAN'S WIVES,
by Tracy Sinclair,
available in March!

She's friend, wife, mother—she's you! And beside each
Special Woman stands a wonderfully
special man. It's a celebration of our heroines—
and the men who become part of their lives.

SILHOUETTE... Where Passion Lives

Don't miss these Silhouette favorites by some of our most distinguished authors! And now you can receive a discount by ordering two or more titles!

SD#05786	QUICKSAND by Jennifer Greene	$2.89	☐
SD#05795	DEREK by Leslie Guccione	$2.99	☐
SD#05818	NOT JUST ANOTHER PERFECT WIFE by Robin Elliott	$2.99	☐
IM#07505	HELL ON WHEELS by Naomi Horton	$3.50	☐
IM#07514	FIRE ON THE MOUNTAIN by Marion Smith Collins	$3.50	☐
IM#07559	KEEPER by Patricia Gardner Evans	$3.50	☐
SSE#09879	LOVING AND GIVING by Gina Ferris	$3.50	☐
SSE#09892	BABY IN THE MIDDLE by Marie Ferrarella	$3.50 U.S. / $3.99 CAN.	☐ ☐
SSE#09902	SEDUCED BY INNOCENCE by Lucy Gordon	$3.50 U.S. / $3.99 CAN.	☐ ☐
SR#08952	INSTANT FATHER by Lucy Gordon	$2.75	☐
SR#08984	AUNT CONNIE'S WEDDING by Marie Ferrarella	$2.75	☐
SR#08990	JILTED by Joleen Daniels	$2.75	☐

(limited quantities available on certain titles)

AMOUNT	$_____
DEDUCT: 10% DISCOUNT FOR 2+ BOOKS	$_____
POSTAGE & HANDLING ($1.00 for one book, 50¢ for each additional)	$_____
APPLICABLE TAXES*	$_____
TOTAL PAYABLE (check or money order—please do not send cash)	$_____

To order, complete this form and send it, along with a check or money order for the total above, payable to Silhouette Books, to: In the U.S.: 3010 Walden Avenue, P.O. Box 9077, Buffalo, NY 14269-9077; In Canada: P.O. Box 636, Fort Erie, Ontario, L2A 5X3.

Name:_____

Address:_____ City:_____

State/Prov.:_____ Zip/Postal Code:_____

*New York residents remit applicable sales taxes.
Canadian residents remit applicable GST and provincial taxes.

SBACK-DF

Silhouette®
TM